THEFT OF MAGIC

THEFT OF MAGIC

THE LEIRA CHRONICLES™ BOOK 6

MARTHA CARR

MICHAEL ANDERLE

LMBPN Publishing
PMB 196, 2540 South Maryland Pkwy
Las Vegas, NV 89109

Version 2.01 July 2020
Version 1.01, October 2020
eBook ISBN: 978-1-64971-053-6
Print ISBN: 978-1-64971-054-3

THEFT OF MAGIC TEAM

JIT Beta Readers

Thomas Ogden
Sarah Weir
Paul Westman
Alex Wilson
Kelly O'Donnell
Larry Omans
Erika Everest
Erick Cushman
James Caplan
John Ashmore
Tim Bischoff
Edward Rosenfeld
Micky Cocker

If we've missed anyone, please let us know!

From Martha

To everyone who still believes in magic and all the possibilities that holds.

To all the readers who make this entire ride so much fun.

To Louie, Jackie, and so many wonderful friends who remind me all the time of what really matters and how wonderful life can be in any given moment.

And finally, a special thank you to John Nelson of the Austin, Texas Police Department who patiently answers all of my questions. I hope I made you proud. Thank you for your service.

From Michael

To Family, Friends and
Those Who Love
To Read.
May We All Enjoy Grace
To Live The Life We Are
Called.

CHAPTER ONE

Leira stood in the center of the cavernous PDF warehouse looking around at the small circle of people, carefully measuring her words. Her hands were dug into the pockets of her favorite worn brown leather jacket where no one could see her clenching her fists. "You all heard me. Take a seat and someone start talking. Nana, I elect you. You brought the plus one." She glanced at Jackson, falling back on her instincts as a federal agent and assessed the situation, sticking to the protocol. It's what she did whenever a situation was quickly becoming a shit show. I see the resemblance. It could be true.

Leira gave her grandmother the same patient look she used in any interrogation as a detective. The inevitability was obvious. The information was going to come out. It was just a matter of when and patience, but Berens women all had a measured amount of patience that could quickly hit a wall. Her partner, Hagan looked around at everyone counting the seconds in his head. "This is a new kind of shit storm," he muttered. "He does not look old enough to be your father."

"He doesn't look clean enough to be anyone's father." Correk grimaced, his feet in a wide stance and his arms crossed against his chest.

"He's an Elf who's been on Oriceran. It's like its own magic potion. And believe it or not, Correk, in his day he cleaned up pretty well. This hermit routine he picked up in recent years." Mara pushed Jackson further into the center of the warehouse.

The air in the large metal warehouse felt still and close as everyone froze right where they stood. A large black fly buzzed noisily over the long table set up down the middle of the room. Leira gave a sidelong glance at her grandmother to see if she was casting a spell to slow down time but Mara was avoiding her glance and her skin wasn't glowing. An icy breeze blew across the back of Leira's neck. The warehouse was never airtight, and Austin was in the middle of a rare cold snap.

Hagan finally found his voice and cleared his throat. "This has got to be the definition of awkward. So, in other words, a normal family get-together." Leira's eyebrows shot up as she looked at him, but he just shrugged. "I think honesty is going to be your friend here, partner. Your long-lost father showing up from another world in the middle of a large dinner ranks right up there." He held his hand high in the air. "Moments like this we usually make sure everyone has checked their weapons, which is a little tougher in this crowd. Weapons being built in, and all. Kind of wish Lois was here. She wields a mean wand."

"That won't be necessary." Symbols flashed along Leira's skin, subsiding as Jackson's eyes widened in surprise. The silverware along the table rattled and clinked and rose in the air a few inches before settling back down.

"The energy is telling her what to do next," gasped the Elf. "It's predicting the inevitability of outcomes…"

"No fucking kidding," whispered Mara. "Your daughter has a few magic tricks we've never seen before."

No one moved from their spot, turning their heads to look at Leira to see what she was going to do next.

No one except Jackson who gave the same familiar one-sided smile as his daughter, Leira, his green eyes half-closed. It hid the even mixture of panic and anger roiling through him. Correk noticed the Elf working his hands by his side even as he tried a casual stance. He looked over at Leira and saw a familiar pain in her face. Bits and pieces of lost family coming together again. This time not by her reckoning. An old hurt echoed through his chest for what he had lost.

"No one's going to sit down at the table? Okay, we can start right where we are." Leira blinked hard a few times, her chest rising and falling. Breathe. For once, don't say what you're thinking. She was twisting the sapphire ring on her finger. "Nana, you care to explain? I thought you said he was dead and best forgotten."

"That stings." Jackson scowled at Mara. "I should have known that would be your general description of me."

"More of a hope mixed with a truth… for a while. What I told you in your shack was true. Hate me," she said, pointing at Leira, "she's still your daughter."

"More of a cabin than a shack and I can't stay in this world forever. Left my dog alone."

"Already trying to leave. Now, that is familiar." Mara's Texas twang grew thicker, a short burst of anger crawling up her spine. "Think you have enough time to at least help out your only child? She needs the information inside your head."

"See? Regular family dinner…" Hagan gave another shrug and wiped his face with his handkerchief, pulling out a chair. "I'm sitting and if no one starts making sense soon, I'm eating." He opened the box sitting on top with the familiar Home Slice logo to see what kind of pizza was inside.

Jackson worked his jaw as he looked at Leira locking eyes with her. She held his gaze, defiantly lifting her chin.

"I've seen that look before," said Jackson, evenly. "You get that from your mother. Fight your way out of a corner with a rusty hair pin if you had to."

Leira looked past Jackson to her mother on the far side of the table.

"Mom? You knew he was alive and kicking?"

Don squeezed Eireka's hand as she licked her dry lips, buying a little time. She raised her chin and chose her words carefully, eyeing Jackson. "You left me before I could tell you about Leira. Vanished. I was hoping that meant you were dead."

"At least you women are all consistent in hoping I'm dead."

Mara cleared her throat just as alarms went off overhead. There was more footage on the screen of the troll in action in a bar with a barely distinguishable view of Hagan behind him just as Hagan turned and the letters PDA appeared on the back of his nylon jacket.

"Well, fuck me." Leira stood in front of the magical screen hanging high in the air, watching the video of the troll standing well over six feet tall in a dark bar in Austin, growling at a trio of over-muscled meatheads. The comments were piling up underneath with people guessing if it was a fake or there were now Yetis in Austin, Texas. There were even comments about the fat dude behind the hairy beast. "The other kind of trolls of a human variety making themselves known," said Leira.

"This is going to make it hard to go back to Barfly's. That's my favorite hidey hole. Best cheap beer in town…" Hagan let out his own growl and slapped his hand down on the pink Voodoo doughnuts box, bending the top.

"Hey!" The troll peeked his head out from inside the box, his mouth full of chunks of chocolate doughnut as he looked up at the screen. "Uh oh, that's not good." Crumbs tumbled from his shoulders and belly, down around his feet. "Huh?" Yumfuck licked a finger and pressed down on the stray bits of doughnuts, popping them into his mouth. "Yummmm…"

A loud growl filled the room, echoing from the video. The

troll looked up at the screen, surprised. "Hey, I look good. Nice angles." The troll let out a cackle and dove back under the box as it jiggled across the desk. Hagan looked at the box and back at the screen, taking his handkerchief out of his back pocket and wiping his forehead. "Not Barfly's," he moaned.

On the screen, everyone watched the video of Yumfuck dragging his oversized claws across the bar letting out a roar. In front of him was a man in a sleeveless plaid shirt with hairy arms, snarling even as his eyes grew wide with fear. Leira felt a certain amount of satisfaction and dread. Always nice to put down a Jughead but not in front of the world.

The number of views was rolling in the lower left-hand corner, quickly climbing to three million views and hundreds of thousands of shares. She felt the tension grow in the pit of her stomach. The desks across the room rattled for a moment as if the ground was shaking. Leira took a deep breath and let it out. That's new.

"Maybe no one will know it's Barfly's." Hagan licked his lips just as the neon flashed by the side of the bar. Barfly's sputtered in bright red with a Budweiser in blue glowing beneath it before the whole thing sparked and fizzled out.

"Great…" Hagan let out a deep sigh. "I suppose there are other watering holes in Austin with the same appeal."

Leira looked at him, slightly amazed. "I take it you mean early decrepit with a solid C rating from the Travis County Health Department. Maybe just a few dozen"

"You are looking at Texas vintage," he argued. He opened the top pizza box and pulled out a slice, folding it in half and taking a big bite.

"Hagan, you manned up more when you were shot. How about we focus on the real problem here. You're blowing our cover, which won't sit well with the General. I kind of like our job and I'm thinking anonymity is a key part of the job description."

"That's not something you see every day. An oversized troll taking care of business on Earth. At least not since the gates slammed shut." Jackson scratched his chin through his scruffy beard as he walked closer to the screen. Closer toward Leira.

Mara cleared her throat and reached out to tap Jackson on the shoulder. "Uh, Jackson… most of these people just met you. Including your…" The word caught in her throat for a moment. "Your daughter." She choked out the words.

Leira felt the hairs bristle along the back of her neck. Of course this is the way I meet my father. She rolled her head, stretching her neck. After all these years. An ache rolled through her chest. She kept her attention on the screen making a point of not looking at her mother or grandmother. Not yet.

Correk slid in between Jackson and Leira, taking a wide stance, nudging Jackson over a few feet. Leira noticed and thought of his father, wanting to reach out and take his hand. Not now.

"We can come up with something. The world already knows about magic, thanks to Rhazdon and the prophets. The video misses the part with the troll growing and Hagan is in the background. Hard to tell who he is, mostly… PDA won't register with anyone."

Leira turned around to glance at Hagan who looked sheepish as he grimaced with a hard swallow of pizza. "All kind of happened pretty fast. If it makes you feel any better, we stopped an old Wizard at the bar from using his wand."

Leira gave him a dead fish look and looked back up at the screen.

CHAPTER TWO

Turner Underwood looked up from the ancient Oriceran manuscript on his desk, moving the large magnifying glass to the side and turning off the small light on the side of it. The letters on the page quickly faded, leaving the page blank. He lifted his chin and listened for a moment, a smile coming over his face even as the concern never left him.

"The next phase has begun. This is good. I can work with this. The seer's prophecy is rolling right along." Turner cupped one hand over the other in front of his chest and whispered into his hands, slowly pulling them apart as a blue ball of light grew to the size of an orange. "Big enough to do the job." He waved his arm over the ball of light as it vanished with a pop and found its target, hovering just under the bumper of the green Mustang parked outside the warehouse.

The troll pushed up the lid of the pink box, swallowing the remains of a jelly doughnut as he jumped off Hagan's desk. He scrambled across the warehouse and up Leira's leg as she reached down and held out her hand, placing the troll on her shoulder. "I'm a celebrity," he chirped, letting out a cackle.

"Your lack of concern is doing nothing for me." Correk drew his mouth into a thin line and watched the video loop, his hands on his hips and his elbows out at his side even as the troll shrugged and sat down on Leira's shoulder.

Jackson let out a short laugh as he sized up Correk, taking a step back behind him. "Okay, big fella, I can take a hint." He ran a hand through his thick hair, creating more tall peaks along the top of his head.

Correk took a whiff of the air, wrinkling his nose as he looked down at Jackson's boots and up at the different stains along his tunic. He looked straight at Jackson and slowly crossed his arms across his chest. Leira shook her head and went back to looking at the video. "Some kind of male Elf posing. Suddenly, I'm back in a squad room again." She pointed at the screen. "Look, this isn't a problem. Not yet." She puckered her lips. "Not unless the Silver Griffins decide to make it a problem. Only a handful of people know what PDF or PDA really stand for."

"You think the Silver Griffins will care enough to do something about this?" Eireka spoke up from the far side of the long table, still holding her boyfriend, Don's hand tightly. Leira looked over at her mother and saw the tremor pass through her shoulders. I can finally return this favor. Comfort her. Leira's bright green eyes glowed as she sent out a thin stream of magic, curling around her mother's shoulders to hold her in an embrace that hummed with energy.

"Not if we can get to the General to explain things before they have to come looking for us. Hagan did everyone walk out of there under their own power?" Leira ran her hand through her hair in the same way as Jackson had just done, giving Correk a start.

"In a manner of speaking."

Leira gave him a long look, waiting for more, knowing there

wasn't more coming. She'd done enough cases with him by now to know what he was about to say.

"Never complain, never explain. Not to anyone but Rose, of course," he said. Leira mouthed the words along with Hagan.

"That's a classic, Hagan. Haven't heard you use that one in a long time."

He took another large bite of pizza while the troll jumped up and down on Leira's shoulder, leaping into the air toward the pizza box as Leira caught him and put him back on her shoulder.

A tiny "Motherfucker!" filled the room.

"Haven't stepped in shit this deep in a long time." Hagan wiped grease off his face with a small white paper napkin. "This one will take an extra-long shovel. Any chance magic could handle this?"

"As far as I know, never was never will be doesn't cover the globe or we could solve a few things before pizza."

"That has to be getting cold." Mara waved toward the long table set with dishes and silverware and the pile of pizzas at one end.

"Mom is right. Nothing's going to get explained to anyone's satisfaction in the next hour." The words came out slowly as Eireka looked pointedly at her mother. "We should eat first."

"You want to sit down at a table and eat like nothing just happened? That's a lot to swallow, even for me." Hagan watched carefully, reading the room. "Everybody staying calm? No itchy fingers?"

Mara threw up her hands, her long, thick dark hair moving along her shoulders as she grabbed a handful of Jackson's tunic, dragging him along with her. She went to the near side of the table and pulled out a metal folding chair. "Sit. You're about to try one of this world's finest inventions."

"That's it?" Jackson lowered himself into the chair, a smile spreading across his face, deepening his dimples. He pulled out a long, thin leather strip, smoothing back his hair and tying it in the back. The women watched closely as he flexed his arms, tying a knot as Correk rolled his eyes.

Correk took the seat one down from Hagan and leaned in to mutter., "Apparently they haven't gotten past the mullet on Oriceran."

"Is this some kind of Earth custom. One last good meal together before the body slamming?" Jackson looked up at Eireka and Don, giving a nod of his head. "You're looking good. This your mate?"

Correk let out a grunt as Jackson leaned forward in his chair, stretching his arm across the table. "Don't believe we ever got around to introductions. I'm Jackson, an Elf of sorts."

Leira glanced back at the screen as Eireka waved her arm, archiving the video. "It's too late to stop the video. It's sitting on too many phones at the very least. Give it a day or two and everyone will move on."

"Elf of sorts?" Correk slowly put out his hand and shook Jackson's hand tightly, feeling a strong and familiar hum. It reminded him of the energy that ran through Leira but with less power. Still…

"I think that's why Mara dragged me through a portal… To explain. Or at least start to explain. Strange thing to work at keeping a secret for well over a hundred years and now I have an audience to spill it to."

"Quit dragging it out, Jackson. Just tell them." Mara made herself look at Leira, but she was intently watching Jackson. I hope I did the right thing.

Jackson blew out a deep breath, puffing out his cheeks. "Fine." He spread his hands flat on the table.

The troll leapt down to the table and scrambled in front of Jackson, smiling. "You're a Jaspar Elf. Rare!"

Jackson opened his mouth to say something and shut it again. He grimaced as he said, "What the little furry guy said."

"Not a surprise. Turner Underwood already broke that news.

You came all that way just to say that?" Leira could feel the frustration growing. So many questions.

"Turner… The Fixer." Jackson's smile grew tighter. "You must be in the middle of a few things for Turner to be making an appearance. Not the only reason I came."

"And not the only reason I went to fetch him."

"Without saying anything to me." Eireka's eyes glistened as she leaned back in her chair. "A heads up would have gone a long way."

Mara looked pained as she looked at her daughter. "There was no time to explain everything. You don't understand what's going on here. I could tell you, which would have taken days, trust me. Or I could save Leira."

Yumfuck took advantage of the distraction and crawled toward the tower of boxes, easily scaling them till he was at the top. He tugged on a large slice topped with pepperoni, pulling it out of the box with as little noise as possible. He glanced over the top of the box and saw Hagan looking in his direction. The troll gave him a smile and a wink and ducked back down, giving one last hard tug as the slice came out in one easy slide acting like a hot, greasy toboggan. The troll jumped on board, holding on to the crust as the pizza hit the table, flopping over, rolling the troll inside. Yumfuck chewed his way through the top and quickly stood up, wearing the pizza around his waist, his hair slicked back with grease.

"Never seen him look happier," muttered Hagan. He reached over and got another piece and offered the box to Correk. "Go ahead. Good pizza has helped more than one bad party get going." Hagan stood up and started passing the rest of the boxes in both directions. "We're all family here… of sorts. Let's start with that and a little pizza."

Leira took a seat between Correk and Hagan and pulled out a slice with mushrooms on it, passing the box. She chewed her lip, ignoring the slice as she took a look around the table. "There's a lot of people at this table that I love and some I almost lost this past year. Two of you I had to fight like hell to get back." The words came out choked as Leira took a deep breath and let it go, slowly. She looked over at Correk, squeezing his hand for a moment. "I've had enough of losing family, even if it's to anger. Nana, you're going to explain all of this in great detail. I'm guessing you fucked something up royally. For now, tell me how I'm in danger of dying and we'll deal with the rest later."

Mara looked back over at Eireka again but Eireka looked away. She wasn't ready to let it go as easily.

"Okay, fair enough. Frankly, this is actually a better reception than I thought we might get. It's true, Leira is not a Light Elf. She's part Jaspar Elf, a large part, which explains the power she possesses."

"And it takes a few rules to get the energy to work with you. Otherwise, it can get away from you pretty quick and cause some damage to the user as well as the surrounding countryside." Jackson pulled out a slice of pizza and bit, slurping up the melted cheese. "Damn, that is good," he said, as he took another large bite.

"There's a twist, though. It's why I was in such a hurry to get Jackson. Leira is also part human on my side of the family. Not all magical beings come from Oriceran." Mara let the boxes stop in front of her as she folded her hands over her plate. "There's an old legend about human beings that some have one different chromosome that acts like a sentinel waiting for the right mixture of DNA to turn it on like a switch."

"Wait! I've heard this story before. Toni told me about it one night at the Jackalope. But it's supposed to be a myth." Leira rubbed the top of Yumfuck's head with a napkin, wiping off as much grease as she could from his green fur.

He kept on chewing as his head bobbed around and Leira moved on to wiping his ears. "Yummmmm..."

"How did you manage to get it under your arms?"

"I'll show you," he chirped. The troll lowered his head and started biting at the piece in front of him, doing a slow crawl through the pizza. Leira plucked him out of the middle before he could get to the end, wrapping him in a paper towel and setting him back on the table. A large grease stain steadily spread across the brown paper.

"That one's on me. I did ask you."

"It's not a myth," said Mara. "But most people never know they have it. It lies dormant till it's mixed in the right genetic soup. Even then, it might give someone what feels like heightened intuition or really good luck. Nobody connects the dots."

"Mixing Jaspar Elf with my human side connected all the dots..." Leira looked up at Mara as the realization grew across her face.

"You knew... you knew all along, didn't you?" Eireka rose up out of her seat. She jabbed her finger in the air in the direction of her mother, her eyes wide with amazement. "You did this!" She looked over at Jackson and back at her mother. "Wait... wait..." Her arms were stretched out in front of her, her fingers spread wide as if she was protecting herself against some unseen onslaught. "Jackson, did you stand me up? All those years ago, did you... did you get my message?"

Jackson looked at Mara for a moment as he answered. "I'm going to give a qualified no. Truth be told, I liked to drink a lot more back then. There's a chance I got it and it just didn't register."

Mara looked relieved as Jackson leaned closer to her and whispered, "You owe me."

"Can we get back to the present day? How is Leira in danger? Turner Underwood was already teaching Leira how to handle the energy," said Correk.

"Not handle, I'll bet. More like avoid. Am I right?" Jackson leaned over the table to grab one of the boxes in front of Mara, pulling out another slice. "I'm sorry I didn't take to portals a long time ago," he said, as he took a large bite.

The troll rolled himself into a fur ball and careened down the center, bouncing off a bottle or two like a pinball until he landed in front of the pizza boxes and crawled inside one. A loud trill echoed off the walls of the box as it jiggled.

Hagan stood up and reached across Correk for one of the pizza boxes. "Don't mind me. Didn't want to disturb your indignation." He sat back down opening the box and found the troll sitting in the middle, smiling up at him. "You licked all of the slices, didn't you?" The troll let out a cackle as Hagan sat back. Correk arched an eyebrow at him and passed another box to him.

"Very kind of you," said Hagan. "This is one of the more interesting family dinners I've ever been to. Go back to what you were doing, continue."

Jackson abruptly stood up as Correk leaned forward, his muscles tensing. "Easy big fellow. I'm just stretching. I was never a danger to anyone here. No one comment on that," said Jackson, holding up his hand. "Alright, avoidance of the energy is only going to get you so far. Leira, right? Strange having to ask my own grown daughter if I got her name right. Look, the energy you feel is vast. Thought to be endless. Let's just say no one has ever found the limits of magic and lived to come back and tell the rest of us. You can keep tamping it down, but something is going to happen that will catch you off guard and the energy will soar through you like a hurricane across the Sea of Rodania. When that happens, you may not be able to avoid anything."

Correk stood up, stretching to his full height, his long silver hair hanging down past his shoulders. "But learning the rules would help her."

Jackson eyed Correk with his chin tilted and looked over at Leira, the crooked grin returning to his face. "Save her. The rules would save her."

"What are they?"

"Not that simple. Magic is never that simple. This is more of a show and do kind of lesson."

Hagan scratched his chin and pointed at Jackson, taking in his entire appearance. "You mean to tell me, you've been living by these rules this whole time?"

"This look has taken me years to achieve and yes, I have but I still only have some of the energy that Leira must possess."

Eireka rose out of her seat and placed the tips of her fingers on the table as she spoke slowly. Don rose to stand next to her, his arm around her shoulders. "This extra chromosome in our family line. You knew about it." She looked pointedly at Mara. "And you knew about it?"

Jackson shrugged. "Mara, she's got me on this one. Yes, Eireka I knew all along, but your mother asked me to keep it to myself. A lot of Oricerans feared Jaspar Elves. I was told at an early age to keep that one under wraps and I heard the stories." He shook his head in disgust. "Might not have been true and probably weren't. I mean, how could anyone capture a Jaspar Elf long enough to…" He squeezed his eyes shut. "Thing is, magical beings feared that little quirk about humans just as much and a human being is a lot easier to capture on this world or the next. One thing I didn't know about of course, is that the two lines had come together."

Don slid his arm around Eireka's waist and pulled her closer. "This is clearly a long story. Longer than one weird family dinner."

"You're right." Eireka rested her head momentarily on Don's shoulder, briefly smiling at Leira as pain crossed her face. "We can't add any more to the story and Leira, it looks like you need to talk to your boss. We're going to leave."

"Eireka."

"Not now, mother. Not here." Eireka's voice was strained but she did her best to smile at her mother. Family sticks together, especially when it's the last thing I want to do. She took a long look at her daughter, instinctively sending out a thin stream of energy to wrap around her only child, checking on her. Leira felt the warm embrace and let it roll around her shoulders and run down her spine. It was as much to comfort her mother as it was something familiar and sane.

Leira looked at the two women as Correk leaned closer. "What are they doing? Are they reading minds all of a sudden?"

Leira rested her elbows on the table, leaning her chin on her hands. "Kind of. We have one family ethos that seems to be coming up a lot these days."

Correk interrupted her. "If it's the last good thing we do…"

Leira looked up surprised. "You remembered from our fight at the Driskill. This is going to be a hard one to work through, but they will."

"You all will, but you're not angry?"

"Royally pissed off. Wish there was somebody I could run down and put in handcuffs right about now. It's why I'm going to wait a beat or two to ask a lot more questions of anyone I'm blood related to. Less likely I'll do something I'll have to think about at night."

"So, that's your father. Explains a lot."

"Careful Elf. I have a lightning bolt with your name on it."

"Not in any Elf's arsenal. You know, Berens, even when things get very freaky, you're still a very lucky woman with a family like that."

Leira turned and looked at Correk with a crooked smile. "Freaky is in your vocabulary now? It's the troll's influence, isn't it? Careful or those rounded ears won't need a glamour anymore." She looked back at her mother and grandmother. "This one may take some time to unravel. My father is alive and an Elf. A Jaspar Elf." She startled and looked up at Correk. "We're not cousins…"

Hagan looked back and forth at everyone around the table

and leaned back in his chair. "I am definitely going to have to read Rose in. This is better than one of her soaps on TV but with magic." He pounded his chest with the flat of his hand as he let out a wet belch. "Oof, ate that last piece too fast. This dinner theater may do me in one of these days."

Leira looked over at Hagan and took in a deep breath, letting it out slowly, puffing out her cheeks. "Mom's right. Hell, Hagan's even right on this one. This is bad theater. No way anything else is getting settled here today. Not like this. I say we call it and let everybody take a breath. Jackson comes with me." Leira scooped up the troll in a pile of paper towels and held him out in front of her as she headed toward the door.

Hagan looked at Correk surprised. "You're not going to insist on going along?"

"Leira's armed and she has very powerful magic. She'll be fine." And there's somewhere else I need to be right now.

"Wasn't Leira I was worried about."

Mara got up to go as Jackson tried to stop her. "You're not even going to protest or ask me if I mind?"

"There's no point in arguing with my granddaughter when she gets that look in her eye. Besides, this is why I brought you across the divide. Might as well get on with it and then you can get back to your shed and your dog."

Turner Underwood looked down at the Breguet watch on his wrist. "Right on time. Of course, I would expect that of a Light Elf."

Correk marched across the patio as a few small stray leaves swirled around his cowboy boots.

"I heard about the family get-together. Jackson finally made his way to Earth. Surprised it took this long." Turner Underwood looked out over Lake Anna from his well-manicured lawn as the sun set, turning the large Texas sky red and purple.

He was dressed in a long dark wool overcoat, the bottom flapping in the cold breeze. A brown fedora with a striped ribbon around it was clamped down on his head. "Tempting to use a little magic and let the wind blow right around me. Would certainly be warmer. But then, what's the fun in that? You try to make everything comfortable all the time, in my long experience you end up missing out on some great moments. Besides, it's Austin and by tomorrow we'll be back to balmy. I suppose this is our idea of a change in seasons. Would hate to miss it."

Correk came and stood next to him, his hands clasped behind his back. He was dressed in his tunic and jeans, his eyes watering from the wind. The troll poked his head out just as the faint smell of pizza mixed with the air around him. Turner turned and smiled at Yumfuck. "Some guests enjoyed themselves at the dinner."

"I won't waste our time by asking how you could already know about Leira's father showing up or even how you know him. Doesn't matter, at least not to me. But you can answer a question for me that's been bothering me." Correk turned to look at Turner. "Are you equipped to help Leira learn everything she needs to know given her special circumstances?"

Turner pursed his lips and leaned on the silver handle of his cane. "Jackson has his doubts. Not surprised. My role was to mentor Leira, to be a guide and not to ensure anything. That is an assumption you were making. No one can guarantee that and if someone tries, thrash them with a fireball for being a damn liar. Dangerous business."

Correk folded his arms across his chest. "Tell me about the Jaspar Elves."

"I will answer your question, mostly because you won't be able to focus until I do but it's the last one today. I asked you here to discuss something else that is more important." Turner easily made his way up the stone steps to the patio, tapping his cane on each step. "Take a seat." He slowly lowered himself down into one of the wrought iron chairs around the large glass-topped table and settled back, adjusting his coat. "Where to start, exactly?"

Correk sat down across the table from him as the troll jumped out of his pocket and down his leg, scampering across the lawn to investigate the bushes. Turner smiled broadly as he watched, balancing his hands on his cane. "Some of the smartest creatures… Some would say smarter than an Elf. Definitely cagier." Turner Underwood jabbed at the air letting out a hearty laugh, but he could see Correk was not in the mood. He arched an eyebrow and started into the story again. "I suppose I could tell you about the times when Jaspar Elves were more common."

"I'm only interested in the parts that affect Leira."

Turner shut his eyes, nodding his head. "A good sign for our eventual conversation. Fine, I will cut to the chase, then." His deep-set eyes opened slowly as they narrowed, studying Correk as he talked. "Magic is another name for energy. It's like electricity in this world. It's unseen and all around us, all at once." He waved his hand in the air, dragging streams of colored light that formed into different shapes of dragons, pixies and trolls, scattering into sparks that floated up into the sky. "It isn't until someone can harness it that things change." He formed a ball of light in his hands and reshaped it like a pillow, sliding the light behind his back.

"A first-year child on Oriceran knows all of this." Correk was growing irritated and his eyes glowed momentarily as the old injury sent an ache through his body.

"Don't interrupt a fucking old Elf. I'll tell the tale the way I want to, Correk. You came to me for answers. Try trusting that I know how to set the truth free. Where was I? Ah yes, the energy of it all. Magical beings are all like the hose from a garden. Energy passes through us but isn't ours to keep for very long. Some beings can let more energy pass though and others are better at manipulating the hell out of what is available to them. But not one of them ever merges with the energy. Turn it off and you are back to your regular self. You see it now, right? That comparison to electricity was necessary."

Correk gave him a hard stare, waiting for the next part of the story. His lips were pressed together in a thin, determined line.

Turner tapped his cane hard on the grey slate in frustration. "Do not act as if this is a crisis, Elf! It's a sure way to cause harm. There is always time to pause and think before you act. Always."

Correk bristled and snapped, "I did what had to be done against Rhazdon."

"I would agree. Again, you assume without gathering information. There is a lot for you to learn, still. But first, let me finish answering your one question," Turner said, pointedly.

The troll suddenly rolled swiftly out from under a bush covered in peat moss as a mouse peeked out from the rhododendrons and just as quickly disappeared again. The troll let out a cackle and set off to follow it.

"Jaspar Elves are the same as any other magical being. They don't absorb magic, but they can channel a far larger quantity and are very clever at bending the shit out of it. I long suspected Jackson was really at least part Jaspar. Damn clever of him to keep it quiet by living in humble surroundings. There's far more he could do if he ever chose to."

"Says even more about him that with all his gifts he chose to be a scavenger."

"Just one more of nature's recyclers." Turner held his arm out wide. "Another clever ruse. His ability to detect the more powerful artifacts would be even more keen than even your own skill set. Yes, it's true. Get your fucking hackles up if you need to, won't change a thing. You might miss a detail like that, but he wouldn't. Sometimes I wonder what's buried out at that cabin in the woods. But, that's another day. He's even been able to teach a lot of his finer skills to his young protege, Louie. Be glad he's on our side now. That young Wizard has some mad skills. Alright, I'll get on with it, but patience will be required of you in the coming days, mark my words. Leira brings an ancient spark of humanity into the mix and this combination is even more rare than a Jaspar Elf. It was rare even back then and..."

Turner hesitated, letting out a gruff cough and clearing his throat. "There are no stories of anyone living to be an old Elf like myself who had the combination but..." He held up his hand to stop Correk. "There's also a good reason why that might be. A wise parent would have hidden the child and spirited them away. It's the same way that the few remaining Jaspar Elves have managed to live amongst the Oricerans peacefully. It's possible…"

"But not likely." Correk finished the sentence for him. "The power got away from them at an accelerated speed, didn't it?"

"Most likely. The light drew them in until they merged with it. That's the point of this tale. The combination of that spark of humanity means that Leira doesn't just take energy in and then let it go. She is slowly becoming one with it. Her very being is becoming a vessel for the magic."

The color drained from Correk's face as his eyes widened. "You're saying she's becoming a living artifact." He gripped the sides of his chair.

Turner nodded his head. "The most powerful kind either world has ever known, if she survives the transformation. That would be the tricky part. The unknown element."

"How fast does all of this happen?"

Turner's bushy eyebrows shot up as he wrinkled his forehead. "More unknowns. But Leira doesn't have an illness. She's not sick. Don't take that attitude. It won't help her."

"Is there a possibility we can stop the melding from happening?"

"I'm going to say with some confidence… No. That should not be our goal, anyway."

Correk pushed back the chair abruptly, scraping it along the slate. The troll emerged from the middle of a bush, looking around for trouble. He took a seat on the end of a twig and kept watch, sensing the tension in the air.

Turner tapped his cane hard again. "I didn't say that meant the end of Leira," he said, tersely. "Sit down and pay attention. We are after a different goal. To guide Leira so that she can become the conductor of the energy on a level we have never seen before. I tell you, it has to be possible," he said in a hushed tone.

"How can you say that?" Correk spit out the words, pounding his fist on the glass, rattling the table.

"Because Leira exists and therefore all things are possible, including a good outcome. But only if we focus on it to the obliteration of any other ideas. We must, or we are certain to fail. We must be sure that every decision we make is aimed at succeeding and not at preventing failure."

"There's the slimmest of differences."

"True but it will make winning this campaign possible. You had best decide right now if you have what it takes to see this all the way through."

Correk's brows knit together as a spidery trail of anger crept back up his spine, lighting up the symbols on his arms. "I think I've already proven that."

"This venture will take even more than what you have already sacrificed because it will take time and require restraint and the hardest of all, exactly what I've said all along. Belief in a good outcome." He pointed his finger at Correk, his gold cufflink twinkling in the last of the light. "It will shade what we do by the thinnest of margins but could be what changes everything."

"I understand what you're saying, you know. I won't be able to rescue her. Not again. In the end the choice will be Leira's."

"But we can teach her balance in the meantime. Don't underestimate the power of a guide. Her father will be of use as well. He may hold small details to what it's like to actually be a Jaspar Elf that could prove crucial."

"I don't trust him."

"Not a requirement. Let it go and focus. There's something else that's interesting about Leira. There's a measure of belief inside of her already that acts like a compass. It's built into her and even after everything she's been through, it's still there. A most remarkable and extraordinary thing."

"Is that part of being a Jaspar Elf?

"Does her father strike you as having that same quality?" Turner shook his head with a laugh. "No, not to me either. It's not part of that spark she was given in her DNA, either. Made her a great detective, even without any abilities and is serving her well as an agent. Leira innately believes a solution exists. I feel very good about all of this. Yes, indeed I do. Now settle in, we have something else we need to discuss and it's time we got to it."

"Tell me about Harkin." Correk said it quickly, trying to catch Turner off guard.

The Fixer didn't answer right away, studying Correk carefully. "You're hoping for a particular answer. I may not have it for you."

"I'm gathering information."

"A valuable trait that will bode well for you in your next adventures." He sat forward in his chair, leaning on the top of his cane. "Your father was an interesting Light Elf. A mixture of traits I don't see often. He was always carrying some piece of machinery in his pocket that was the start of new idea and in another pocket, there were always candy of some sort. He had a sweet tooth for a lot of things."

Correk looked out over the lake, resting back against the chair. "A fondness for women. I know already. You don't have to spare me."

The troll had found a slope along the thick green lawn and was curling himself up into a ball and rolling down, landing under the rhododendrons.

Turner wrinkled his chin pushing out his bottom lip. "I believe in that old adage of not speaking ill of the dead." He lightly tapped the cane on the slate. "Frankly, I don't have any ill to say about Harkin. He loved life and just about everything in it." He sat up straighter, looking in the same direction over the lake. A lone kayaker was pushing an oar through the water, passing effortlessly in front of the estate. "You in particular. You were the light of his life."

Correk jerked his head up, a slim reed of anger passing through him. Turner waited but the younger Elf said nothing. The Fixer tapped his chin. "I'll tell you a story about him. One of my favorites that I don't get to share much anymore. Magicals have very long memories. One of the perils of living for so long when the memories are not entirely accurate. Most aren't, you know. We tend to select something and magnify it and it stands in for the entire picture,"

Turner pushed himself to his feet, shooting out his arms to adjust the gold cufflinks with interlocking circles. "Come on, let's go down by the water." He got up and quickly veered off the carefully paved area, not waiting for Correk, tapping the cane against the soft ground. "Must have been well over a hundred years ago. You were fairly young." He snorted and lifted his cane in the air. "We were traveling together down the coast toward Maticaw. I had business with the witches that lived in that area. Your father was in search of a part or an old artifact."

They got close to the water and Correk took in a deep breath, letting his shoulders drop, but the Fixer saw the symbols flickering along his arms. "I loved hearing about what he was working on next. I have to say I didn't always understand the mechanics of it. That's what made him so unique. He saw how everything interconnected even back then."

"To the exclusion of everything."

Turner held up his free hand. "Don't fuck with me in the middle of a story." He cleared his throat. "We all make mistakes we can't fix with time, Correk, and as Elves we pay quite a price with all the years to look back." His tone softened and he put a hand on Correk's back. "You know, perhaps I will choose to stay here in the present with you today. Always a better choice. All the magic we have right at our fingertips," he said, holding up his hands, sparks dancing across his fingertips, "and the only place we are effective is in the present."

"I still miss him. All the time. But it's hard to remember him or honor him because of what he did."

Turner nodded his head, shutting his eyes and letting the sun warm his face. Yumfuck let out a squeal of delight behind them.

Turner opened his eyes and smiled gently. "What he did to his best friend or what he did to you when he left without a word? No need to answer. I'll tell you this about your father. In all the years I knew him, I never once saw him do something to harm another. Not even casually. There must be more to the stories than you know."

"I may never have more." The wind picked up off the lake, blowing Correk's hair off his shoulders. "How do I make peace without him?"

"Ah, we are getting to the root. Forgiveness. It's not on your shoulders to create it, only to accept that it's already there waiting for you to take it in. Let go of all the endless questions."

"There are rumors he's still alive."

Now it was the Fixer's turn to look surprised. His bushy eyebrows waggled, and he tapped the cane hard against the grass. "You must believe there's a grain of truth in there or you wouldn't be mentioning them. Well then, you have the answer you came here for. A grain is enough to go and search for more. But, remember what I said. Let everything from the past go if you want to be able to clearly see what's in front of you."

There was a sudden splash and Correk looked up to see the troll in the lake, holding on to the back fin of a yellow perch, slicing through the water. "I'll leave Yumfuck at home."

"I don't know. He's very good at finding just about anything."

CHAPTER FOUR

Charlie Monaghan showed up thirty minutes early to Kellari Taverna to stake out a table and take a seat facing the entrance. The restaurant was convenient for meetings at the White House less than a mile away and featured some of the best seafood in Washington. It was located on K Street along the power corridor and was already filling up with lobbyists with toothy smiles rubbing elbows with aides to Senators and Congressmen chatting up their cause. Charlie loved taking in the atmosphere as he laid a cream-colored cloth napkin across his lap.

So close... push a little harder. You want to win, don't you? The buzzing, crackling voice in Charlie's head made it hard to hear anyone else at times. It whispered to him, encouraging him to work the angles even more than he was used to doing. There were actually lines even Charlie wouldn't cross but it was all getting blurry and he found himself arguing out loud in the car or the shower. His wife even caught him shouting angrily at the yogurt in the refrigerator, tightly gripping the door. He came back from the moment feeling like he had been somewhere else and wasn't even sure how long he had been gone.

Then there was Wolfstan Humphrey and all his demands. Trying to take over his territory that he had spent years solidifying. His stomach was swirling with the turmoil. Charlie squeezed his eyes shut, licking his dry lips.

The same feeling was starting to come over him as the fast-moving waiters and chatting diners began to fade, and he listened to the crackling hum. No one means what they say. Have to be careful. Protect yourself at all times. Or else… An inky blackness crept into the irises of his eyes, momentarily dotting out the honey brown color as Charlie was lost in a swirl of anger, reliving every slight he'd ever felt.

"Charlie, good to see you! I see you got us a great table." The Senator from Oregon gave a large grin as he turned and waved at different familiar faces, letting everyone know he was in the restaurant. He clapped Charlie on the shoulder shaking him out of his dark reverie, too busy giving a wink and a nod to the Senator from Maine at another table to notice the darkness fading from Charlie's eyes. He took a seat opposite Charlie and settled in, laying the napkin across his lap. "Just coffee, please. Long workday still ahead, of course."

Charlie felt the rush of adrenaline subside inside of him, his heart slowing down just enough to get a clear thought. He blinked hard a few times and wiped the sweat off his lip with his napkin, forcing a smile as he put out his hand. He was back in the restaurant, a slight film of panic still roiling around in his gut, as he wondered how long he had checked out this time. It's getting worse. "Senator Bleeden, so glad you could make it."

An elderly man with a slight stoop wearing a dark grey pinstripe suit and blue silk tie came through the crowd, shaking hands as he went and resting a heavy hand on the occasional shoulder leaning over to whisper something conspiratorially. The top of his head caught the light from the oversized, round chandeliers overhead, shining through the thinning silver hair neatly combed over to one side and trimmed just above his ears.

Senator Thatcher made his way to the table back by the wall, making a point not to look at who he was meeting until he was almost on top of them. "Charlie Monaghan, glad I could find the time! Senator Bleeden, good to see you too." He nodded his head, keeping the smile on his face but the warm sentiment failed to make it all the way to his eyes.

"Nice to see one of our senior statesman." Senator Bleeden made a point of rising halfway and pulling out the elderly Senator's seat partway as he sat back down. It was all a show put on for each other and anyone else who might care enough to watch. Courtly manners as entertainment so they could settle in and get down to business.

Charlie watched it all unfold, waiting for the maneuvering to be finished. He had seen it played out a thousand times before and even on a good day only reluctantly played along. Today he wasn't in the mood to do more than give his signature smile, showing his even, white teeth. The waiter came brushing by their table as Charlie quickly glanced up and gave a gentle shake to his head. "Not yet, we have a few things to discuss. Bring these gentlemen their usual. We'll let you know when we're ready for more."

"The coffee's enough for me, Charlie."

"Nonsense. This is an important day. We can celebrate a little. Surely you already know how you're going to vote and both of you have drivers waiting for you to take you back to the Hill." The smile slipped off Charlie's face for a moment as he felt a twinge from somewhere deep inside. "Fortify yourselves." The smile returned to his face as he took a sip of the bourbon served neat. "Are we all in agreement on that vote, gentlemen?" He dropped his voice to just above a whisper, lifting his glass to take another sip.

Senator Bleeden waited for the waiter to put the crystal glass with gin and tonic firmly on the table before he raised it, his hand shaking making the ice cubes clink. He took a large swallow, grimacing from the cold temperature against his teeth and set the glass back down. "I don't see why not, Charlie. Makes good sense. If Axiom finds an artifact first, they should have the right to use it as they see fit."

"As long as it doesn't run contrary to American interests," Senator Thatcher quickly added, drumming his fingers on the table. It irritated Charlie that the Senator was always looking for loopholes to be used later at his convenience. Not to be trusted, not this one.

"Of course, goes without saying. We could even talk about leasing the rights to some of the artifacts for government use if the need arose. A new kind of defense contract or even do some good works if one of them turns out to cure something or make something grow faster." Charlie waved his hand impatiently. The memory of his loss in the last boardroom meeting to Pearson Cowley slithered into his mind like white smoke filling every corner. He looked at Senator Thatcher, barely containing a sneer. "So, we have the necessary votes?" He glanced down at his watch.

Senator Bleeden cleared his throat. "We do, enough with the games. Plain and simple, we do. You've been a gracious and generous host for some years now and it's noted and greatly appreciated. I would ask that you keep the mayhem to a minimum when discovering these artifacts or that could become an issue."

"It's in our best interests as well to get in and get out as cleanly as possible. Does this mean the government will back off their own excavations?"

Senator Bleeden let out a deep-throated chuckle. "Oh no, not at all. I appreciate your asking for the moon, Charlie. Be glad you got hold of a few stars. Our government has its own plans. Don't ask me about them..." The Senator raised a wrinkled hand, the knuckles knobby and twisted. "Goes even above my pay grade. You may run into them out there."

Senator Thatcher shifted uncomfortably in his seat as his junior colleague glanced sideways at him.

"You should drink down that liquid courage, Senator Thatcher. Be mindful when you're out there, Charlie. You harm a government employee and the world hears about it and it will be more difficult to protect you from the slings and arrows of the public. And when they gather together in sufficient numbers they can actually wound."

"Understood. Our teams have their instructions to be as circumspect as they can. They will not start anything…"

Senator Thatcher looked like he wanted to add something to the conversation but thought better of it.

Senator Bleeden gave him a look and cleared his throat. "I hear there's a new player on the table. This Fleeker is making some bold moves."

"I'm aware of them." They're coming for you. Be wary. "We are looking for ways to work together." Charlie shifted in his seat, swallowing the rest of his drink and holding up his hand for a refill.

"Good," said Senator Bleeden, "then I'll have the Lavraki and we can talk about the dinner Axiom is hosting for me." A waiter appeared at his side as he lifted the menu. "We can celebrate everyone's success in this new age of magic."

CHAPTER FIVE

Leira pulled up in front of Estelle's and easily slid into the spot just in front of the gate. Jackson loosened his grip on the dashboard and shifted in the seat, clearing his throat.

"You played on Turner Underwood's wet lawn this morning, didn't you?"

Leira looked at the troll as he stood up between the seats and let out a sneeze. He wiped his face on Leira's jacket, leaving a greasy smear.

"Really?"

Yumfuck let out a cackle and slid into her jacket pocket before she could stop him. "Dry cleaning will not get out troll snot," she said, still trying to wipe away the sheen.

Jackson flexed his hands, taking a look around at Rainey Street. "Gotta say, I'm a little surprised that you'd take a stranger along in this metal wagon on just your grandmother's word. You have no idea if I'm dangerous."

"You have no idea that I actually can be and it's part of my job. And this is a Mustang, not a metal wagon. Come on, you've never seen a car before?"

"I don't get out as much as you'd think."

Leira turned and looked him up and down, narrowing her eyes. "You and Mom never came through a portal to Earth? You know what, never mind. Not going to open that line of questioning today. Save it all for later." Leira felt a shudder pass through her as she opened the car door. "Metal wagon," she muttered.

Jackson got out of the car and stretched his arms over his head, smelling the air. "Where exactly are we and what is that smell?" He rubbed his belly, looking around for the source. "Come to think of it, I haven't eaten since..."

"You're fine. Those are food trucks for another time. Right now, you're going to tell me everything you know about Jaspar Elves and why I'm in danger."

"I could have done that back at the party. Wasn't that your office? This looks like a pub."

"It's a bar and I live behind it." My father is coming over to my house. I'd really rather be in a shootout right now. She bit down on her lip. "Fuck, let's do this." Leira looked over her shoulder to see if anyone was watching from Estelle's. "A lot of the people in there are my friends and they have no idea that the monsters in the closets are real and then some. You don't say a damn thing when we walk through there, and you just keep walking."

Jackson followed closely behind Leira as she headed for the gate, her chin tucked down. "I had an idea that parenting would be a lot like this. What?" He held up his hands in protest as Leira scowled at him, opening the gate. She buried her hands in the pockets of her jacket as she marched along the edge of the patio.

Estelle was standing on her step stool behind the bar and watched the pair head for the guest house as she blew a long stream of smoke out the side of her mouth, taking another long drag creating a cloud as everyone at the bar turned away from the smoke.

Leira opened the door and dropped her purse on the red velvet chair, stepping aside to let Jackson in before she pressed the door shut. She slid out of her jacket, resting it on the back of a kitchen chair as she scooped out the troll and carried him over to the sink, holding him under the faucet and squirting dish soap on him.

"Motherfucker!" He bristled as the cold water hit his neck. He grew to fit her entire hand.

"Like a fucking chia pet. Hold still. I can't wait for you to lick off the grease this time. You'll leave a trail wherever you go."

Jackson took a glance inside the bedroom and around at the living room. "Not a bad space. Nicer than my cabin. It's about the same size, though you have more toys in yours." He stopped at the kitchen door and leaned against the frame. "Don't you know you're not supposed to water them or feed them after midnight?"

Leira grabbed a dish towel and wiped off the troll as she spun around, her eyes wide. "I knew you had been to Earth before." She shook her head, frowning. "Why lie about it?"

"No lies. I've never been to Earth but doesn't mean I'm unaware of all this."

Yumfuck stood on the kitchen table and shook his entire body, spraying a fine mist in a foot-wide radius. "You could have just asked. I would have obliged," he chirped. "Oooh, lavender scent!" He licked his fur and scrambled off the table, bouncing on to the chair and scaling down the leg, running out of the room.

"His shows are on. He discovered Law and Order." Leira put down the dish towel and took a seat at the table. "What do you know that Turner Underwood can't teach me."

"It's something I have to show you more than tell you." Jackson moved cautiously toward the table, pulling out the chair.

"That's going to get annoying pretty fast. Look, we're strangers to each other and you have information I need. That's all this is right now. Show me what you know."

"Fair enough." He stretched his arms across the table, his hands open. "Take my hands." He gave a short, one-sided shrug. "You want to know, take my hands."

Leira startled as he did the same impatient twitch she did at least once a day. She put her hands into his as he grasped her fingers tightly and his eyes began to glow, the energy pulling in from the ground and up through his body, lighting up the symbols. The magic sparked between their hands and shot through Leira, lighting up her skin, casting a glow around her entire body. "What the fuck?" She looked at her arms and legs, the hairs on her arms standing on end.

"Give in to it. Fighting it will only make it harder for me to show you. A little trust will be necessary."

Leira took a deep breath, doing her best to let go. Think of your favorite places. Interrogation. She felt herself relax a little picturing the middle-aged banker who killed his wife and shot himself trying to cover it up. He eventually confessed but not until after Leira and Hagan carefully laid it all out for him. Good times. Favorite things to do. The familiar sound of handcuffs closing made her laugh.

You and I are more alike than you know.

Leira heard Jackson's voice inside her head as she instinctively pulled her hands back, but Jackson's grip was strong, and the energy was holding them together. He rose out of his chair, his chest across the table as he pulled against Leira and sat back down. Welcome to a Jaspar mind meld. It's unique to our kind. We can connect on a deeper level.

His energy was mixing with hers, intertwining as his voice rolled through her head. Haven't been able to do this since I was a kid. Don't run into too many Jaspar Elves anymore. Met a very old Elf who showed me Oriceran's past in a way that gets under your skin. The battle with Rhazdon's followers... That was a bloody mess.

Wait, you were there? How?

You'll see, hang on.

What does that mean? Leira loosened her grip around Jackson's hands but the energy still sealed them together.

Okay, this is where it gets a little tricky.

Leira felt her muscles tense under their own power as the energy surged through her. She resisted at first, wary of losing herself.

We won't let it get that far. I can feel what you're feeling. If you try, you can do the same.

Leira looked into his eyes and felt her energy open up as Jackson's thoughts came rushing into her head. Dude, slow down! His memories unreeled, spilling out without any order, filling every inch of her thoughts. Images of Oriceran spun through her mind as she watched the gargoyles in the post office fly swiftly overhead, their wingtips barely missing each other. They gracefully swooped and rose, opening the small brass-framed cubbies and inserting the mail, just as quickly darting away to gather more, their leather pouches flapping against their backs. The memory compressed into a rose-colored swirl, elongating as it looped and swirled away, replaced by a field of tall yellow flowers with blooms the size of a large melon. Underneath were entire troll villages with small houses built out of mud and shaded by the flowers. Trolls of various sizes ran between the mud houses, cackling and rolling, while others sat back and watched.

A pang of loneliness rang through Leira's body as she realized Yumfuck must have come from a village but just as quickly the memory flattened out in a swirl of yellow and zipped away. Leira took in a sharp breath as she overlooked a sharp drop down a rocky cliff, another memory. He's a scavenger.

Jackson's voice filled her head again. That's right. A noble profession. I bring back to life what others have lost or forgotten. She heard the edge in his voice and took in a deeper breath, amazed at the view over the Conca, the winding river far below. "I can feel the wind in my face," she said, amazed. Her eyes were wide-open, glowing as they darted back and forth but all she could see in front of her was the wide open-terrain of Oriceran and the sharp drop below.

It's part of the memory. I remember that venture. Not surprised it came up. There were a few hairy moments. Really seared itself into my memory.

"How much further?"

A familiar voice echoed in the memory as the image shifted away from the cliff's edge and Leira found herself looking at the Wizard, Louie, grinning as the wind ruffled his hair. His cheeks were red, and he was covered in sweat and a fine brown dust.

That was his first venture out with me. He was a fast learner.

Before Leira could say anything, the image broke into small prisms, pieces of Louie's face breaking apart, the light shining in every direction inside of her mind as it turned to colored dust and blew apart. "Fuck me…" She turned her head trying to follow the images. But just as quickly another started and Leira felt herself slip inside of the memory, forgetting where she was inside of her kitchen, sitting at the table. In front of her was a younger Eireka, laughing and running down the main pathway outside the royal gardens of the Light Elves. She was dressed in long, layered pale silks and sandals and her dark hair was tied behind her in a long braid. She looks so happy.

She was happy. That was the best time of my life.

Leira heard the pain in his voice. My father. The thought slipped into her bones.

Eireka twirled and sang as the nearby reeds bent toward her, following her voice. A sense of belonging filled Leira and held her close for a moment, dissolving with the image. That was so easy, like I could take it for granted.

That was the love we felt for each other. I wanted you to feel that for yourself. It was real.

Leira's eyes shined with tears. I've seen enough. She gathered her own energy through her feet, letting it surge up through her body, pushing at Jackson to let her hands go.

"No! Not like that!" He was shouting as a loud tear that sounded like fabric being rent slammed into both of their heads.

Leira squeezed her eyes shut from the pain and lifted her shoulders toward her ears.

A wall of energy hit Leira square in her chest knocking the wind out of her and knocking over her chair, breaking the connection with Jackson as their hands came apart. The troll rolled over onto the black and white linoleum squares of the floor and grew till his head dusted the ceiling, the tips of his fur tinged blue. Jackson looked in horror as Leira gasped for breath and a rip in the world in between appeared. Her foot dangled in the void as the troll pulled at her leg. A loud, wet sucking sound pulled at her foot, dragging her toward the world in between.

Jackson crawled over the top of the table, landing on top of Leira, one hand on the stove as he called on his own magic and pulled her away. He turned in time to see a dark mist rolling through the world in between, seeping into their world, sticking to Leira's skin and wrapping around her foot.

The troll roared in anger, shredding the mist with his claws as he pushed Jackson aside. The mist wrapped around Yumfuck's head, blinding him momentarily as he reached out and lifted Leira easily into the air, moving toward the living room. The black mist pulled at his furry head, back toward the world in between with each step as the troll strained against it, pieces of light shining through to direct him. He shook the guest house with each step as he pounded across the floor, his fur turning a darker gray blue.

Jackson summoned the energy through his feet, letting go of control as his arms lit up and the symbols rolled across his arms. He reached out and shoved the troll with the force of his magic, pushing him just beyond the reach of the dark mist as he landed right at the edge of the darkness. He felt his mind start to cloud as he scrambled backward like a crab across the small kitchen away from the tear in the world, slamming into the door of the oven. He watched in amazement, his mouth hanging open as the hole gradually dissipated, the mist leaving a black film along the floor. "What the fuck was that?" he muttered, his heart pounding.

He shook his head hard to regain his senses, wiping his face with his sleeve as he got to his feet and ran to Leira. The troll was already shrinking in size, his fur still a blue hue. "That's not supposed to happen!" he shouted. He ran a hand through his thick hair, clamping his palm down hard on top of his head, his eyes wide in amazement. "Even with your spark of humanity that shouldn't be... I mean, I've never seen anything... The troll turned blue goddammit!"

Leira was sitting up, her head resting in her hands, her elbows on her knees as she sucked in air as fast as she could to clear her mind. A wave of nausea came over her and she swallowed hard to keep down her stomach. "The...the dark mist." She was having to spit out words in gulps. Her entire body seemed to be trying to regroup.

"In some ways..." she took another breath as her stomach turned over and she let out a loud retching noise. "In some ways... you're a really great father and in some other ways your parenting skills could use some fine tuning..." She took in another deep breath and held it for a moment, slowly letting it out. "Not a good choice of first games to play with your daughter there, Dad."

Jackson was bent over, his hands on his knees peering closely at Leira as the troll stood on her shoulder, quivering from head to toe.

"You alright little guy?" Jackson put out his hand to rub Yumfuck's head and the troll growled at him, baring his sharp, tiny teeth. Jackson pulled back his hand but stayed where he was, watching Leira struggle to breathe normally. "Leira, I should have told you more before we did that, but I never would have guessed you have that kind of power. It's like you won the genetic jackpot."

"Doesn't feel like I won something. Feels like the bends. What just happened?"

Jackson stood up straight, throwing his hands up in the air. "Fuck, it was like an ocean of energy came rolling through and tore at the connection we had just because you willed it. It was too much of a power surge and flipped what your world calls a breaker. Damn thing opened up the world in between. After that, it was a freak show with some dark blob rolling out to get you, and the troll turning blue. You do know what the fuck that means when a bonded troll turns blue, don't you? It means you're inches from death… from leaving this world… from being no more!" He was waving his arms, his eyes wide and some of his hair was sticking up straight. "Your mother and grandmother would cut me up into little bits very slowly if I got you killed on our first outing! And that tall Elf, the way he looks at you… He would figure out a way to throw me into the world in between if I ever harmed you. Yeah, I noticed."

"Not sure I'd see that as the worst part of the story in that scenario and Correk is my friend."

"Sure, let's go with that."

"Because that's what it is." Leira's breathing was finally coming back to normal. "You know… if I'm dead." She gave her father a crooked smile and leaned back against the couch. "Do you know that's not even my worst encounter with the world in between?"

"What the fuck was that? I've never seen the world in between go hunting for guests."

"That is what I like to call the dark mist. It doesn't exactly hunt as much as go toward the light." Leira shut her eyes for a moment and waited for the ringing in her ears to subside. "That large surge of energy combined with the sudden opening must have pulled the dark mist toward me. It felt like an enormous weight sitting on top of me."

"I'm not sure that was the dark mist. You were ramping up the emotions there for a second after you saw your mother and demanded the magic help you. It was a winning combination. Fuck me." Jackson bent over again and took in a deep breath. "Glad you have a ferocious little friend, there or we'd be spending an eternity together, just hanging out."

Leira looked up at Jackson. "You would have followed me in."

"More like been dragged behind you but yeah, I would have gone in swinging. Oh, motherfucker this one is going to take a few minutes to get over. I almost killed my only child I just met…" Spit flew from his mouth in the excitement. "That was worse than tangling with the black octopus off the coast of Trevilsom Prison."

"Aloha," chirped the troll as he blew Jackson a raspberry.

Jackson looked at the small troll. "That can't be good."

"It can mean more than one thing," said Leira, as she let out a relieved laugh. "Not how I pictured father daughter outings either, but I have a feeling this is the norm for me. Now, tell me what else do I have to know about this energy in order to stay on this side of the veil."

Jackson looked sheepish as he sat down on the couch. "Keep your emotions in check. I thought I was going to be able to show you some good memories and help you ramp up the energy slowly without pushing it all the way through the floor. I had no idea it would upset you that much. I mean, I figured you had a good childhood. I know Eireka would have seen to that…"

"Mom wasn't around for a good chunk of it. Long story. Better saved for another time." Leira's voice grew strained.

"There's so much more I have to show you, but I need more background before we try again. That was too dangerous. For now, there are two ways I know of that you can pull back when the energy is running away from you. One is to connect your mind with another Jaspar Elf and let them tamp it down with you."

"You're the only other Jaspar Elf I know of…"

"You have the ability to sense them around you, especially when your emotions are running high. I can teach you how to do that. The other way is to use a certain kind of artifact. This is where your old dad is really going to come in handy. One of the reasons Mara was so intent on finding me." He smiled broadly, the creases around his eyes deepening but he was still sweating, and his hands were gripping his thighs. "I've heard about these artifacts before…"

"But you've never seen one. Great."

"Let me finish. I've seen one…" He got up and paced the room. "Just didn't get close enough to hold it, much less take it with me. They're rare and highly desired, if you know what I mean. The only thing I know of that can hold back magic. They date from the time when Jaspar Elves and Atlanteans were thriving and their magic was dominating everything. Enemies came up with a way to enhance common objects to siphon off energy from magical beings. There is a catch."

"There always is…"

"An artifact can only siphon off so much before it will implode and crater everything around it. You have to either find a way to leech out the magic back into the Earth or into someone else."

"Or I learn to control the energy."

"That's not exactly a possibility. You're becoming one with the energy and it's endless. You don't want to be endless."

"You said not exactly."

"You would have to be able to resist using your magic to its full potential all the time. Every time you push it, you blend a little more. The temptation grows. It's a damn rush."

"I don't believe that's the only answer."

Jackson stood there mystified. "What do you mean, you don't believe it? You think just because you say it that makes it true? That attitude comes from your mother's side of the family."

"I don't believe it. There's always a way and I'm going to find it. You said it yourself that beings like me are rare and everything you know is from stories or myths or legends."

"Pretty sure those are all fancy words for the same thing." Jackson sat back down on the couch with a whomp.

Leira set her mouth in a determined line, pressing her lips together.

"Alright, fine. I recognize that look already. You want to look for some other way, fine. But, in the meantime I'm going after one of those artifacts. Might keep you from becoming one with the universe just long enough to pull off a Berens miracle."

"Won't be the first time."

"I have just one small favor to ask. Don't tell your mother about what happened here, okay?"

Leira let out a laugh and leaned over to pat her father on the back. "Now you sound like a normal dad. Sure, we can let this one near death experience go. Of course, the troll might be a problem."

Yumfuck looked up and let out a cackle. "I can be persuaded."

"Don't worry. He likes to be paid in doughnuts."

Correk came bursting through the front door, stopping in the center of the room when he saw Jackson sitting on the couch.

Yumfuck came bounding out of the kitchen and ran across the floor, scaling the couch and climbing onto Correk's arm.

"Sorry, what? Am I on your bed?" Jackson stood up slowly as Leira watched the two move slowly around each other.

"You're still here. Didn't you have a dog to feed?" Correk pulled the couch away from the wall and reached behind, pulling out a leather tunic.

"Hello to you too." Leira stood in the kitchen doorway, her hands on her hips. "Why are you storing your stuff behind the couch?"

Correk shook out the tunic and reached under a cushion for a pair of soft leather pants.

"I can't wait to see where you hid your tall boots," said Jackson.

"Coat closet," said Correk, hustling over and pulling open the door. He pushed aside the collection of leather jackets and reached into the back for his boots.

"I can give you a drawer in my dresser, you know."

Jackson opened his mouth but Leira gave him a dead fish look and he closed it again, crossing his arms over his chest.

"Are you taking a trip? Spill, please." Leira cut him off before he could head to her bedroom to change. "I need details."

Correk looked back at Jackson who held up his hands, and back at Leira. "I need to go look for… for something."

Leira studied his face and shook her head. She plucked the troll off his shoulder and set Yumfuck on the couch. "You're with me," she said, taking Correk by the hand and pulling him into the bedroom, shutting the door. "You're looking for Harkin."

"How… what…"

"I was a very good detective, but it's not hard to tell. You've got an Oriceran starter kit in your arms and you look different. That's not the look of someone expecting trouble."

Correk suddenly smelled the air. "What in two moons is that?" He put his clothes down on the bed and stepped closer to Leira sniffing her hair. His heart began pounding. "It's in your hair. That's the same rancid odor from the world in between." He looked toward the door and back at Leira. "That black tide came looking for you here?"

"I feel we're off topic now."

Correk wrapped his arms around Leira, holding her tight. He felt the hum of her energy pass through him.

"Okay, we're doing this." Leira gently patted him on the back, her face buried in his shoulder. "It was nothing. We kicked its fucking ass. Yumfuck packs a scary punch. Okay, full disclosure, he turned a little blue, but it's already done. Not even a scrape."

Correk let go and took a step back, not saying anything.

"It's okay, I still do not need or want a babysitter."

"I'll only be gone for a few hours." He still wasn't moving, his brow furrowed.

Leira put her hands on his chest and was momentarily taken aback when her magic jumped forward twining around his. Her face reddened even as she got out the words. "I can go with you. We can look together."

"What about Jackson?"

"Father daughter day is about over. We did the usual. I showed him where I live, he met my troll, we battled the darkness in another realm in my kitchen. All that was missing was an awkward dance with everyone staring at us. That's enough for today."

"We're headed into the deep parts of the Dark Forest. Perrom heard something interesting. It may lead nowhere."

"Enough of a lead for me. Look, you have followed me anywhere to try and save my family. Let me do the same for you. Yeah?" She clapped her hands together, excited. "I'll go tell Jackson and scoop up the troll."

"You're going in that?"

"Don't start. I'm sticking with leather and jeans. It's worked this long. Get changed, we have travel plans. When we get back, I'll clean out a drawer."

CHAPTER SIX

Correk stood at the edge of the Dark Forest peering into the tangle of trees and ferns.

"This is where I found the trail. No one enters the Dark Forest from here." Perrom adjusted the long bow strapped to his back. "Crawley vipers are common in the underbrush. One bite can take down an elephant."

Leira stood between them, her eyes already glowing from the energy in the ground. "Good information. How do we avoid these vipers?"

"Don't step over dead logs or tree roots."

"So avoid ninety-five percent of the Dark Forest."

"Now you see why no one enters from here, but someone has been making this a regular route." Perrom crouched down, his irises looking over the ground. "An older Light Elf. Ely caught a glimpse of him and swore it could have been your brother."

"Harkin," muttered Correk.

Yumfuck was sitting in Correk's outstretched palm. The five inch troll stood up and cupped his paws around his mouth. "Aloha motherfuckers!" he yelled.

"Interesting guide you have there." Perrom stood back up.

"It was Leira's suggestion. Yumfuck gets a chance to roam on his home turf again."

A golden macaw rocked back and forth on a high branch calling, "Aloha motherfuckers." Its long tail dipped below the branch.

Correk arched an eyebrow and set Yumfuck on the ground. "That's why you did that. Don't wear out our welcome. The Gardener knows we're here."

Perrom stretched his arms over his head, the muscles rippling and the scales along his skin flipping back and forth.

"Thank you for coming with me, both of you." Correk looked off in the distance at the spires of the Light Elves castle.

"I've been your best friend since we were small. Of course I'm here."

"I will always be here when you need me," said Leira. Perrom tried to hide his smile, turning his head to look into the forest.

Correk pulled in magic letting his eyes light up and the symbols along his arms slowly flipped over, unsure of what to report. He scanned the ground and saw the beginning of a thick residue from a magical trail layered in different shades of dark blue. He crouched down and watched the light inside of it bend and twist. "This one must be about a week old." He put out his hand, letting his fingers pass through and felt the vibrations, aligning his magic with it for a moment. "I've never seen anything like it."

"Would you recognize Harkin's magic?" Leira stepped into the dark blue stream, letting what was left of the magic swirl around her. It feels like mixed messages. The magic pulls in different directions.

Correk rubbed his chin. "That's what I was hoping." He shook his head, unsure. "There's something familiar about it, but I can't say why."

"I thought magic trails never changed their signature."

"They don't," said Perrom. "But there's been a lot of things lately that were said to be impossible."

"We're here, let's see where it leads us. What's a few vipers between friends?" Leira set off in the forest not waiting for the others. The troll picked up speed, running alongside her.

Perrom let out a laugh and looked at Correk as he shook his head.

"That's Leira being cautious. She's not running ahead. She must be taking the viper thing seriously."

"I can hear you. Come on, an adventure awaits." She stepped carefully around a tall tree's large roots that spread across the forest floor.

They made their way through the dense foliage, the troll rolling underneath most of it. He was easily keeping up with everyone, running ahead most of the time and waiting till the group caught up with him.

The forest gradually grew denser and the light faded, unable to shine through the dense canopy. Correk lit up three balls of light in his hand, throwing them into the air and watching them zip in place above each Elf, casting a soft ring of light in three concentric circles.

He was lost in thought, listening to the chorus of wood frogs and crickets, lulling him into a peaceful reverie. A small, furry creature came leaping out at him in the darkness, his arms and legs outstretched, startling him.

"Beetlejuice! Beetlejuice! Beetlejuice!" Yumfuck grabbed onto Correk's long ponytail, swinging wildly.

"Two moons! Why is he yelling about bug juice?" Correk turned in a tight circle, trying to catch the troll who was holding on with his front paws, his legs stretched out behind him. His mouth was wide open, gulping in air broken up by a loud cackle.

Perrom and Leira turned around, their eyes aglow, ready to fight, but Leira quickly broke into a crooked smile.

"Two moons are the only swear words you know. I've tried to teach him, Perrom. I've done my best." She tilted her head with her hands on her hips, watching the pair dance together.

"Stop spinning and he'll have to land somewhere," said Perrom, with a laugh.

Correk finally stood still and Yumfuck came in for a landing on his shoulder. "Nailed it!" The small troll took a knee, holding his arms over his head. Correk tried to swat at him over and over, but Yumfuck easily jumped over chanting, "I had a little sports car. A two-forty-eight." The troll jumped again. "I drove around the corner and slammed on the brakes."

"Who has he been hanging out with now?" Leira finally reached over and grabbed the troll by the fur on the back of his neck, setting him on the ground in front of her. "I suggest you run. Run very fast. Faster than a fireball with your name on it."

Yumfuck let out a cackle and a wink and took off at a run. A faint, "Aloha motherfuckers!" could be heard echoing somewhere far ahead of them.

"It's like he's christened the woods."

"Damn pest," muttered Correk.

Leira waited for him and put her arm across his back. "You know you love him. Come on, he took your mind off just about everything there for a minute."

Perrom watched the two of them trudging through the dark forest, side by side and smiled. They came to a clearing where streaks of sunlight broke through, dappling the ground. The trail of energy was covered in a sparkling green magic that spread out over everything.

"It's the Gardener's protection," said Perrom, crouching down, to move it aside. The smile dropped from his face as he pushed the energy gently away. Underneath the dark blue trail splintered and then disappeared altogether. "Whoever this is, the Gardener's magic has wiped away the rest of his trail. He's not known for his benevolence…"

"Which means whoever it is means something to the Gardener," said Leira.

The troll suddenly reappeared, his cheeks bulging, clutching something close to his chest.

"What are you eating out here?" Leira crouched down. "How did you find candy out here? It's like your own weird superpower. What is it? I smell strawberries. Come on, hand over one of them. That's an order."

The troll reluctantly let go of one of the green Haribo gummy bears. Leira held it up in the light, turning it in every direction. "I remember these from when I was a kid. This is Earth candy. Why did they make the green ones smell like strawberries?" She saw the look on Correk's face, and her eyes widened. He held out his hand and she put the candy in his hand. "What is it?"

"Hope," he whispered, as a sliver of happiness took its place inside the ache in his chest.

"Do you want to keep going?" Leira's eyes began to glow and the symbols along her arms started to spin.

"If the Gardener is involved, we won't find what we're looking for without a lot more energy." Perrom swept aside more of his father's energy, his brow furrowed.

"I can supply that."

Correk put his hand on Leira's arm, stabilizing her magic. "No, you're still learning how to control the surges. This is enough for today. We'll find another way to keep searching, but for now, let's head home."

Mara looked at the cards in her hand and at the troll sitting across from her. She narrowed her eyes and looked at the pile of mini chocolate donuts in front of him. "Entenmann's. High stakes. Hey, why do some of them look shiny?"

Yumfuck held his cards up over his head and blew a raspberry, sticking out a green-colored tongue. He lowered the cards again, hiding his face.

"How did you get a green tongue? Nevermind, I don't want to know." Mara finally gave in and laid down her hand. "Two Light Elves and a Kilomea over two Gnomes."

Yumfuck let out a squeal of delight and laid down his cards. "Two Wood Elves over three Light Elves with a moon in the background. I win again." He crawled onto the table and pulled the red licorice toward his pile, biting on the ends of each one.

Mara pursed her lips. "Hey! What if I win those back?"

"You can have these." The troll pushed a pile of spicy pork rinds toward Mara, kicking one with his foot. "They have ghost pepper," he said, with a wink. "Even better."

"You're not fooling anybody. Those things will hollow out your insides." She picked one up and smelled it, blinking her eyes. "Has to be a Kilomea that came up with this recipe."

"Last hand." The troll stood on the table, mixing the cards in a pile. He stopped momentarily to look up at Mara. "Unless you want to get more snacks for your pile."

Mara arched an eyebrow. "Very funny. I know I'm losing. We're done, for now."

Yumfuck gave a shrug and sat down in the middle of one of the little donuts, rolling over to bury his face in the chocolate.

Mara reached for a piece of licorice while his head was down but was startled by sparks hissing across the hard wood floor of her apartment. She grabbed the licorice, holding it close to her chest.

Yumfuck abruptly raised his head, a halo of chocolate framing his face. He took one last bite, opening his mouth wide and filling his cheeks before standing up.

"Sonofabitch. Someone is opening a portal. What happened to a knock on the door?" Mara took a bite of licorice. "What? Consider this a hostess gift. How about we focus on the uninvited guests." She pulled in the magic through her feet and let it roll through her body on a low frequency.

The troll shook his head, sneezing out chocolate and taking a wide stance on the edge of the table. "I'm ready."

A slim hand shot through the opening, reaching out and waving around for something to grab onto. It opened a little wider to reveal the face of a female Light Elf with jet black hair, holding tight to a small Elven girl. The familiar foliage of the Dark Forest of Oriceran was behind them but not in a section Mara recognized.

Mara reached out and took the Elf's hand, helping her step into the living room.

"Who are…" Mara couldn't get out the words. Tumbling right behind the Elves were three Gnomes wearing matching outfits, pushing and shoving each other to climb through the portal. "A troll!" shouted the first one, drawing back his arms in horror, knocking against the others.

Mara rolled her eyes as her phone chimed and the portal closed, sending sparks skittering everywhere once again.

Thirty point two six seven two north by ninety-seven point seven four three one west. Two by three. Hold for safekeeping. The text ended with an emoji of two quarter moons.

A chill ran across Mara's shoulders. "The sign for sanctuary. Now they send a text. A little late, fellas. I thought I was out of that game. How in the hell did they know I'm out?" Mara looked up at the Elven woman. "You're a refugee? What's your name?"

The woman's blue eyes shone. "Travi, and this is my daughter Cari. We barely escaped in time."

"What's happening here?" The troll scurried back and forth along the top of the table.

"Yumfuck, you wanted the details of how I got myself caught in the world in between." Mara held up her hands at the small group crowding her living room. "Welcome to the underground transport for descendants of Rhazdon followers. I was hoping the persecution would have died down by now."

"I've heard of you," said the middle Gnome. "The name is Harry. These are my brothers, Weezer and Lincoln."

"Your mother not really care for Weezer?"

"You can hear him breathe. All. Day. Long." Lincoln elbowed his brother.

"How is that my fault? I'm just breathing? Ooh, what are you playing over here? Deuce to Seven Triple Draw?"

"Texas Hold Em, of sorts. Why is there a small party in my living room out of the blue?"

"Things have gotten worse. Rhazdon's coming out party just stirred things back up again," said Harry.

"My neighbors turned on us and burned down our cottage. We barely escaped." Travi pulled the small Elf closer to her. The child looked like a miniature duplicate of her mother.

"You're the one who used to run most of the pipeline," said Harry, his brow furrowed. "I heard you were dead."

"In a battle years ago," said Lincoln.

Weezer drew a line across his throat. "Finito."

"I get it. Dead. I was still alive, just… held up."

"Held back, held in, held out…" The troll smiled at the group. He put a paw to the side of his mouth. "The world in between where you're everywhere and nowhere all at once." He shivered from head to toe and followed it up with a cackle. Everyone looked at Mara, their eyes wide.

"Okay, okay. It's over now. I'm fine and in one piece. How did the sanctuary find me?"

"You were seen recently near the Dark Market with an Elf," said Harry. "They put a tracker on you. You should really check your stuff when traveling." He shook his head. "You never know these days."

"I'm getting that now."

"And there was no one else. We were told to stay with you till the next host arrives to pick us up."

"Sleepover!" yelled Yumfuck. He picked up a licorice stick and hopped off the table, racing to the small girl. "Have you ever seen E.T.? You'll love it. All about a friendly alien. Like us. E.T. phone home." He held up his arms till Cari picked him up and held the troll in her palm close to her face. He reached out and rubbed his soft green fur against her cheek. "You're safe now," he trilled, holding up the candy. "I can share."

Mara let out a sharp laugh. "Ease the child in to your sorta truths." She waved her hands at them, shooing them apart. "No need to stand bunched up in the middle. You may as well find a seat. If it's like the old days, this could take a while."

"How can you be sure we'll be safe?" The young Light Elf looked up at Mara.

Mara put her hands on her hips and pursed her lips. "I have something for you Cari." She reached into her pocket and pulled out a cicada. "It looks real, but this is an old artifact of mine that's been magically enhanced. If you're ever in trouble, whisper where you are into it and set it free. It'll always find me, and I'll know how to find you."

"You'll always come?"

"That's a Berens," squeaked Yumfuck. "They always show up."

"Go find a seat, Cari," said Mara, as the child carefully held onto the cicada. "Weezer, I don't know if I'd eat that. The troll licked it. No? Okay, take two. You may fit in on this planet really well."

***

Hagan stayed behind, cleaning up the pizza boxes and breaking down the tables. His mind was working overtime trying to figure out a way to explain the video to Rose. "Just the kind of thing they'd run on Access Hollywood for a hoot. She loves that show."

He paced around the table, taking a bite of cold pizza, chewing down hard on the mouthful, looking for a creative answer. He stopped and swallowed hard, giving a shrug. "On the other hand, this could be my excuse to finally tell her the truth, the whole truth and nothing but the truth." He shrugged, feeling a little relieved and took another bite of the pizza. "Even good cold. Hmmph. This could work."

The doors to the warehouse burst open, the door slamming against the wall and ricocheting back toward General Anderson as he marched into the room, followed by his aides.

Hagan startled and quickly dropped the pizza slice he was holding and wiped his hands on the tablecloth, swallowing as he looked around for a napkin for his mouth. The alarms went off on the virtual screen warning of approaching visitors as Hagan rolled his eyes. "Yeah, fuck you too," he muttered in the direction of the screen.

Alan Cohen brought up the rear, dressed in a plain blue windbreaker and looking grim. He made a point of not looking directly at Hagan.

"Sir! What can I do for you? Agent Berens isn't here at the moment…"

"Here to see you, Agent Hagan." The general walked to Hagan's desk and carefully laid down his hat at one corner and sat in the chair.

I can actually feel my colon tightening, thought Hagan.

"I suppose you've seen the video?" The general spoke in clipped words that Hagan had seen him reserve for only the worst of occasions.

My balls are actually trying to rise out of the way. "Yes sir, I saw it." Never complain, might have to explain… this time. "Some bullies were bothering the patrons and I didn't see the girls with cell phones."

"Whiskey Tango Foxtrot! That sounds like a long explanation for you fucked up!"

"That would neatly sum it up, sir."

"You know, there's only one really good reason why you're not losing your job tonight. Care to know what that is?"

"Yes sir, I'm thinking I definitely would." *My pension would, Rose will be interested, my pride could use a good reason…*

"You were the least of our damn exposure." The general's head shook with anger as he got up and marched toward the couches. Alan Cohen picked up the remote Lois and Patsy created for non-magical beings to turn on the screen and change the symbols to English. Images appeared lining up in neat squares along two rows of the troll riding a bull, the troll dancing on stage behind a guitar player, the troll dancing on someone's shoulder wearing a cowboy hat and tiny red boots, the troll waving at the cameras in front of a nursing home. The last image was of a supersized troll roaring in the face of hairy, overgrown bullies in a dark bar with Hagan right behind him. Symbols scrolled along the bottom as Alan tried to find the right button to translate. Hagan glanced up and was able to read just enough. *Well, fuck me. Some smartass thinks he's got himself a story about a dangerous alien pet. Leira will want to see this.*

"Someone put two and two together. Or five inches and eight feet." Hagan scanned the images looking for a watermark to show who bought the images.

"I'll save you the trouble. These were all compiled by a reporter at the Austin Statesman. His name is Blake Johnson and he's doing his best to convince people that the tiny little dancing fellow and the large roaring fellow are the same magical beast."

"That green hair is probably not helping." Hagan brushed a few crumbs off his tie, straightening it out. Alan shook his head behind the general, waving his hand under his chin to stop talking.

Hagan smoothed his tie down over his belly and cleared his throat. "Sir, unless he can find the troll, he can't prove anything.

It's too easy these days to create fake videos like that. Frankly, we can put out there that it's all for some action adventure movie."

The general let out a snort as Alan looked up at the steel rafters. Hagan held perfectly still. *Shit! Did I just talk him into firing me anyway? I suppose I could go back to looking for killers. Maybe it's time to retire…*

"That's not a half-assed idea at all, Hagan. Hell, we can probably get someone to actually make the damn movie! Say it was some skinny guy from Fresno in a blue bodysuit against a green screen that they squeezed into the videos."

"What about all the witnesses, sir?" A blonde with a swishy ponytail neatly pulled back spoke up, arching an eyebrow as she stared at Hagan. Hagan frowned but said nothing, waiting for the verdict.

"We make sure the late night shows get the idea to do a few jokes about the wild Yeti seen on the city streets and his tiny pal." Alan Cohen spoke up, doing his best to back up Hagan. "Or we get the tabloids at the checkout to write a story and compare it to the old blurry black and white photos. Come up with some catchy name. Say the yeti is the punk version updated."

"In the meantime, maybe I could do a little old school detective work and keep an eye on this Johnson and warn Yum… uh, the troll to lay low."

"And you'll stay out of that bar and anything anywhere near that bar? That may sound like a question but I'm only looking for confirmation."

Hagan felt a pang but nodded. "Yes sir, nowhere near. Never again."

The general smiled for the first time, putting out his hand to Hagan. "Good. Glad we could resolve this. Good man. One of the things I really value about your team."

"What's that, sir?"

The general strode over to his hat and placed it back, firmly on his head. He looked up at Hagan. "You firmly believe in solutions. One way or another we can get the job done. Need more like you."

"Yes sir, thank you sir. Uh, one more thing…"

The general stopped right at the door and turned around as Alan briefly shut his eyes and let out a sigh.

"I have a wife… her name is Rose…"

A shiny black patent leather purse with a brass clasp and a stiff, patent leather handle was positioned next to an ornate wooden box on Lacey Trader's desk.

Lacey sat behind both of them in her office on an upper floor of the Water Tower building in Chicago.

"No time like the present." She picked up the purse and set it on the ground, snapping open the clasp. The older witch began tugging at the sides, pulling it apart until there was enough space to fit her inside of it. She gently picked up the wooden box off her desk and held it close, stepping into the purse and onto the circular stairs hidden inside. "Just brilliant," she said, smiling, disappearing into the purse, as it reshaped and snapped shut behind her.

She pulled out her wand and circled it, lighting the end and casting a glow down the stone steps, deep in the recesses. "Just brilliant. Amazing. You think you've seen everything and then… poof!" She shook her head, circling round and round, going down and down the stairs, making sure the box stayed level.

Waiting at the bottom of the stairs was Mabel Garner, her hands folded one over the other in front of her, grasping her wand.

"Agent Garner, just brilliant. You, my dear are going to go far in the Silver Griffins. Whatever made you think of fitting an entire vault into a purse?"

Mabel's face warmed and she ducked her chin even as she put

back her shoulders and stood up straighter. "It was from a story my Nan told me and it wouldn't have worked without all the senior Silver Griffins adding in their magical horsepower. Team effort. It was necessary after what happened with the necklace."

"Just goes to show what can happen when we all work for a common cause. We left enough fairly dangerous artifacts in the old vault to stop anyone from searching further if someone ever tries to breach us again." Lacey stepped off the last step and into the new foyer of the vault. The old employee bathroom had been replaced by a reflecting pool of swirling waters, slowly going in a clockwise pattern.

"We have a new addition to the vault?"

"Yes, a very special one. Why don't you do the honors and see us in."

"Oh, me? Sure, well, yes, of course," Mabel sputtered, stepping forward and carefully leaning over the side as the water stilled and she her reflection began to appear. "Silver Griffin number two hundred and eighty-five, Mabel Garner," she said quickly before the water was completely still.

The water slowed and began swirling counterclockwise, sparkling bright enough to illuminate Mabel Garner's face before settling back again to a deep sea green and reversing the flow. The recognition spell had worked once again. Mabel stood up straight and blew out the breath she had been holding, puffing out her cheeks. A shudder passed across her shoulders and she pressed her lips together.

"That one always gets me too," said Lacey with a wink, startling Mabel. The far wall began to split apart with a sound like rushing sand, leaving a space just wide enough for the two witches to pass through. "Come on, it won't stay open long," said Lacey, nudging the younger witch. They passed through to the iron balcony that sat far above the repository containing the thousands of carefully curated artifacts.

Mabel walked quickly to the pedestal on the left and placed

her hand firmly on the large opaque glass ball. Lacey cradled the box under one arm and placed her hand on the other glass ball.

A virtual dashboard appeared between them. "Silver Griffin number two hundred eighty-five, Mable Garner."

"Silver Griffin number one, Lacey Trader."

"Silver dragon from Oriceran that has been artificially… Oh hell, that has been maimed and to be placed in our care."

Mabel's mouth opened to a perfect 'o' but she kept her hand where it was while the dashboard spun until it blurred, skimming over all the inventory till it came to rest in a new section of the mammoth side vault. "Magicals falling all over themselves over technology when we can do this," muttered Lacey. "Come on, let's get going. The dragon has suffered enough."

Lacey removed her hand and the screen faded. Mabel paused, looking to Lacey. "This is your show, my dear. You helped us to protect the vault."

Mabel blushed again and stepped forward, placing her hand flat against the metal door, pressing gently and waited for the spell to recognize. The air shimmered around the door and there was a click as Mabel pressed a little harder, opening the door.

She stepped inside, instantly feeling the cooler temperature of the vault with a reverse air flow and a lower pressure. Lacey passed through, the doorway scanning her body and passed Mabel, stepping up to the railing. "Hop to. We have to do this part together."

"Yes ma'am."

They each put their hands firmly on the metal railing in front of them, feeling it warm against their skin, making their hands glow an ocean blue as it read their individual biometrics. The stairs began to move with a loud creak from the center of the railing over to where Mabel and Lacey stood as the railing in their hands vanished.

Lacey started down the stairs, proving to be remarkably agile despite her years, still careful to hold the wooden box level.

Mabel came right behind her easily keeping up as they made their way down all the stairs. They turned in front of the spiraling stacks and headed for the oversized hangar door.

Mabel stepped up to the door and pressed her hand firmly against it. The laser emerged and shined a pinpoint of light into her eye and to the back of her skull. Mable held perfectly still, holding her breath till it was finished and abruptly blinked off. "Almost there," said Lacey, "at last."

Mabel removed her hand and let out the breath as the colossal door rose, pulled along by chains attached along each side and in the middle.

"Just brilliant," said Lacey, striding forward, past the whale armor.

Mabel was right behind her till she noticed the shimmering frost climbing up a far wall. "That wasn't here before. What is that? It's so colorful."

"What?" Lacey stopped and turned around to look in that direction. "Good eye. I can feel the chill from here. Behind that rolltop door is our other new installation. There are glaciers back there, rescued from the polar ice cap. They come in every color. They were made from magical waters and frozen for safekeeping long before we were even keeping records."

"What does the water do?"

Lacey chuckled. "That is open to speculation. Some say powerful healing, others say terrible diseases. Maybe it's both, it's hard to say. Don't worry, we replaced them with standard frozen water in the same size and shape. No one will ever notice." Lacey was briskly walking again, headed toward the submarine. "Come on, we have work of our own to do."

Mabel took one last look, breathing in the icy air and took off at a trot to keep up with the head of the Silver Griffins, passing the submarine and the oversized CAT scan. They came to another tall, rolling door and this time Lacey stepped forward without a word. She placed her hand against the door and waited as the laser emerged and entered her eye, venturing to the back of her skull. It blinked off and a solitary door appeared within the rolling door. "That's new," muttered Mabel.

"Clever, right? The rolling door is a ruse. We can never be too careful. Not down here, and not with this. This, my dear Mabel, is our new top secret." Lacey pushed the door open and a cacophony of noise echoed into the large chamber. Lacey smiled and stepped aside. "Ready?" she said, gesturing to Mabel.

Mabel stepped forward, her eyes wide and breathed in the warm, sweet air. "That's Oriceran!" She hurried through the door and into the dense forest, stamping her feet on the thick, dirt all around her. "There's no ceiling!" She tilted her head back and looked up, marveling at the puffy clouds far overhead. "Those are old growth oak trees and that's moss growing everywhere. This is the most amazing thing I have ever seen," she said, breathlessly. "How is it even possible?"

"Said the young agent who came up with the idea to put a giant vault in a purse I can carry anywhere. Welcome to a simulation of the Dark Forest. The Gardener even helped us install it along with his mate, a powerful Dryad. We needed a place for some of the more exotic animals that have been tortured."

Mabel's eyebrows shot up, but she didn't say a word. Instead, she waited as Lacey turned the box's opening toward the forest and slowly opened it.

The light was immediately sucked out of the room, throwing them into complete darkness. Mabel put out her hands and turned her head in every direction, ducking when she heard the loud whoosh of oversized wings flapping and a faint clicking, whirring noise.

The light gradually began to return, and Mabel looked up to see the dragon flying high overhead, its wings outstretched and the sunlight shining through the gears and engine parts. Mabel couldn't take her eyes off the creature, watching with equal measures of horror and delight. "How did that happen?" she finally managed to get out.

"Very good question. An ongoing project and part of why this room must stay a secret."

"This is a room?"

Lacey snorted, one hand on her hip, pleased with the new installation. "A room of sorts. The sky is an illusion, much like the purse. You inspired us with your idea, and we figured out how to take it even further. Sometimes solutions are right in front of us if we can only take a step back."

"All this space for one dragon…" Mabel's head was still tilted back, watching the dragon soar through dense clouds and emerge on the other side.

Lacey let out a troubled sigh. "That is the difficult part of this adventure. This place is so large because this dragon will probably not be its only resident. Something is wrong out there beyond our walls and someone is causing it. But we have been unable to figure out who, yet. Perhaps another sharp mind like yours will spot the clues we've missed and put this puzzle together, and soon." Lacey took a long look around the forest, her face strained. "If it's the last thing I do, I'll stop this menace."

CHAPTER SEVEN

Turner Underwood slowly swept his arm across the fire pit, curling his fingers one at a time into a fist, raising a warm blue flame as the sun set over the lake. "Nothing like a Texas sunset. Going to be another cold night in Austin." He looked at Correk warming his hands by the fire. "Do you need a cloak? I might have something from my travels that would fit you. These days I prefer the stylings on this planet, but I kept a lot of Oriceran clothes for nostalgia."

"The fire is enough for me. You never talk about your days on Oriceran…" Correk let the thought go, waiting to see if Turner would pick it up and tell him more. Turner was never someone to push into corners he didn't want to be in.

Turner leaned one hand on his cane and held his other near the fire, still watching the sunset as he let out a contented sigh. "Not much to tell, really." He let out a chuckle and rocked back on his heels, ducking his chin. "Not that there weren't adventures or that things didn't happen… Like I've said, the past is done and despite how much human beings like to dig it back up, the past cannot predict the future. It can only make it harder to clearly see

64

the next path. I take it you followed your path and found your next clue?"

"It's possible. Enough to keep wondering." Correk pushed his hands against his knees. "Do you ever miss your life there? Your friends or just that it's easier to create magic there?"

Turner looked at Correk, studying him. "Ah, that is the crux of your inquiry. Can you be happy somewhere new and different? This is a land where you're considered an alien even though Elves have been here for thousands of years."

"In disguise. It's not the same thing. Everything here is similar but not quite the same. There are the underground lands but they're like a third world."

Turner tapped the side of his nose, smiling at Correk. "It can be better if you can let go of the idea that you're losing something and start looking at what you're gaining. Just to be clear, I mean look beyond fast food and Dr. Pepper or giant warehouses full of things to buy."

A smile grew on Correk's face as he scuffed a boot along the slate. "Those are not bad things either."

"If that's where you set your bar then finding a lot more to love about this planet should be pretty easy. But there's more to it than that. Human beings are really wonderful creations, and this is their giant playground." Turner held out his arms expansively. "Oricerans like to point out that humans don't possess the ability to create magic on their own. Even that rare gene that sometimes heightens magic in our own kind doesn't kick in until it's mixed with magical blood. But I know that's wrong. Their magic is in their ability to cooperate and work together. Amazing things happen when you least expect it and they can overcome foes, even magical ones." He shook his head. "The trick is to get them to work together. But that does not really answer your question. Can you let go of Ossonia?"

Correk looked away, out over the lake, setting his jaw as he folded his arms across his chest. "Ossonia is not mine to let go or to keep. We have no promise to each other."

"And then there's Leira…"

"I was sent here to guide and protect Leira as an assignment."

"That young woman is a spitfire who runs toward danger the second anyone's in trouble. And look out if it's someone she cares about." Turner shook his hand in the air. "Even without magic, Leira Berens could take down a city block if it meant protecting the innocent. Not too hard on the eyes either."

Correk didn't answer, keeping his thoughts to himself. Leira is in too much danger for me to think about anything else but how to protect her.

Turner stepped back toward one of the Adirondack chairs near the fire and slowly eased himself down, sending out a stream of light to scoot the chair underneath him. He sat back, letting out a relaxed sigh, settling the cane between his legs. "Given that Leira is hardwired to protect and serve, the best way you can do your assignment is to help Leira learn how to protect herself."

Correk startled, glancing over at the old Elf to see if there were symbols running along his skin that would tell him if the old Fixer had learned how to read minds. There was nothing. "I would agree, and I intend to complete my mission, come what may."

The Fixer made a steeple with his fingers, resting his hands on his belly. "Yes, you've already proven that intention, above and beyond. Alright, we will put a pin in that idea for now and come back to it one day." Turner Underwood chuckled. "That wasn't a threat. There will come a day when you will have to choose to stay or go and not because you were told to be here. And it may come sooner than you think. I have a proposal for you. I am growing older and I need an apprentice."

The hairs along Correk's arms rose and tingled, glowing in

the night as he felt a rush of energy suddenly pour through his body and the muscles in his arms tensed. He sensed what was coming with a mixture of amazement and dread.

"Correk, I want to hand the role of Fixer to you. To teach you all the magical secrets I've learned over the years and to share the tomes I keep in a very special library to watch over the Oricerans who choose to live on Earth."

"I think the Gnomes would have something to say about you sharing valuable ancient books with me…"

"I spoke with the Gnomes already about the idea. Yes, it's true. Your work here has seasoned you and you have become a trusted warrior. You chose someone else's life over your own and yet, still survived it all. I don't want an answer now. It's a lifelong commitment and as an Elf that means hundreds of years. It will also answer your query about where you will plant your flag."

"I need to focus on other things right now."

"They're one and the same. Don't miss that point. If you accept, you will gain tools to better assist you in this assignment and when it's done, branch out to watch over more Oricerans. Think of it! You'll watch over the start of the opening of the gates after thousands of years. You'll be a part of helping Oricerans come out of the closet, so to speak and integrate with all of mankind when magic returns."

And give up on ever living on Oriceran again. The weight of what Turner was asking weighed on Correk and he stared into the distance at the moon, trying to picture the two moons of Oriceran and the reeds gently moving in time with Queen Saria's voice. Perrom, my friend.

"I can't be everywhere, despite the legend of the Fixer," said Turner. "And Leira needs one hundred percent focus. I need to become two… Think about whether or not you can step up?"

"Let me live with the idea for a while." Correk felt the chill pass through him, making the bones that had healed from the last battle ache from the cold. He passed his hand over his head, pulling in the warmth from the blue fire around his body. "I am honored to be considered..."

"Keep in mind, it's a job, a big job... Some of the shit I have seen has turned my skin green and back again. It will not always feel like an honor and at times more of a duty. But if you accept, you will learn deeper layers of magic than most ever get to know. Only the Gnomes of Oriceran have as much knowledge and only the Fixer actually gets to put it into practice. Of course, that can be fun at times, as well. The Elven ladies love it." He let out a laugh and gave a wink.

Turner Underwood held out his arms and he quietly whispered into the night air. A ball of light whizzed out toward the lake, skipping across the top like a stone creating images of the lakes of Oriceran and the large silver and red dragons that lived in their depths.

"Think about it... but not too long. I will need to start training my replacement soon and not just anyone will be chosen to be the next Fixer." Turner rested his hands back on his cane and smiled in the darkness. At least this part of the prophesy is coming true.

Perrom walked deeper into the Dark Forest till he got to the oldest stand of oak trees. It was twilight and the sun was finally going down, casting shadows on the few places where the light managed to come through the tops of the trees. Perrom was waiting patiently by the largest tree, idly letting his irises wander, watching a yellow lizard with bulging eyes studying him in return. A frog hopped over his foot, letting out a sneeze and a sigh before disappearing under the large leaves of a nearby fern. Dragonflies circled just above him, resting lightly for a moment on his head forming a buzzing crown and taking off again just as quickly, breaking formation and flying in different directions.

"You always did love the Dark Forest, just like your father." The voice was coming from the old oak tree. A female face emerged from the bark followed by arms and shoulders as a Dryad gradually freed herself. She was honey colored and wearing wide strips of bark across her torso with no boots and her dark hair spilled out over her shoulders. Flowers and vines trailed along her arms and legs.

"Hello Mom. Dramatic entrance as usual." Perrom smiled at his mother, the scales along his skin flipping over to his natural state of honey brown.

"It's more fun, don't you think?" she asked with a laugh. "I talk to so few magicals…"

"But get a kick out of scaring so many of them."

The Dryad arched her back, stretching her arms over her head. "I'm your father's alarm system. I cause alarm and stop Elves and Witches from traveling too far into the forest. It works rather well, especially since so few know I exist." The Dryad took a seat on an old tree that was rotting on the floor of the forest. She tilted her head and looked at her son. "Why are you here? You're too pragmatic, like your father," she said with a nod, "to visit without a reason."

Perrom laughed and clutched his chest. "Ouch, I visit you all the time."

"And I'm always delighted to see you. Spill it. Why are you here in the depths of the Dark Forest at night?" She studied her son more closely. "It's a female, isn't it? At last."

Perrom let his scales flip over to resemble the trees behind him, making most of him briefly disappear.

"You've been doing that since you were little, Perrom. I'm a Dryad. I can still pick you out of any background in the woods. I let you win at hide and seek. A mother's duty. Come on, give me details. I've waited a hundred years for this." She let out a laugh that echoed in the woods, shaking bats out of the trees that took flight, silhouetted against the rising two moons.

His scales flipped back, and he reappeared, his irises focused on his mother. "It's Ossonia, the Light Elf. I want to tell her how I feel."

"Isn't she Correk's intended?"

Perrom's dimples in his cheeks deepened and the Dryad smiled, the flowers on her arms opening their petals even in the dark. "Not anymore," said Perrom. "He's found someone else, an Elf on Earth."

"The plot thickens. Correk has relocated. Permanently? I suppose it doesn't matter." The Dryad stood up and took Perrom's face in her hands. "You are a wonderful being and not too hard on the eyes. You have your father's passion rolling through you."

"I'm pretty sure mothers are not allowed to point that out."

"When have I ever been like the other mothers? This was where you went to school most of your life," she said, laughing, throwing her arms wide. The flowers on her opened and shut, bending toward her voice.

"Tell her you want to court her. You've watched her from afar long enough. I've seen how she watches you when you two have walked along the edges of the forest. You have nothing to fear. She'll welcome the attention. Bring her to the forest to tell her. I will make everything bloom for you." The Dryad wrapped her arms around Perrom and kissed him on the cheek, leaving behind a smear of gold pollen. "I'm off to see the Gardener. I trust you can find your way out of the forest even with your eyes shut." She was already headed down a path, disappearing into the darkness.

"Other mothers have names, you know," he called after her, a familiar game.

"You call me, Mom, your father calls me his love. Who needs more labels?" she called back.

"You're the original flower child," he said, but this time there was no answer. He turned to head back in the other direction and let out a loud laugh. His path was lined with blooming flowers. "Thank you, Mom," he shouted.

"You're welcome," echoed through the forest, stirring the birds from their roosts.

CHAPTER EIGHT

"Has anyone seen the troll?" Mara looked around Leira's small kitchen, listening for the sound of paper rustling or a foil wrapper being peeled off, or crunching and slurping. Nothing. It was quiet as Eireka and Leira looked back at her from the other side of the small table. "No one worried? He's gone out for a constitutional. Nobody?"

"He can handle himself." Eireka held her mother's gaze.

"He's proven that on more than one occasion. Besides, he's been going out at every opportunity all along. I don't pin him down to one location anymore." Leira brushed her bangs off her forehead.

"That was before we knew about a reporter piecing the whole Yumfuck story together…"

"Quit changing the subject." Eireka took a sip of the warm coffee, peering at her mother over the edge. "Start explaining."

The silence returned to the room as Eireka and Leira sipped their coffee, patiently waiting out Mara. "You two would be great busting balls just by sitting there."

No one answered her.

"Okay, fine… I'll start. I did a horrible thing for all the right reasons. I knew what Jackson really was, and I mean that on a lot of different levels. Hell, I could have lived with the idea that he was a scavenger." Mara pointed her finger. "And you know that comes with a certain lifestyle of wandering and danger that was never going to change. That's the life you would have had."

"I ended up spending fifteen years in an asylum, instead."

The color drained from Mara's face. "Point taken. But I also knew he was a Jaspar Elf and Jackson is the one who swore me to secrecy. We were old friends before you two met, Eireka. This aging thing on Oriceran… Technically, he's a lot older than you are but…"

"Get on with the story, Nana."

Mara arched an eyebrow and pressed her lips together momentarily. "You have got to be one helluva detective. Fine, I kept his secret because he asked me to… gave my word, no less! And then, he saw you." Mara reached across the table and touched Eireka's arm, a spark of energy passing between them. Eireka's face softened but she said nothing.

"Well, that was it. Before you, Jackson was known for loving them and leaving in the middle of the night. He went out on scavenger hunts to get away from some angry Elven women as much as to find more treasure. But the look in his eyes when he was around you. I knew about the spark of humanity our family carried, of course I did. And Eireka, don't act like you were completely clueless. Berens' women have been able to weave magic like nobody's business far too easily for you to not have an idea."

"An idea, yes but you never talked about it and it only meant I could conjure up things more easily here on Earth. Hell, it wasn't enough to even get me out of the psych ward."

"Did you ever try to tell those doctors Mom wasn't crazy?"

"That hurts that you'd even ask me that, but I get it… Many

times, over and over again." Mara grew angry at the memories. "I even went to Oriceran trying to get the Gnomes to help me with a spell to just have everyone forget my beautiful daughter had ever talked about Elves or a floating castle. Of course I did! But no one would listen. They said it would expose them all."

"So, why did you lie about Jackson, the Jaspar Elf? My father…"

Mara looked down at the table but quickly sat up straighter, putting her shoulders back and lifting her chin. "I thought I was preventing something that was already coming to fruit. You, Leira… You were already on the way but that day I made sure Jackson never knew about the meeting to go to Earth, I had no idea Eireka was already pregnant. No one knew. By the time we realized it months later, Eireka was starting to get over Jackson…"

"Not true… That took years." Eireka's eyes were shining with tears. "Every time I looked at Leira and realized what she never had, the pain shot through me."

Mara looked stricken as she reached across the table, one hand on Eireka and the other on Leira's arm. "I'm sorry, I'm sorry. I did cause that. I had no business deciding for you, no matter my reasons. I was trying to prevent my grandchildren being taken by the light or the darkness. I was wrong, and I'm sorry."

"You didn't see there was a solution. You didn't even try." Leira said the words quietly.

"Yeah, that was a lapse in judgment that the world in between really knocked out of me. Imagine how much time I had to think about everything I had done."

"Wait…" A realization came over Leira's face. "That's why you were going back and forth to Oriceran. You were trying to set Mom free."

"Well, that and something more. By then, I knew it was only a matter of time before your powers started to show and I had no idea what that would even look like. But the palace was already ignoring my requests. So were the prophets, the Wood Elves, the Gnomes. I even tried the Silver Griffins. No one would listen. There wasn't a chance in hell I was going to ask them about what to do with a young Jaspar Elf with the spark of humanity inside of her."

"You were looking for Jackson." Eireka sat back in her chair as Mara nodded.

"Yes… that's the truth and almost the whole story. I got a lead on where Jackson could be found and, in my excitement while doing something else I didn't pay enough attention to what I was doing and tore a hole in the portal. The world in between sucked me right in."

Leira shuddered but tried to hide it. *The damned place is still looking for me and the light wants to be my BFF.* "You said almost…"

Mara bit her lip, carefully choosing her next words. "Children should never have to pay for the crimes of their parents."

"Interesting start. I can't tell if you're the criminal in this story or someone else." Eireka swatted Leira, shaking her head. "What? It's Nana, it's possible," said Leira.

"She's not entirely wrong," said Mara. "But no, I'm not the criminal. You might even say, I'm the hero in this long story." She held up her hands. "Don't worry, I'll give you a very short version. A long time ago, Rhazdon had an entire legion of followers…"

"This isn't starting out well." Leira leaned her head on her hand.

"I'm just going to plow through the unruly comments… The followers that survived the great war had children, and they had children. Most of the descendants wanted nothing to do with Rhazdon or those old ideas of purity and magicals coming first. But not everyone else felt the same way and the persecutions began."

"I remember hearing about those. A lot of Oriceran magicals were chased down and killed," said Eireka with widened eyes.

Mara let out a deep sigh. "All true and many others lost everything and had to go into hiding. It became impossible for some to live on Oriceran." She shrugged and held up her hands. "That wasn't good enough for me. No one deserves to be hunted down because their grandparents were fools. So... I started a rescue mission and began illegally transporting refugees from Oriceran to Earth," she blurted, letting the words hang there.

Mara looked at Leira and Eireka who were both staring back at her. "Blink one of you. Come on, this isn't really that wild of an idea. Eireka you were locked in a psych ward, I got stuck in the world in between and Leira is hanging around a royal Light Elf and is permanently bonded to a troll who she's taught to swear. And that's a description of a normal Tuesday for us."

Eireka blinked her eyes and opened and shut her mouth, finally narrowing her eyes. "How were you pulling this off by yourself? How long were you doing that? While I was locked away? How many refugees are living on Earth?"

"You really got your engine warmed up. That was a lot of questions. Let me see if I can answer them in order. I don't do any of this alone. There are hundreds of hosts on this world and about as many who help out on Oriceran. I was helping the underground portals for about five years before I got sucked into the netherworld, so yes, you weren't here for part of it. I wasn't going to turn my back on them. And I'd guesstimate there's about a thousand here by now. I hear they've kept doing it even while I was away."

Leira finally spoke, shaking her head. "You weren't away. You were in a void of time and space made up of jello and dead people."

"Not everyone was dead."

"How do you know they're still conducting transportation,

Nana." Leira arched an eyebrow and leaned forward, waiting for the answer.

"I can see you already think you know the answer and you're only half right. A Light Elf and her daughter and three Gnomes transported themselves into my apartment."

Leira and Eireka went back to staring at her.

"Oh come on, like either one of you wouldn't have helped out if they had asked you first. Leira, you run toward burning buildings that shoot death rays, not away from them."

"I don't know about death rays."

"And Eireka, I've never seen you walk by someone in need."

"She has you there, Mom. Wait, Nana, where are the travelers now?"

"Their next contact picked them up. They're in safe hands."

"And you're planning to do this again."

"Maybe. Probably."

"I hear definitely. Berens women, what are you gonna do?"

"Until we can get Oricerans to forgive the past, I suppose I'm going to keep helping. I was on my way to help and make a pit stop to see Jackson when I fell into the world in between. There, that's the whole truth."

Eireka's brow furrowed. "Why didn't you tell me all this a long time ago?"

"I was too busy meddling in your business." Mara froze, waiting to see her daughter's reaction. Eireka tried to put on a scowl but it broke into a smile and she shook her head.

Leira reached out with her hands, grasping onto her mother and grandmother. "We've all paid enough for everything that's happened in the past. It's done and it's over, well, most of it. Nana's apparently still fighting the good fight and trust me, we will talk more about that later. Turns out I have an interesting magical father. You know, a few months ago that would have been hard to take in but now it seems just about right." Leira gave a crooked smile as the magic pulsed through her hands without her summoning the energy. It circled through the other two women and came back to Leira on a lower voltage, more contained. Leira gently let go of Eireka and Mara as a smile spread across her face. "Fuck, did you feel that? Nana, there's always a solution and we all may be part of it."

"Seriously, is no one worried about where the troll has gone off to?"

CHAPTER NINE

Perrom stayed just inside the line of trees inside the Dark Forest, moving easily along the brush. The entire forest was second nature to him and felt like home. The scales along his arms and neck flipped back and forth, blending in with the foliage. The irises in his eyes moved in every direction, looking for predators in the branches overhead and along the uneven ground, at the same time keeping an eye on Light Elves walking down a path on the other side of the trees.

The castle was visible in the air, hanging against the deep blue of the sky. Clouds floated near the spires at the top. Perrom looked up in time to see a heavyset Elven woman shake out a rug from an upper window. Brightly colored weaving moths scattered from the rug, their translucent wings catching the sunlight. They were no longer needed, finished with repairing a hole.

Perrom stopped short just under a thick branch of trees and watched a trio of hissing frogs the size of a small dog leap over large roots and into a dead log. They weren't deadly but the venom in their tongues could leave an Elf paralyzed in their hands or feet for days. He slid by cautiously, careful not to jostle the log and picked up his pace. He got to the beginning of the path he was looking for, unseen by anyone else and he turned, delving deeper into the Dark Forest.

He stepped carefully, barely missing a large spider's web capable of trapping a man's head and suffocating him, and watched a family of trolls frolic under the large, flat leaves of an osiris plant, cackling and trilling as they pulled each other over and rolled in the foamy dirt. A herd of antelopes sensed his approach, despite his ability to fade into the background and they spooked, taking off for deeper parts of the forest. At last, he arrived at the edge of the sanctuary within the Dark Forest where the sunshine split through the heavy, green layered canopy in thin streams of light.

Perrom took out the small cloth pouch and pulled open the drawstring, releasing the fireflies as he blew the dust from a glowing rachel flower onto them, enhancing their light. They flew in formation just ahead of him, lighting the way as he ventured further into the darkness. Only someone who had grown up in the Dark Forest would ever venture this far on purpose.

He stepped, sure footed, feeling the ground easily through his thin-soled boots, stopping and waiting whenever he heard anything amiss or too close. The fireflies stopped with him, hovering in place. At the junction of the great trees where the oaks and the elms and the maples all stood tall in a large grove, overshadowed by the mighty ancient redwoods, planted the last time the gates were shutting, complete darkness fell except for the fireflies. Their light extended only as far as two feet around. The rest of the forest was pitch black.

Still, Perrom was perfectly comfortable standing there, at home in his childhood playground.

"What brings you this far into the sanctuary? You haven't paid me a visit in here in quite some time."

Perrom turned toward the voice, giving an easy smile. He couldn't see who was talking but he knew exactly where his father was standing. It was never a simple trick to get along with his demanding father, but he still loved him, and it showed. The fireflies responded to the sound of the Gardener of the Dark Forest's voice and swarmed over his head, giving him a halo of light cascading down around his face. Perrom was sure his father taught the small bugs to do that on purpose. It only added to the legend the few times others thought they had seen the mythical Gardener.

"I came about the sanctuary in Texas."

The Gardener gave out a light whistle and more fireflies appeared, swarming overhead casting a soft glow that extended even further lighting up where they were both standing. Perrom marveled once again at the thick carpet of moss that ran all over the ground like rolling waves of deep green water. Here and there night flowers sparkled from the light, closing their petals slowly, preferring to open only in total darkness.

"What's happened to the sanctuary?" He snapped out the words, throwing out his chest, the vines growing through his dreadlocks crawling and twisting.

"Nothing…yet. You can relax, too. Trying to look larger to scare someone off doesn't have quite the same effect on your son." All of Perrom's irises slid forward together to look at his father. "You need to come through a portal and meet with some friends of Correk's. A human who calls himself General Anderson. He has power over some of what goes on in the country you chose for your sanctuaries and he can help to protect us."

The Gardener shook his head hard, scowling. "That sanctuary has been there for years and we've been able to protect it without outside help. No… no, bringing in humans only leads to disaster. Over half of the fauna and flora in this large sanctuary were taken to keep them from extinction on their home planet."

"The general wants to help us. I believe him." Perrom pounded his chest with his fist, a common symbol by a Wood Elf that he was giving his word.

"I'm sure he does, for now. And when his interests change, so will his ideas about helping to protect the sanctuary."

"Times are changing, people on Earth know about magic and the gates will start opening sooner rather than later. You're going to have to trust someone for the sanctuaries to survive and thrive. Let's start here. Correk will help. Come through the portal with me and meet the general. If I'm wrong or you at least think I'm wrong, we can wipe the visit from his memory."

"Give me one good reason to go…"

Perrom smiled, remembering the lesson from when he was young. His father was already halfway convinced if he was choosing to bring up the game.

"In the end, the only way all of the birds and insects and animals and great trees and reeds that you've saved will survive after you're gone is if enough beings want them to. We will need to teach them to care, instead of making them afraid for their lives if they venture into the Dark Forest and meet the bogeyman. Also known as my father."

The Gardener let out a deep laugh that echoed through the forest. Perrom knew that children talked about the sound and told each other the Gardener laughed when he caught an Elf or a pixie who wandered in too far, never to be seen again.

"Come with me to the other sanctuary and meet the general. Start letting humans in on your secret. If the prophesies are right and all of this will have to move, we had better get started. It will look like we're restocking their planet and you'd rather they saw that as an opportunity to do things right this time and not an all you can eat buffet."

The Gardener bristled and the antlered lion who was never far from his side growled somewhere in the darkness. "I'll go, but one misstep, one talk of bringing more humans or letting the world know and I'll erase his memory myself and leave him standing on a small island wondering how he got there."

Perrom smiled. "Fair enough. We maroon the general if he

turns out to be an asshole. I'll come and get you when the meeting is arranged." Perrom formed a ball of light in his hands, pulling his hands apart as the portal opening appeared and grew.

"I heard you saw your mother."

"I see my mother all the time."

"I heard you want to court a Light Elf."

"Just ask me, Dad."

"Nothing really to ask." The Gardener hesitated, surprising Perrom. It wasn't like his father to ever hesitate about anything, whether he was right or not. But suddenly he was grasping his son, hugging him tight and patting him on the back, all at once.

"This is weird, Dad. I'm just asking Ossonia if I can court her."

"That's the start," boomed the Gardener, throwing up his arms. "Have I ever told you about courting your mother?"

"Not even once."

"It's a great story. Your mother tells it better. It worked out well."

"Was that it? No more verbs or adjectives or fatherly advice?"

The Gardener looked puzzled and rubbed his face. "Listen as if your mind could be changed."

Perrom's brow furrowed. "Not what I expect from you. Don't glare at me, Dad. I'm not giving you new information."

"I listen extremely well."

"It was the change your mind part I was talking about."

The Gardener arched an eyebrow, the vines in his hair rolling and turning. Perrom waited for the tension to pass and was startled when his father let out his booming laugh. "I'll come with you now and check on the sanctuary." His father reached out and laid his large, strong hand heavily on his son's shoulder, transporting them both through the opening and onto the grounds of the sanctuary before Perrom could say anything else. Perrom held still for a moment, waiting for his head to stop spinning. Never can get used to that extra twist.

They stood on the edge of the grounds, watching the cars in

the far distance driving by, no one slowing down to look. The magical cloak around the property was holding. "The sanctuary is safe."

The Gardener looked around at the rolling hills and the forest behind him as an elephant trumpeted. "Only because I defend it."

What does that mean? Perrom's irises moving in every direction scanning the ground. "Are there secrets buried here?" Bodies?

"Don't ask questions you don't want the answer to, Perrom. It's a good rule in life. Now go, I have work to do here. Come alone to tell me of the meeting and then we'll all meet." The Gardener turned and whistled as a young unicorn emerged at the top of the hill, galloping toward them. The Gardener climbed on his back, holding on to the mane as the unicorn whinnied. "You're part of this family even if no one on Oriceran knows it. Some day when I'm gone this will all be yours." He rode off without waiting for Perrom's answer.

"That's what worries me," said Perrom, even though no one was left to hear him.

CHAPTER TEN

Blake Johnson was having a pretty good day. He knew it from the moment he got up and the neighbor's dog wasn't barking. For once. There was even just enough coffee left to make one pot and no accidents on William Cannon Drive on his way to work. His old Ford pickup was making a strange noise, but he cranked up the music and sang along and decided to forget about that for the day. Leave it till tomorrow.

I'm early! He got to the parking lot at the Austin Statesman and found a spot in the third row back. Never happens!

The morning's paper was on his desk, along with an assignment to cover the Gardening Show and find some new decorating tips. "Not even going to dent this day," he muttered.

"What are you so happy about?" asked his editor, Doug Freidell, who was passing by with a clipboard holding a layout of the day's stories. He was wearing a short-sleeved yellow button-down shirt and a wide striped tie in various shades of brown.

"Didn't even know they still made those things. Leftover from the '90's?" Blake tapped the clipboard, smiling as he tilted his head to the side. "Do you leave it next to your CD collection with Wham and Duran?"

"Don't be dissin' paper. You make your living off analogue, my friend. Seriously, what's got you so giddy? It's unnerving. You're not even the guy who thinks the glass is half empty. You're the one complaining about who must have stolen the other half."

"Got a hot story I'm working on." Blake set his ten-year-old backpack left over from college down on his desk. There were still gummy outlines from where Pokemon stickers used to cover it.

"Do tell. Don't hold back from your editor. I've got a hole to fill. You have eight inches worth of words?"

"Not saying a word. Nope! Not a word until I have more. Too easy to write off."

"Awww, come on Johnson, it's not that Yeti story, is it? You do see where you're working, right? We don't do those kinds of stories. That's the real fake news."

"Not since those aliens came through a hole in mid-air outside that California restaurant. That makes this real news."

"The government said that was smoke and mirrors."

"I thought we were supposed to be the ones to figure out the news."

"Good point, we are and today your job is to ferret out the real news behind planting the best suburban garden to make all your neighbors jealous. Leave the yeti story for your off hours." His editor tapped his ball point pen impatiently against the clipboard.

"Seriously dude, no tablet? Hang on, hang on, I got a call." Blake saw the unfamiliar local number and felt his stomach knot up, wondering what had gone wrong. No, no, this is my day, dammit! "Hello?"

A high-pitched trill came through the phone followed by a loud cackle. "I hear you're looking for me." Yumfuck was using one of the burner phones Mara kept giving to him to call the reporter.

Freidell could hear the loud troll and smirked, waving his

clipboard at Blake. "Hang up, it's a prank! Someone saw your YouTube video. This is company time," he said, tapping the face of his watch. "Garden Show, fifteen inches by this afternoon. Make me proud." He was walking backward, still tapping his watch. "See if you can find something about decorating with vegetables. Alicia in Obits says that's a hot thing these days." His editor turned and waved his clipboard at another reporter as Blake rolled his eyes.

"Look, whoever this is, it's not as funny as you hoped. No one's ever heard of a talking Yeti."

"Not a yeti. They're more of an Earth thing," squeaked the troll.

"Okay, enough." Blake had his finger poised in the air to cut off the call, feeling the edges of his good mood fading away.

"I'll prove it!" Yumfuck let out another cackle and hung up, quickly taking a selfie of himself using a selfie stick to push the button. He was standing on top of a pink box in front of Voodoo Doughnuts front window. The tall emblem with an outline of the voodoo doll doughnut logo. He texted the picture to the reporter and typed, 'see you soon', hopping off the box and sliding the phone under the lid, lifting it all over his head as he moved quickly down the street.

"Busy day," he chirped to a couple walking by, holding hands. They looked at each other and shook their heads.

"Keep Austin weird," the woman said.

"Now, that is lazy," said her husband. "Getting your tiny dog to pick up your doughnuts. What do you think that was? Some kind of teacup chihuahua?"

"You'd totally do it if you weren't so lazy you wouldn't take the time to teach the dog."

"Totally."

A man walked by the troll, his sunglasses firmly on his face after a rager last night and stopped to watch the bobbing box till it turned the corner on San Jacinto Boulevard. "That tequila was a little more potent than I thought." He scratched his head and went into the shop, walking up to the counter. "I'll have whatever the little hairy dude was having and some strong black coffee."

Harkin emerged from the Dark Market ducking past a wizard holding aloft a long wooden pike with different artifacts attached to it, shouting about his new finds. He jostled a magical in a cloak, shoving him hard into one of the last tables.

"Excuse me, my mistake," he said, keeping his tone even. Too many in the Dark Market would bring out weapons for far less. The magical turned and Harkin felt a chill all the way to his bones. "Wolfstan Humphrey," he hissed.

"It seems both our deaths were merely rumors." Wolfstan gave a sly smile. "Good to see you doing so well. I trust you found everything you needed?"

"What the hell are you doing here? I know what you're trying to create?"

"Trying? Say hello to Correk for me. Oh no, that's right. He thinks you're dead. I tried to tell him, but he wouldn't listen. Hardheaded like his old man, which means you can't help him," he sneered.

Harkin lunged for Wolfstan, his hands reaching for his neck, but Wolfstan was ready and pulled the shadows around his body, easily slipping away. Harkin was left grasping at air and wondering if his old cellmate was finally coming out into the open. "Maybe it's time I did the same."

CHAPTER ELEVEN

Blake came running into Voodoo Doughnuts waving his phone. He pushed past the line that was starting to form in the late morning and shoved the picture of the troll smiling at the camera at the young man behind the cash register.

"That'll be eight and change," said the man, ignoring Blake's phone as he helped the customer in front of him. He looked more bored than anything else.

Blake leaned on the counter, breathing hard and waited till the customer slowly took their change and counted it, putting it in their pocket and picked up the bag of doughnuts.

"Next!"

A woman in shorts and a puffy coat walked toward the counter.

"Wait! I have to know and then I'll leave you alone. You see this... this... furry guy in here today?"

"I don't talk to cops and I make a real point of not talking to crazy cops. What'll you have?" The man turned his attention back to the new customer as she unzipped the front of her coat.

"That's not a cop," said the woman, looking Blake up and down. "Cops don't wear hoodies." She peered over the edge of his phone. "Yeah, sure, I've seen the little guy in here a few times. Loves the doughnuts but never carries a wallet. Someone always helps him out, though. Cute! You must have missed him a little while ago."

The color drained from Blake's face. Even he wasn't sure if the story he was chasing was true. He looked at the woman, his eyes shining till he noticed the t-shirt underneath her puffy jacket. She was wearing a green t-shirt with a surveillance camera on the front and underneath was printed, they're watching.

Blake shook his head at her, annoyed. "Really? I'm trying to do a serious job here, lady."

"Okay! That's enough." The cashier waved at Blake with a large, sweeping motion. "Move it along, buddy. You're not even the weirdest thing I'll see today but it's a little early. Come on, go pester someone else."

Blake stormed off toward the front, still waving the picture of the troll, angry that he was duped.

"Hey, hairy little dude! You got a picture!" The man in sunglasses smiled as he took another sip of his coffee. He was carefully leaning back against the wall near the front of the store right by the small stage. "You think you could send that to me if I give you my number?"

"You saw him?"

"Saw him and the box of doughnuts he rode out of here." The man smiled again, briefly shutting his eyes. "Long night, if you know what I mean." He sat forward and sipped his coffee. "Good stuff, black gold."

Blake licked his lips, feeling hopeful and foolish all at once. "You see which way he went?"

"Oh sure, headed down San Jacinto last I saw him. Moving along. Strong little dude. Box never tilted." He held his hands up in the air over his head to illustrate.

Blake ran out to the street and jogged to the corner looking in both directions but there was no sign of the troll. "Dammit!"

His phone pinged and he look down. Another selfie but this time the troll was standing outside of Cheer Up Charlies, flanked by two large drag queens getting ready for the cabaret brunch show. Blake ground his teeth in frustration and stared at his phone. He ran back to his car and took off, gunning the motor. He had to know.

The cashier saw Blake's car speed by the front window, the tires squealing and shook his head. "That man is going to give himself a stroke. Needs to ease up," he muttered. He looked up and yelled next, still talking. "Little furry hamster is in here all the time," he said to a trio of girls visiting Austin from a small town in Oregon who were busy trying to figure out what to get. "Finally had to start comping him a few so he'd stop licking them all to figure out what he'd like. Gotta love Austin. We do our best not to hate on anybody. What'll it be?"

CHAPTER TWELVE

Charlie Monaghan was losing bits and pieces of time. He was sure of it. He found himself gritting his teeth, biting down hard trying to remember what he was just doing. Can't be a stroke. Someone else would have noticed. It was making him work even harder at controlling whatever he could around him. Never let 'em see you sweat, Charlie, old man. He carefully wiped his forehead with a starched white cotton handkerchief, careful not to muss the front of his hair. Not when you're so close.

Charlie had plans… a lot of plans. At the center of all of them was Oriceran. He smiled at the thought. "Always good to be first at cornering the market on anything. Thank you, Langston Rogers for needing a favor so badly. Thank you, Louie for your services." He raised his glass of two fingers worth of aged bourbon and took a large gulp. His cufflink twinkled in the light. "It's good to be the king, despite Pearson Cowley." He sneered as he took another swallow. So the board had voted against Charlie. That damnable Wizard will give me enough of what I need. The board will thank me when this is done. Charlie was always sure he was right, but lately there was an inner voice that was urging him on and making him feel he couldn't lose. It helped him with his ambitious plans.

A few groups deep within Axiom Industries were quietly shifting gears away from their old lines of business and refitting to be able to do experiments on longevity, grow more food faster, and even build a better weapon. Even if the weapon was part animal and part artifact. But they all were operating off the books, funded with money Charlie had been siphoning from the company for years, one penny at a time. Too small for anyone to notice but it had all added up to millions of dollars.

A war chest! That's the key to everything! Charlie stood by his window on the top floor of the building, looking out over the Richmond, Virginia skyline. "We need to get to the artifacts first." He looked down at his tie, straightening it out and saw that a button had chipped. Imperfection. "Tsk, will have to get rid of this one." It bothered his wife every time he insisted on throwing something away because of some flaw that sometimes only he could see.

He saw it all as necessary if he was going to maintain control over the three separate projects.

Each of the groups operating within Axiom knew nothing about the other and operated at black sites, removed from any official company sites in plain buildings that looked shuttered from the outside. Workers were bussed in for their shifts, so no cars would be suddenly parked around the locations. Updates were funneled through several layers of managers who only knew the name of the contact directly above them. At the top layer they all reported to one person who passed on anything interesting or of note to Charlie. He was the only person who knew of Charlie's involvement in any of it or the connection to Axiom. Not even the connection to Charlie knew where the funding was coming from for the artifacts or the research. Only that there was a lot of it and it was at their disposal, as long as they produced results.

He was also the only person Charlie was sure would not betray him.

He set his glass down and looked through his phone, dialing the number marked Kyomi. "Hello, anything to report?"

The tall Elf on the other end of the line looked up from the liquid pool of silver in the stone basin in front of him. He was summoning images from each of the hidden locations, watching them work.

Kyomi was still nursing hurt feelings after everything came out and he was removed from the Prophets. Not even an apology to Queen Saria or the King or even Correk encouraged the group to keep him in the end. No one trusted him and they said it was better if he left. A rumor was started that he had introduced Rhazdon to the prophets in the first place. Over time, his loneliness grew as he found himself without friends or purpose.

All lies. Bitterness began to creep into his heart. Eventually, he had found his way to the Dark Market, and heard there was someone on Earth looking for someone with leadership capabilities to help clear the way for when the gates opened again.

Charlie Monaghan was doing his best to play to his audience and sell them on what his projects could do for them. Sell them the sizzle instead of the steak. "Are we on target?" He jingled the coins in his pocket nervously.

Kyomi had smiled when he heard about the project from some old scavenger Gnomes working out of the Dark Market. They were still willing to talk to him but only because they had a grudging respect for his alliance with Rhazdon. They believed the lies. Kyomi did his best to hide his anger and disgust and got what he needed to find Charlie Monaghan and his projects. It wasn't that hard after that to convince him of his motivation for staying on track and keeping things to himself. No one would have listened long enough to hear him out anyway.

But this was a way back into everyone's good graces. The three projects held his redemption. He believed the prophesy that

Oriceran's time was coming to an end and his people would need to emigrate. He wanted to be the one who rescued them all.

Charlie Monaghan was a convenience he was sure he could ultimately control.

"Progress is being made but there's nothing new. We will need more artifacts soon. Stronger ones. Can your source deliver?" Kyomi had suspicions about who was the magical being that was helping them, but no real proof. Had to be one of the scavengers from the Dark Market. One of the better ones.

"He has so far, hasn't he?" Charlie's voice sounded cold. He could feel the darkness creeping over him as a wave of panic crept up his spine. "Do you have everything you need in your secure location?" He was spitting the words out as fast as he could, knowing he was about to black out and come to just minutes later with no memory of what he might have said in the meantime. He gripped the phone tighter as his eyes grew entirely black.

"There's more supplies here than I need. I don't even know what half of these things are for." Kyomi wasn't going to mention his trips through portals back to Oriceran. He still had a certain loyalty to the Light Elves. Everything is just a misunderstanding that will straighten itself out. Time to take a little trip. Travel to where the veil is thinner and we can meet. "Charlie?"

"I'm sure you won't want to let us down."

"Us? Who else are you talking about Charlie?" The same familiar chill came over Kyomi. The memory of watching Rhazdon transform from a Gnome into an Atlantean swept through him. "What else don't I know?"

"Huh?" Charlie felt the fog lift and a dull headache beating in his head. He felt like he was forgetting something, some important detail. A trip was in order. Check with my assistant. He felt the sweat up the middle of his back. She'll have a note on it. Just a momentary slip. Kyomi was still sputtering in his ear about telling the truth. "What?" He did his best not to sound startled, but the headache was making it harder to think. "There's nothing else. No, no, I'm the only one. I created this. The ideas are all mine." He looked down and saw a message from Wolfstan Humphrey, making his head pound more. Charlie felt a surge of pride and tapped his chest hard. "If even one of these projects succeeds, it will be big and become a new way of life. Improve the quality of life for millions."

Not for Oricerans. Kyomi kept the thought to himself. The advantage was all his. He knew more about each of the projects than Charlie Monaghan. All the information filtered through him. And best of all, he had magic on his side. A winning combination, he was sure of it. "Of course, Charlie. All is well. Everything's on track. I'll send the updates as I have them. Soon."

Charlie hung up the phone, his mouth dry even as sweat trickled down the middle of his back. He didn't see the transparent bubble creating a soft spot in the veil pushing into this world, a dark mist creeping around the edges. "Nothing can trace back to me." His head jerked up. He could have sworn he heard someone answer, nothing will, trust us.

CHAPTER THIRTEEN

"Patsy, did you get all of that?" Lois pushed her glasses up her nose, her eyes wide. Her wand was aimed at the overhead screen watching Charlie Monaghan pace his office.

"Wooeee, that sent chills through my whole body that a nice Excaliburation spell couldn't even touch!" Patsy was sitting in her office chair, just under the screen, her head tilted back so she could take it all in.

"Like those two are plotting the end of the worlds." Lois leaned closer toward the screen. She was sure she saw something peculiar in Charlie's eyes for just a moment. Whatever the hell that was, it's passed. Still… may have to chat with Lacey Trader. Her face tensed for a moment, but she put back on a smile for Patsy. No need to start rumors. Not this kind, anyway.

"Well, as we know it." Patsy loaded up her mouth with the green peanut M&Ms from a baggie in her pocket, chomping down hard.

"I'm telling you. Fools to the left of me, traitors to the right. Here I am…"

"Lucky to be here in the middle with me." Patsy flinched, anticipating a magical poke from Lois.

Lois let out a laugh and a snort, her glasses sliding part of the way down her nose again. "I wasn't going to poke you. Geez, that was a lot to take in, and you haven't seen a lot of battlefield action."

"Well, lately. It's starting to add up," said Patsy. "I wonder what became of that dragon."

"Best not to wonder about any of it. I doubt we'll ever know." Lois raised her wand toward the overhead screen as a thin electric blue stream of light fed into it scrambling the images into symbols that compressed into a square and zipped off to the side. "Sent! General's got his report and we can relax, like that's possible after all that nonsense! They always think they're so smart." She shook her head. "It's why I'm of the opinion that criminals are morons and most other beings are basically good, especially my Earl. Keeps me optimistic in general."

Lois wandered back to her desk, tearing off the spell of the day page from her calendar and glancing at the spell for making potent itching powder. "Ah, a classic. Haven't used that in years...," she muttered to herself.

"I see what you mean. That young Wizard could have kept his yap shut about his customer list even if we did have him dead to rights on scavenger hunting in our neck of the woods."

"Darkness like that has a way of coming out. Trust me, I've seen it happen all the time in cases over the years." A sour look came over her face. "And by the time we had the details that kind of darkness would have seeped inside of him. Louie made the right choice on more than one level."

"And may never even know it! Foolish human. Knows about magic and it never occurs to him we could be listening in this whole time."

"I don't think that Charlie Monaghan is doing a lot of deep thinking these days."

Patsy pointed her wand at a nearby wall, sending out a stream of magic that pushed off, sending her rolling chair across the wall. She came to a gentle stop near her desk and opened the drawer, pulling out her reserve Twizzlers.

"Patsy, if you're going to keep eating candy like that you might want to consider at least walking across the room to get them."

Patsy crossed her arms across her chest, tucking her wand in where it couldn't be seen and briefly considering giving Lois a nice jolt of a magical what-for but let it pass. "You may have a point." Patsy suddenly sat up straight, throwing her arms in the air. "What a plot twist! An old prophet turns out to be a traitor! General Hospital couldn't have done a better reveal! I almost expected some forgotten twin to show up halfway through their conversation." She bit down on a red licorice and chewed excitedly.

"So tense! I was on the edge of my seat listening to those two conjure up a twisted new world…"

"Here, let me help you out. Sit back in your chair a second." Patsy waved her wand in a rolling wave as the back of Lois' chair began to undulate and massage her. The top of the chair reshaped itself into two hands, gently rubbing her neck.

"The best… How do you think the world would feel if they knew we stood between them and that kind of dark mess?"

"I'd say nervous, Lois."

Lois swiveled in her chair, the meshed hands growing out the top of the chair still massaging her neck. "Someone should let Pearson Cowley know what's happening under his nose."

"The Silver Griffins will take care of that one. Report's on its way to the general. We can relax! Hey, there's a few minutes left of Hoda and Jenna on." Patsy waved her wand toward the screen. "Today's the makeover day! We should see about getting a couple of those."

"Patsy, if I wanted a makeover I'd wave my wand. This look has taken me decades to perfect. Righteously badass suburban Witch."

"Yeah, the sparkly cat pin on your favorite sweater set really finishes off the look. Didn't know kilts were still a thing among the senior set."

"I'm not changing a thing," she said, as she finally let out a small zing, poking Patsy in the ribs.

CHAPTER FOURTEEN

Jackson walked nervously along the road toward the Dark Market, looking over his shoulder and glancing into the nearby forest.

"Expecting company?" Leira felt the magic surging through her like a vibrating hum now that she was back on Oriceran. She opened and closed her hands, flexing her fingers.

"No, just not used to approaching the market with somebody working for some government agency and, by the way, she's my daughter. Been wondering if I should introduce you as kin or let it go."

"Let it go… for now. We have bigger things to worry about."

"Tell me again why we had to cross worlds to find Louie and you couldn't contact him through your what is it, PDF?"

"I don't want to explain that magic has become an itchy finger on a loaded gun for me. They wouldn't take it well. And if I asked too many questions about Louie they'd want to know why. I do my best to keep lying to the bare minimum and only with felons."

She opened and closed her hands again as the symbols along her arms briefly lit up and died down.

"What was that? What are you doing?"

"Not used to this much magic right at my fingertips. It's like it's always there on high. Why didn't I feel this on other visits?" She picked up the pace, feeling her heart rate quicken, fighting the instinct to run it off.

Jackson gave her a look up and down, stopping at her blue and orange Merrell running shoes.

Leira always liked to have on her favorite pair when walking into unknown trouble. An outing with her father to the Dark Market fit the bill.

"Some pretty colorful shoes you got on there. Resist the urge to take off running. I'm in no mood to keep up with you." He scratched his head, tucking the shorter hair behind his ears. "Magic isn't like the fairytales. It isn't just there or not there at the same levels all the time. People who can access it have to be willing to take it in, give the energy access. Magic isn't something you do as much as something you feel and you grow into it, especially if you're a Jaspar Elf. Didn't Mara tell you any of this?"

"Nana may have been waiting for the right moment and then shit happened. She took a detour into the world in between trying to find you."

"You have a pretty good potty mouth going there. Another gift from Mara."

"Thanks for noticing, motherfucker." Leira gave him a dead fish look but kept moving. "And you have a mullet that isn't popular anymore on two entire worlds."

"Nice touch. Explains a lot about the troll. I'm going to assume you said that with some affection. You dig in deeper when challenged. You get that from me."

Leira stopped in her tracks and felt her legs shake for a moment as the energy settled down, feeding into the ground. Nearby, a doe nudged her fawn back, deeper into the forest, glancing fearfully at Leira as they bounded away. The animals can feel it pulsing off me. I need Correk, or even Hagan here right now. Not this stranger. "Jackson, I get that you are probably my father, but I just met you. I might have gotten green eyes or your chin but that's about it. Don't rush this whole thing. I'm a grown ass woman who has an entire life on a different planet and I was told you were dead."

"That wasn't my doing." Jackson set his jaw, his hands on his hips.

Leira recognized the gesture she had made herself a thousand times and rolled her eyes. "Let's just start with finding this arti-fact that can slow the magic down and we can work from there." She walked on, taking bigger strides as she watched the trolls rolling through the grass away from the path. The trees gave a loud rustle and birds took to the air, flying away from her.

Jackson looked up at the flight of the geese overhead and reached out, grabbing Leira tightly by the arm, flowing his own magic into her, leveling down the energy. Leira was about to pull back when she felt the energy get easier to control and some-thing more. She looked up at Jackson, startled. "I felt your inten-tions. Damn, that was weird. You really are trying to do this father thing." The tall grass at the edge of the path straightened up as the energy slowed. The edges closest to her stayed bent in a perfect circle. Wonder if that's what made crop circles.

"Call it instinct. Not bad at having a dog either. We have to stop by my cabin and look after Roscoe. He's too old to stay alone for very long. Not big on long walks anymore but he needs an ear rub every so often. What? Keep talking to keep 'em calm. That's what the parenting book said." He let go of Leira's arm slowly as she took a deep breath, waiting to see if the energy surged through her system again.

"You're using a parenting book on me." Leira let out the breath she was holding and gave a crooked smile even as she shook her head. "I'll give you some credit, Jackson. You are trying pretty hard, here."

Jackson reached into a deep pocket of his tunic and pulled out a handful of caramels. "I even have these just in case…"

"Just in case I throw a tantrum at the Dark Market?" Leira let out a snort of laughter and took one from his hand. "You may have to just get to know me and let the Dr. Spock stuff go." Leira saw a horse and buggy coming around the bend, packed with Elves and Gnomes and even a Kilomea headed in the direction of the market. She turned and started walking for the market, stepping to the edge of the grassy path as the buggy passed them. The Kilomea looked over the side at the grass circle and up at Leira, grimacing.

"That was not a friendly grunt."

"They don't do friendly very well. If he's not raising a weapon at you, just ignore him. They aren't very subtle creatures."

Leira felt her chest expand easily, taking in air. "See that's the kind of fatherly advice I can use. Thanks for the assist back there. It helped. The energy flow has slowed down."

"It can be tricky for any magical creature coming into their own who didn't grow up on Oriceran. When the gates finally open there will be a lot of people losing their shit trying to get their sea legs."

The market came into view, the large colorful tents taking up most of the horizon and the chatter from the market carrying all the way to them. The horse and buggy that had passed them on the road was making a turn coming back this way with a new load of customers. Leira stepped aside again with Jackson right behind her as they came closer to the entrance.

Jackson walked up to the table out front and knocked hard on the top. "Ronnie, wake up. I know you're in there. Ronnie!" He pounded a little harder, shaking the stones on the top. "Does Louie know you sleep under the table with his wares spread out. This isn't the best neighborhood."

The old Gnome poked his head out from under the table, rubbing his eyes. "Louie isn't here. Come back later."

"Not exactly the best sales pitch, Ronnie."

"Not exactly a good salesman." Ronnie looked up into the

sunlight as he crawled all the way out from under the table and stood up. "Oh, it's you, Jackson. Same answer, Louie's not here. He's off on some mission or adventure. Not really sure." Ronnie opened his mouth wide, yawning. He reached under the table and pulled out a battered bowler hat, brushing off dirt and placing it on his head, tilted to one side.

Leira stood to the side, picking up different artifacts and holding them in her hands, feeling the hum of the stored energy. Ronnie kept taking sideways glances at her, interested as he spoke to Jackson. "Not sure when he'll be back. He doesn't keep a regular schedule."

"Tell him I'm looking for him and it's important."

"Where can he… Hey, I know you." Ronnie pointed a stubby finger at Leira. "You're that Elf chick from Earth that Louie likes. You have some badass power or something. No wonder you can handle those stones like they were marbles." Ronnie smiled, placing one hand to the side of his mouth and saying, conspiratorially, "He told me not to tell you, but he kind of has a thing for you. Louie likes women who could kick his ass."

Jackson stared at the Gnome. "That's my kid." He hitched a thumb over his shoulder at Leira.

The Gnome's eyebrows shot up and wrinkled his forehead. "Well, then this is awkward."

Leira gave a crooked smile watching Jackson glare at the Gnome. "It's still weird," she muttered.

"You want to find Louie, ask the kid here. He's working for you now, isn't he?" The Gnome's voice rose to a defensive whine, trying to regain some ground with Jackson.

"Not me, exactly and I'm not in charge of watching him this week." Leira absentmindedly picked up a blue glass stone and held it closer to get a better look at the silver veins running through it. The stone rattled in her palm as rays of piercing silver light shot out in four directions, illuminating the nearby tables and bushes.

Leira quickly dropped the stone back in the box and took a step back as Jackson stepped between her and the table. Confused vendors looked up, trying to find the source of the light and customers stood around, their mouths open. Jackson noticed the Kilomea from earlier looking in their direction, squinting his eyes. He held his gaze and planted his feet, his hand resting on the hilt of his knife.

"What the... did you see... how the hell... you captured light..." The Gnome spun around and around, looking at Leira and Jackson, words sputtering out of his mouth.

"Silence," hissed Jackson between clenched teeth. "Stop moving or I'll nail your hairy feet to the ground." He looked at Leira who was standing firmly, keeping her eye on the Kilomea. "You okay?"

"Doing just fine. I can hold my own in a battle, you know." Leira gave a low growl, her eyes briefly glowing.

"Probably better than me, I'd wager. Let's not find out today. You get the message to Louie." He swatted at Ronnie, closing his mouth for him. "Stop gaping like that. You're attracting the mealy gnats." He jabbed a finger into Ronnie's chest. "I know you have ways to contact Louie on this world or the other. You tell him I said it was go time. He'll understand, and you forget what you saw here. Don't mess with my kid." His voice was menacing.

"Oh brother." Leira rolled her eyes and set off back down the road at a fast clip. The sooner I get away from the market, the better.

Jackson looked up, surprised and took off at a jog to catch up with Leira. "What now?"

"Don't mess with my kid? Really?"

Jackson put out his arms at his sides. "Seemed natural to say it."

"I'm usually the one doing the messing, and I'm not in need of defending. You keep saying you know Nana. She would have kicked your ass for good measure if you said something like that around her. You're gonna need to fine tune your routine or we can't keep taking this act on the road."

"Duly noted. Is it okay if I point out we're headed in the wrong direction? Cabin is this way."

"Deep in the woods, should have known. Let's go…" Leira plowed ahead without asking directions. The sooner we can get home, the better.

"This is kinda fun, isn't it? Our own little adventure… I really think there were a few bonding moments back there." Jackson easily kept up the pace right behind her.

"How about you try one of those caramels and we walk in silence."

"Now, see? That's just like me too. Some things are just hardwired."

Leira smiled in spite of herself as they walked deeper into the woods. Behind them at the edge of the road the Kilomea watched them fade into the green forest, carefully studying the pair. Wolfstan Humphrey would be interested in knowing and would pay a small fee.

CHAPTER FIFTEEN

Charlie Monaghan couldn't help himself. He had to make a personal appearance at the gathering. Everything about the meeting was unusual. It was being held in the middle of a remote field in the middle of Iowa among tall green plants not normally seen on Earth. A long low wooden table was set up in the middle of the rows, away from the nearby road where anyone might accidentally see the remarkable sight and worse, film it for social media.

There were enough conspiracy groups building a case that the magic popping up on Earth was actually very real. Along with it came a lot of stories about being overrun by magic that was seeping onto posts and tweets. It wasn't that Charlie cared if the general population knew magic was all around them. But he wanted it done on his terms and on his timetable and after he had his share of the new world order. The one he was determined to create, despite Wolfstan Humphrey and his demands. It was getting increasingly difficult to plow forward with Wolfstan redirecting his every move, boxing him into ever tighter corners. Today's big event were on his orders.

Charlie bristled but kept smiling at the first arrivals.

On one side of the table sat a row of six businessmen from around the world, nervously tapping the table or busy fingering one of the nearby plants, marveling at how it moved with the sound of their voices.

Charlie checked his wristwatch. Thank God, no time is missing. He had taken a large glass of liquid courage before driving to the site from the Axiom headquarters only an hour away from the fields. These were his privately-owned fields, over two hundred acres set aside for experiments the government wasn't as anxious to approve. "The time is nigh, gentlemen..."

He was interrupted by sparks scattering across the table as some of the group ducked or covered their heads with their arms. A portal opened just on the other side of the table in the exact coordinates Charlie had so carefully provided for the other attendees. Out stepped a group of Light Elves with Kyomi following closely behind, closing the portal with a sizzle and a snap.

"Right on time." Charlie gave his best smile, waiting for the Elves to sit before he took his own seat at the head of the table between the two groups. He gave a nod to Kyomi and sat down carefully, his chair wobbling on the uneven ground. "This won't be a long meeting. There is too much at risk to stay out in the open like this." Charlie kept smiling as he chatted amiably, the smile never reaching his eyes. "Let's get right to it. No need for introductions. We all have enough friends. Our aligned goal is to make sure if this prophesy you're so sure is going to happen, actually takes place and there's a mass migration onto Earth that we all come out the winners in the eventual war of magic."

"It's inevitable..." said a man with a trim beard, gravely shaking his head. The Elf across from him studied his face, slowly raising his arms and putting them on the table, his long silver hair falling around his shoulders. The man barely registered a flinch, bracing himself for something that never came. The corners of the Elf's mouth turned up slightly into a sneer.

One of the Elves at the end of the table looked up at the bright sun and pulled in magic through his feet, the symbols lighting up along his arms as he waved his arms overhead, gathering the clouds to hover over them, casting a long shadow across the table. The human side of the table all shifted in their seats, glancing up at the darkened sky and across at their new business partners.

"What do you have to offer us if we agree to work with you?" It was an older Elf with a long pink scar down the otherwise flawless pale skin of his face. "Why would we side with you against our own kind and offer you the assistance of magic?"

Charlie sat forward, excited, rubbing his hands together. "You can offer magic and artifacts. We can offer cutting-edge technology that unlike magic, keeps improving and evolving." Charlie batted his hand in the air at the protests from the Elven side of the table. "Together we can create something that neither side was able to do alone. The perfect synergy of two sides."

Charlie stood up and raised his hand, waving it high in the air. The ground suddenly thundered and shook as something large moved toward the center of the field at a rapid clip. Both sides of the table stood up, craning their necks to see as some of the Elves raised their hands, creating fireballs in case this was an ambush after all as some of them had suspected. Kyomi waved them down, smiling calmly and waited for the beasts to emerge from between the tall emerald green stalks.

Bison rumbled through the stalks, crushing them beneath their hooves, stopping just yards away from the table, pawing at the ground and snorting. Standing next to them was a Wood Elf whistling to them in different pitches, controlling their moves.

Both sides of the table gasped as they saw that the middle of each animal, where there should have been the organs was instead a translucent engine made of artifacts reshaped for the task. All the moving parts were visible as if that was needed to add to the shock and awe. The bison had a wild and crazed look to their eyes, but the Wood Elf whistled to keep them back, his irises moving in every direction so as not to miss a single detail.

Only the older Elf seemed unfazed and instead took a longer look at the Wood Elf, one side of his lip curling in distaste. "Ah, a changeling. How charming."

The Wood Elf narrowed his eyes and focused on the Light Elf but only for a moment, before turning away.

"As you can see, gentlemen and Elves, we have progressed beyond magic and technology to a third element... bionics. Welcome to the new world order of animals and even insects that can serve as the missing link between magic and technology." Charlie paused for effect, watching both sides gasp and marvel at the sight of the animals.

Two of the Elves stood, their muscles tensing and their eyes glowing as if they even now still anticipated an attack. Charlie's eyes darkened for just a moment and the corners of his mouth barely turned up. Just as quickly, he returned to his senses and his smile broadened as he hid the small thread of panic deep inside of himself. "These are just prototypes." He made himself sit there calmly, not rising out of his chair or waving a hand in the air to reassure anyone. "The beginning of a long journey. One day... one day soon we'll refine this process and be able to use the same magicology to lengthen human lives or advance what Elves can do beyond just magic to create empires, to win wars. We can take this organic vessel and make each one ten times stronger, and last longer at any task."

"We would be unstoppable," gasped a balding man who kept popping out of his chair, only to sit back down again in surprise.

"We could do this with humans."

"Or Elves."

"We could replace parts, refine abilities."

"Harness magic in an entirely new way."

"Only if we get there first."

Charlie smiled and waved his hand without looking back as the Wood Elf gave off a long, low whistle and turned, gently nudging one of the beasts as they ran slowly back through the field, trampling the tender stalks under their sharp hooves. "Of course, none of this comes without a price." Charlie's pulse picked up as he kept taking deep breaths, his smile firmly planted on his face. "We will need funding for research and artifacts for our experiments. Both in large quantities."

Charlie stood slowly and leaned forward on the table, looking around at everyone at the table. "Get on board, or get left behind because to be clear, I'm not here asking for permission so I can start. I'm here looking for allies to stand with me to get ready for whatever comes next."

"Wouldn't it be more accurate to say you and Fleeker are ready to start?" The Wood Elf crossed his arms over his chest, glaring at Charlie.

Charlie licked his lips, his smile becoming even more strained as everyone turned to look at him. Normally, one of his favorite moments. "I already have allies," he said, not adding anything more. The Wood Elf let out a snort and took a step back.

A cicada outfitted with a small harness lifted up, unseen from the nearby stalks and hovered for a moment, eventually buzzing off to a far side of the field and into the waiting hands of Perrom. He was standing naked in the field, his clothes neatly piled nearby, and all the scales along his skin fluttering to match the nearby stalks stolen from pods on Oriceran, making him appear invisible as he moved along the rows. The scales along his feet were a deep, foamy brown running along the dirt as he came closer to where the two sides were meeting.

He got there just in time to see the Wood Elf turn and stare into the tall plants, his irises moving in different directions and coming back together again. Perrom held perfectly still, waiting for the moment to pass even as he resisted trembling with anger. He recognized the Wood Elf from a village tucked just inside the Dark Forest. Traitor of the worst kind.

The Wood Elf moved away just as one of the Light Elves opened a portal and Perrom got close enough to see the one with a long scar down his face. Leacham! How…

Leacham was accused of trading in stolen goods from the castle, using Willens to get inside the invisible walls. Worse rumors abounded about him taking the life of another Light Elf over a dispute at one of the many pubs that surrounded the Dark Market, but nothing was ever proven. No one was willing to speak against him. It was the reason he was only banished from the Light Elves' kingdom and not sent to Trevilsom Prison for life. He was supposed to have left for the other side of Oriceran… How did he find his way to Earth? He should have been thrown under Trevilsom. And Kyomi. Traitors!

Perrom didn't recognize all of the Light Elves with him but he recognized the different faded symbols they wore on their cloaks that gave away the villages where they were raised. He stepped back on a twig, letting out a faint snap just as he recognized the eternity symbol on Leacham's cloak. He was a follower of Rhazdon.

Charlie Monaghan looked up in his direction but saw nothing and turned his head back to his guests.

Perrom easily ran back through the field, the slender scales along his skin rattling as it kept up the variations in color and texture as he ran, the muscles in his legs standing out as they turned different shades of green and pale yellow. He got to his clothes and quickly dressed, pulling out the leather pouch full of messenger bugs and whispering into them everything he knew. He set them loose on the wind, watching their small translucent wings open up as they flew off to find their recipient. Perrom set about creating a ball of light, focusing on a destination deep within the Dark Forest to ensure he didn't land anywhere near the returning Light Elves.

He set foot deep into the forest only long enough to open another portal and step back onto Earth onto the sanctuary and in search of his father. It was time for a meeting with the Americans, whether the Gardener was ready or not.

CHAPTER SIXTEEN

Blake Johnson ran out of Cheer Up Charlie's with a long feather boa dragging off his shoulder leaving small purple feathers in his salt and pepper hair. One of the dancers noticed him showing the photo of the troll and dragged him into the spotlight, singing a deep, throaty version of Desposito with their arm around his neck, hugging Blake against their ample padded bosom. The singer didn't let him loose until the last chorus and Blake tripped coming off the stage, spilling someone's beer into their lap as he tried to find his way quickly to the exit.

He stood out on 9th Street leaning against the wall. "Come on Blake, good stories don't come easy. You can't give up now. The damn creature is playing with you. Gotta dig deeper." He stood up and put his hands on his hips, leaning back and looking up into the sky. The Superman pose always gave him a little more confidence. He took a deep breath and let it out, checking his watch and calculating when he absolutely had to head to the Garden Show or risk his editor's wrath.

Just as he was considering giving up for the day his phone pinged and two new pictures appeared on his phone. Yumfuck was upping his game. The troll stood, perched on an old sign that read, Midnight Cowboy Modeling in black and red lettering in the first picture. It was a fairly new upscale bar that could only hold a limited number of people in what used to be a long-standing brothel. Reservations were generally required but on the off chance there was an inch of free real estate to squeeze in another body the light would flash outside and those in the know, knew to run right over.

Its old reputation still somehow managed to follow it and there was a long list of what wouldn't be allowed in the joint along with a reassurance that the wait staff would do their best to make their patrons happy, within legal limits. Blake was well aware of the bar but was never able to get a reservation.

"How did the damn furry monster get inside?"

He pulled up the other picture and saw the troll was standing, hidden in the middle of a propped-up drink menu in a dark leather booth, smiling broadly with all of his tiny, pointed teeth next to a tall cocktail. It was a Lawn Tennis Cooler, made with cognac, lemon, ginger beer, whole egg and cinnamon. The troll's favorite.

"Goddammit, he doubled back to 6th Street. How does something so small get there so fast without growing so big someone would notice?" Blake ran back to his car and started it back up, squealing tires, already knowing he was on the losing side of things but still hoping for a lucky break. "Isn't that what every great story has? Some kind of lucky break that some lucky bastard got because he didn't give up." He gritted his teeth and left his car on 7th Street when he saw a spot, running the last block to the bar.

He got to the front door and tried pulling the handle, but the door appeared locked as he shook it hard before pounding a few times on the frame.

"Try the buzzer." A man with mutton chop sideburns sat on a small lawn chair outside smoking a cigarette. "Gotta push the buzzer or they won't pay attention to you. Kind of a bougie speakeasy." The new owner had even kept the buzzer from the old days. It was marked Harry Craddock and in the old days was used to alert the women in the back to a customer or a raid. Patrons wanting to get in still had to use it.

Blake leaned on the buzzer, jamming his finger against it. A waiter heatedly swung open the door to see who was insisting on getting in and looked down into Blake's sweaty face, holding up his phone with a close up of the troll. "Is he in there?"

"This ain't no damn Sesame Street… Fuck off and go drink your cheap beer down the street."

"I'm a reporter! I'm not…" But that was all he could get out before the waiter slammed the door shut again.

Blake stepped back, blinking, his mouth hanging open.

"They don't take kindly to a lot of ruckus. It rattles the aged scotch and makes the good gin go sour." The man took a long drag on his cigarette and blew smoke out his nose.

"You seen him?" Blake desperately held up the screen, hoping for a miracle.

"He's a regular. Sly one and real patient like. Gets in when no one else is looking. Love his laugh." The man nodded, smiling. "But he bounced a little while back, headed down Trinity toward 5th Street. Good luck…" The man gave a small wave as Blake took off running, not even looking back as the man took another long drag and blew out perfect O's into the air, his eyes glowing for just a moment. "Love that fucking troll."

CHAPTER SEVENTEEN

The general sat up front in the pickup truck bouncing over the rough and uneven back roads into the sanctuary just outside of Austin, Texas. He wanted to take extra precautions to ensure he wasn't seen by anyone on his way to meet with the mythical Gardener of the Dark Forest. They parked on the far side of the forest the Gardener had constructed on the vast ranch and hiked their way through the woods, following the instructions of the messenger bugs that had appeared on his table at an outdoor cafe in Pflugerville, just outside of Austin.

The waiter had moved to swat the bugs with a menu as the general grabbed him firmly by the wrist and gave him a strained smile telling him, "We'll call you when we need you." The general had already noticed something strange about their movements.

Alan Cohen had waited until the waiter had walked far enough away. "What is it? Not a line of ants, I take it."

"Not unless ants have learned Morse Code, can give out longitudes and latitudes and have met Leira." The general kept his eyes on the bugs that were crawling all over his hat, quickly deciphering the message as he moved his lips. "We need to go. We can grab something on the way if you're that hungry." The general had gotten up, gently shaking his hat as the bugs took to the air again.

Alan had shaken his head. "No, do we need the team?" He got up, pulling out his wallet, and had left a five-dollar bill on the table tucked under his water glass as a tip for the waiter.

"Good man," said the general. "I always believe in leaving a little something even if I never get to order. In the PDF that happens way too often. Magical creatures don't schedule very well." It wasn't long before they had reached their destination.

At the edge of the forest they got out of the truck and Alan took a look around as the general checked the coordinates again. "Where the hell are we? I've driven down the highway on the other side of this ranch a thousand times and never noticed these trees," he said, looking up. "They have to be well over a hundred years old... You'd be able to see these for miles."

A swarm of blue bees settled across his shoulders sending a feeling of bliss through Alan that only unnerved him more. He ducked his head and shook them off as they regrouped and flew on in a pattern, zigging right and then left.

"We're still on Earth, right? I didn't miss something back there and we drove into Oriceran?"

The general didn't answer, still pondering the best way to go, confidently setting out, stepping over tall roots of a growth of live oak trees and pushing his way into the forest.

The forest was dense and the general quickly pulled out a small flashlight to help cast a light over the uneven ground. Even though he was short in stature he was able to make good time through the forest, occasionally checking the compass on his phone. Alan stayed just behind him, adding the light from his phone to the trek as he kept a sharp eye out for anything that moved.

A family of hedgehogs crossed his path between himself and the general and quickly disappeared down a mossy hole making

Alan smile in the semi-darkness. I'm afraid of woodland creatures.

He looked to the side and saw three pairs of glowing red eyes staring back at him from the deeper, darker parts of the forest, hovering near the ground. Shit… His expression froze as he kept moving, his hand grazing across his gun, glancing back to see if the eyes were getting any closer. Where the fuck am I? I've fallen into Wonderland…

The general came to a stop at a divide in the canopy where the light streamed in, lighting up a center stone. Alan looked up, his eyes adjusting to the light again. They were under a large bush of trumpet flowers that towered over their heads, some of the yellow blossoms hanging just out of reach. A red and blue parrot vigorously flapped its wings just outside the circle of light and let out a loud caw, making Alan take in a sharp breath and hold it for a moment. I will never get used to this.

The general was unfazed and even took off his hat, patiently waiting for someone to arrive. The undergrowth stirred and he felt the ground shake as a lion quickly emerged, antlers protruding from his head. On his back was the Dark Gardener, scowling, the vines and colorful beetles in his long hair, twisting in and out and flitting around his head. The Gardener slid off the lion's back, holding on to a tall staff of wood. Just behind him Perrom appeared and came and stood next to the lion. He stroked the lion's neck as the animal shook his mane of hair and shut his eyes, leaning his large head against Perrom.

Alan's eyes widened as he watched the lion settle, lying down with a thud, the large antlers rustling the bottom branches of trees. He took in the two Wood Elves, watching the irises of their eyes move around, taking in every detail as their skin adapted to the background, changing texture and color to hide them. Finally, Perrom let his skin take on the smooth deep, honey brown tones of a Wood Elf as he leaned against the lion, one hand on the rack. "We're waiting for two more to join us," he said, his eyes still scanning the woods as he listened for their approach.

The general gave a nod and seemed content to wait even though he was tapping his fingers against his leg, tightly holding his hat at his side. Leira and Correk popped out of the thick growth on the far side of the clearing. Leira's face was flush from running through the woods, letting the magic within her help her place her foot or leap over a large bullfrog. Correk did his best to keep up, his tunic snagging on a bush filled with thorns that gave off a sharp smelling gas when disturbed. He shook off the fine dust that had settled on him, releasing the strong odor again as Leira turned her head away, squeezing her eyes shut for a moment. "You think it's passed just as it knocks your head back again. I think it singed the hairs in my nose."

"Next time, don't run through an old growth forest with me in tow."

The Gardener took a long look at Correk, letting some of his irises stray in the Light Elf's direction and the others look back in the direction that would lead to the lab. So close. He let the thought go. It's not mine to settle.

"Everyone is here now, we can begin." Perrom stood up straight, still stroking the lion's fur.

"You sent the message?" The general looked at Perrom. "How did you know where to find me?"

"Part of the messenger bugs' abilities. We speak our intention into them along with the message. Magic does the rest."

"That is some pretty big magic," said Alan. "They found their way across an entire nation."

"Not exactly. Not the same messengers anyway. They live in large swarms that can darken the sky in Oriceran but given a task…" Perrom opened his hand as gold dust rose into the air and flew gently in different directions. "They split into smaller and smaller groups to deliver the message to as many as required and will even connect to other swarms to cross thousands of miles. That message came all the way from Iowa."

"Why not call?" Alan held up his cell phone as the general hid a smile, shaking his head at him.

Perrom hesitated, pressing his lips together in irritation.

Leira leaned closer to Correk. "You can almost hear him thinking puny human. Take me to your leader."

Correk nudged her, without changing expression.

"No one can listen in to a swarm of messenger bugs and they are remarkably efficient at getting someone's attention. Besides, if you haven't noticed, I'm not from these parts and we don't carry phones." Perrom eyed Alan suspiciously, his irises focusing on him for a moment, making Alan shift his weight.

"Enough of this!" The Gardener's voice came out as a roar, echoing through the forest. The lion lifted his head and let out a low growl, shaking his mane. Alan instinctively took a step closer to the general, putting his hand back on his gun.

"No need for that," yelled the Gardener, his palm outstretched.

"Seems we're not getting off to a good start, here." The general crossed his hands in front of himself, lightly holding on to his hat as he gave a relaxed smile that didn't quite make it to his eyes. "In cases like this I find it helpful to begin again. I was told you need my help. Some kind of protection to our interests. That some are even plotting in case of some kind of war. That got my attention. I'm here. Tell me what's happening."

"There are groups on both Oriceran and Earth that are aligning themselves to incorporate magic and technology to create something…"

The Gardener cut Perrom off. "Something grotesque. They're threatening what I've spent my entire and very long life protecting. I will not allow this!" His eyes burned brightly, energy flowing through him as the symbols spelled out his anger along his chest and neck.

He held the staff into the air, sending out a shower of sparks as the trees fluttered and rustled. Living creatures of every kind were scurrying and flying for other parts of the woods. Small orange and black butterflies emerged from his hair, seeking shelter elsewhere.

The Gardener gave a low whistle and waved his staff again as a bison came into view, its mid-section a display of moving mechanical parts.

For once, the General was at a loss for words and his eyes uncharacteristically widened. "What in the name of Sam Hill…" He stepped around to get a better look, careful to give the Gardener a wide berth as Alan leaned to the side to see the machinery better as well.

"Is the animal in pain?"

"This one is not because I've been able to give it something to relieve it, but I can't say the same for the rest."

"The rest? What in hell has been going on?" The general stood up straight, putting his hat back on, his hands on his hips. "Can someone tell me when we all took a left turn toward Albuquerque into a new kind of hell?"

"It's part of the artifacts race, sir." Leira let the magic light up the symbols on her arms and she sent out energy to comfort the animal. The magic curled around the mid-section of the bison, curious, feeling the suffering. This is new. Leira felt the magic circle back around her, checking in, before it went back out again, seeking out others just like the bison.

Leira looked up in time to see a look of concern cross Correk's face before he looked away. Her skin was glowing in the deep shade of the woods. She reached out and put a hand on Correk's arm, sending the magic through him and tamping it down. The energy pulled back, splitting into different spirals to find all the bionic animals, but only going as far as the edge of the woods.

Correk kept his face turned away as he grimaced from the

powerful surge, gritting his teeth as the muscles in his neck strained. He held on, funneling the energy as it lowered down to a more manageable level. He turned and smiled at Leira.

"This is part of what the corporations wanted the artifacts for…. These experiments." She could hear her voice ringing in her ears, bouncing through the energy field and back out again.

"Experiments." The general spit out the word. "Reminds me of another dark chapter in our history. Are these to be used in some eventual war?"

Perrom watched the bison breathe easier as Leira's magic reached him. He looked up at Correk at the same time, raising his eyebrows.

Correk rested his hand on Leira's arm, regulating the magic. "The experiments have more than one purpose. To create beasts of war that can fight longer or cross greater terrain or gain information but also to find a way to create a kind of fountain of youth."

The general took a step closer to the large animal, slowly raising his hand despite the protests from Alan or the looks from Perrom or the Gardener. He steadied his hand, reaching out to stroke the wiry gray fur. The buffalo snorted, a fine spray dotting the front of the general's uniform. He didn't flinch. Instead, he looked just over the top of the beast's eyes, gently bringing his hand down to stroke behind one ear as it twitched slightly.

Leira suddenly gave an involuntary twitch, surprising herself as she felt a rush of emptiness fill her gut. Her eyes widened as she looked at the bison. He raised his head, his large dark brown eyes looking at her. *I am connecting with the bionic animals. The artifacts are doing it.* She shook her head slowly, confused. *You can feel me too. Not in Kansas anymore. I may have to go vegan. They'll take away my Texas passport.*

"Are you okay?" Correk was standing close enough to Leira that she could feel his muscled arm pressing against hers.

"Just another day in magic land. Need to get to Turner Underwood."

"About that… We should talk."

The general kept his breathing even, continuing to rub the animal's neck. "My people can sometimes be real sons of bitches," he said, softly, his voice catching slightly. "That's when the rest of us have to step up and kick some ass."

"It's not just humans. Magicals are involved too," said Perrom.

The general slowly lifted his hand, backing up a step at a time till he was a few feet away. "This really chaps me," said the general in disgust. He took his hat off again and slapped it against his leg in anger. "Well, how do we make this right? How do we stop these cowards?"

"A complicated question," said Leira. "The answer will take some time to even figure out. The best thing we can do is keep getting to the artifacts ahead of them."

"Then why are we all standing around in the woods together?" The general's anger and frustration were growing even as he kept his voice low.

"To do some good, despite this kind of evil," said Correk.

"Lazy evil is what this is. No worse than any other but there's something particularly cowardly about looking for ways to get some poor dumb beast to do your dirty work."

"The Gardener has a way to get ahead of this Frankenstein operation. To at least save a good number of these animals and protect others before they're taken."

"Proactive! I like that more than being told the problem without an ounce of good goddamn thrown into the mix. Tell me the details."

Correk gave a nod to Perrom and constructed a ball of light sending it into the air over their head, illuminating the area around them. The ground became alive with creeping and crawling insects and reptiles. Small furry animals took cover, waddling and hopping and scurrying back into the shade and insects suddenly appeared in bright shades of color as they burrowed into trees or drank from nearby flowers. The general turned in a slow circle as the light moved around to show different sections. Fuzzy baby birds with new blue and gold feathers squawked in their nests, their eyes shut firmly against the light. A small black monkey with a tan face swung in and out of the light, hanging on to vines that wound around every tree, hanging down at different depths.

"This is all in Texas," gaped the general, his head back and his mouth hanging open. "Greatest nation on earth. Can take that one home with you."

Leira looked at Correk and shook her head slightly. "It's a Texas thing. Just go with it," she whispered. Leira held out her arm as a cockatoo landed, his tail dipping down below her waist. "Perrom showed me this one the last time I was here."

Alan flinched as another large cockatoo landed on his shoulder, bobbing up and down. He quickly recovered and straightened up. "All good here." The bird bobbed and dropped a scattering of broken seed shells on Alan's shoulder. "Still all good." He gave a long sideways glance. "Okay, seeds. All good."

Leira smiled and held out her arm. "We are all standing in a vast sanctuary on Earth that was meant as a safeguard to keep every species alive and intact, hidden from the rest of both worlds."

"To leave them at peace," the Gardener said, his voice heavy with emotion.

"But it's no longer enough. We have the magic necessary to round up the animals but not the space." Leira put her hand on the General's arm, filling his mind with images of the animals already contained within the two sanctuaries.

"This is better than Google Glass." The General took a half step back to avoid a large flamingo running by. A wide grin spread across his face for the first time that day. "Felt so damn real."

"We need to create at least two more of this same size in other parts of the world."

"And you need the government's help to get it done." The general eyed the Gardener. "Why aren't you speaking for yourself?"

Correk cleared his throat and put his hand on Perrom's shoulder. "Wood Elves have a certain innate mistrust of humans. Your kind did their best to kill them off the last time the gates were opened."

"Sir, our general history is one of major fuckups and glorious achievements in equal measures. It seems hardwired into us that each of us has to make constant choices which direction we're gonna run headlong into at any given moment. I follow a code that dictates I protect those around me without regard for myself. It's served me pretty well so far."

"Take us on a case by case basis." Leira locked eyes with the Gardener. She put her hand on her chest. "Part human, part a few other things. Kind of a mutt, I know."

The Gardener held her gaze. "Mixtures make the best of their species."

Leira raised her eyebrows and opened her mouth, ready to give an answer but the general cut her off, not wanting to know how she'd take it.

"I'll take that as a positive step forward." The general rubbed his hands together, excited. "It's been a long time since I've been a part of something massive that was about building something instead of tearing something down, even if it was for an eventual good. Where are these sanctuaries going to be located? I have a million questions."

"The first is in the northern most section of Alaska abutting the Noatak wilderness. We bought it from an old miner named Craig Martelle who hit it big in his day. He was a veteran of a few wars who wanted a place to live where no one would disturb him," said the Gardener.

"A frozen river basin at the top of the world would do it," said Perrom.

"A laudable purpose. Hopefully he knocked off five percent for the cause. No more. Practical in all things."

"Do you want to go there?" Leira gave a crooked smile and put her hand on the general again, not waiting for an answer, as she reached out with her other hand to touch Alan. The cockatoo fluttered and spread its wings with a squawk, taking off for a higher branch.

Alan gasped as he felt himself pulled through a pinhole, whooshing over lands. He gasped for air as he found himself above the Arctic Circle flying well above a glacial melt atop Mount Igikpak in the Brooks Range out to Kotzebue Sound.

"If the government can see its way to letting us use part of the preserve for a variety of animals…" The Gardener absently stroked the bison's head as the lion rested on his front paws. "The preserve is perfectly situated in a transition zone between the northern coniferous forests and tundra biomes. The river basin will serve us well for those beings that fly or swim or crawl better in colder climes and already has one of the larger arrays of arctic flora and fauna. There are already caribou, brown bears, moose, wolves, and more than 150 songbird species migrate through the region."

Perrom looked at his father, surprised. "I don't think I've ever heard you say so much in one breath. Ever."

Leira let the energy pull them over the Noatak River as salmon jumped through the air and large bears stood at the curve, swatting large paws looking for dinner. They swooped down over a ring of mountains as a large herd of caribou seemed to sense a disturbance and ran, thundering across the ground, coming to rest in a green and snowy field.

"There's one last important feature to this part of the world." She could sense it before she saw the deep inverted dry basin. A kemana. The energy swelled up to meet her. She could feel it come over them in translucent waves.

"Take me back to terra firma." The general was leaning forward on his toes, his eyes wide open watching the Alaskan tundra below.

Leira took a deep breath and pulled back on the magic, gradually bringing them back. Alan felt the same whoosh and the wind knock out of him as the dark green of the Texas sanctuary reappeared in front of him. He held perfectly still, taking sips of air, waiting to regain his bearings.

"Best damn trip I ever took!" crowed the general. "Is that what it's like to have magic?" A look of awe was plastered on his face. "Where exactly is that preserve?"

"About three hundred miles north of Fairbanks."

"That's pretty damn remote."

"Then we have your support." The Gardener crossed his arms across his chest. The wariness still crept into his voice.

"You already did as soon as I saw that poor animal, but I appreciate the dog and pony show. Not too many people do such a fine job of it. You said you would need more than one. Where's the other sanctuary? I take it someplace tropical. I'm sensing a practical theme of sorts. I take it even magic has its limits."

"Always..." Leira gave Correk a meaningful sidelong glance. "If we can place animals in the habitats where they belong, less magic is needed."

"Arrangements have been made to secure a chain of smaller islands near Kauai in Hawaii. Completely untouched." Correk kept an eye on Alan as he spoke. Alan was finally taking in a deeper breath, smoothing down his hair as he glanced at Leira. I know that look. Correk arched an eyebrow and lifted his hand ever so slightly, sending a small zing of energy to poke Alan in the back.

Alan started and whipped around to see what was trying him

on for size, surprised to find nothing there. "Are there invisible things flying around in this place?"

"Invisible somethings." Leira glared at Correk. "Play nice with the humans," she whispered.

Correk gave a small shrug and let out a satisfied sigh.

"Completely on board with one caveat," said the general.

The Gardener tensed, his fists clenching.

"We keep this to a small circle. I have some autonomy within the PDF and can give the nod to this project, especially since it involves magic, but this can't become public knowledge. It would get tangled up in congressional red tape that's worse than dark magic. Nothing can untangle it."

Perrom stepped forward putting out his hand, his irises focused on the general. "Then we have a deal."

The general didn't waver and shook the Wood Elf's hand, giving him a hard nod as the scales along Perrom's hand flipped back and forth to a wrinkled peach and back to a smooth honey brown.

"Fascinating…" said the general. "The world has so much more to offer than we ever realized."

"And we are the stewards of it all." The Gardener got on top of the oversized lion as he raised his great head, the antlers raising up, scratching against the bark of a tree stand a few feet away. The Gardener gave the lion a gentle nudge as he turned and took off at a sprint through the woods followed by the bison, rumbling along behind him, the twinkle of light from the machinery in his belly providing a marker until they were completely enveloped by the forest.

"Couldn't have said it better myself." The general turned around and took out his phone, checking his compass. "Basic compass was one of the best inventions ever. Made map making possible. Time to head home everyone. We have work to do. Need to double our efforts to stop these bastards in their tracks and dry up their supplies."

"There's one more thing." Leira glanced at Correk. "We also have to stop the magical source. We have a name and we think he's on Earth, but we can't find him."

"Give me the name," the general barked, glad to have something simple to do. "If he's on this planet, you'll have a location within the hour."

"Wolfstan Humphrey, an old Light Elf," said Correk, grimacing. "It may not be that easy. The Silver Griffins have tried to find him."

"That's okay. We do difficult all day long and still get the job done."

CHAPTER EIGHTEEN

"We're here." Leira ignored the skeptical looks on everyone's face as they piled out of their cars, looking up at the tall metal blue, red and yellow sign with a curvy drawing of a woman on the side and two dice in the middle. Casino El Camino Bar and Grille. World Famous Hamburgers. Hagan got out of the back of the green Mustang and looked up at the sign, squinting, a scowl on his face. "I don't normally haunt the bars on 6th Street. Too many kids and tourists."

"Give it a chance, Hagan. You're in the market for a new hang out."

Hagan crossed his arms over his belly and looked around, still frowning. "That's not something you take lightly. A man's home away from home takes years to find. You have to try a lot of places…"

"How about we just go in."

"You didn't do anything magical to the place, did you? That'd be cheating." Hagan wiggled his fingers, both hands in the air.

"Don't ruin the moment with that. You know how I feel about magic hands." Leira was resting her hand on the handle of the door, her other hand on her waist. "Come on, we need this after our last attempt at a get together. Besides, I saw how hard you took losing your man cave. That's what they call that, right?"

"Close enough."

The sidewalk was filled with people just starting their night, trying to get to the Roaring Fork or the Paramount Theater. Passerby weren't really giving the Casino El Camino a second glance. Fine by me. Wait till Hagan gets inside... Leira felt a sudden sharp lurch in the center of her gut, knocking the wind out of her. The scar on her belly burned from the front straight to her back. She gripped the handle and gritted her teeth, focusing razor sharp on not letting the slightest bit of energy seep out. Not now. Not... now.

She moved her head slowly, looking around for any telltale signs of the black mist seeping out of the sidewalk or swirling around her feet. The muscles in her neck strained as she worked at keeping at least a calm look on her face, her lips pressed together. I know what the fuck this is. This is gonna be a shit show. Her arm was pinned to her side, the other one still stretched out on the handle. Correk... Correk... His attention was caught elsewhere.

He was getting out of the front seat of the Mustang and was looking back at the regulars parking their cars. He could hear them a half a block away.

Leira turned her head back toward the door to the Casino El Camino and slowly shut her eyes. Please don't let anyone come out of this door. Not now.

Craig, Mike, Scott and Paul piled out of Mitzi's small car stretching their legs.

Paul arched his back, wincing. "Pretty sure something poked me in the back and laughed."

"That was me."

"What the hell were you poking me with?"

"Like a damn clown car."

A sharp wind came up blowing dust and grit into Correk's

eyes as he squeezed them shut, rubbing them with his hands. A man in an expensive tailor-made suit brushed past Craig, shoving Mike to the side with his shoulder as he kept walking, his cufflinks glittering in the early evening sun. Charlie Monaghan was making a beeline up the street to the Driskill Hotel. His eyes were a dark black and his expression was blank as he marched toward his destination.

"Hey, watch where you're going!" Mike raised his arm, but Charlie kept going, not even glancing back at him.

"Some people…"

"Let it go. He looks late for an appointment."

"Still no excuse."

Leira felt the darkness ease as the pain along her stomach faded and she could loosen her grip on the handle of the door. What the fuck was that? She looked back at the street, shaken at the thought of the dark mist finding her out in the open.

The regulars were still arguing amongst themselves as Mitzi locked the car with a loud beep, doing her best to ignore them. "I played Abba the whole way so I didn't have to hear them in the back." Correk nodded trying to smile as he wiped his eyes again. He turned to look at Leira, the smile fading from his face. He stopped himself from running to her side and drawing attention to her. Instead, he focused on her energy and felt the traces of dark magic and the glittering trail it left, stretching up 6th Street, following the older man in the suit. Something about him looks familiar. Charlie was in the distance and didn't look to either side. All that could be seen was his bobbing head and dark suit as he got further and further away.

Correk looked at Leira as he worked on an excuse to break away and follow him to someplace where he could use magic, and learn more but Leira shook her head hard, staring resolutely into his eyes. Never wanted Perrom's four-eyes so much before this moment.

Just up the street an older Chevrolet pulled up to the curb and parked, doing a perfect parallel park on the first try. The door opened and the young Wizard, Ernie stepped out, the silver streak cutting a large swath through the middle of his dark hair. An older Wizard got out of the passenger side and looked around, taking in Correk and Leira down in front of the bar. "We need to get going. Our target is not far but we could lose him if we don't hurry."

"Hang on, they're calling. Hello, this is number two hundred and one. Yep, we saw him. There are others in the area. Leira Berens is here. No, no shit, Peter. You're not supposed to talk like that over official airwaves. I don't think she wants your number. Besides, she's with that tall, geeky Elf. You know, the one from the bowling alley. This is how you got yourself stuck on answering phones in the first place."

"Hang it up!" The Wizard was getting testy. Never easy training the new ones even if they did survive the world in between.

"Gotta go! No, I'm not getting her picture. Hanging up now." Ernie hung up, sliding his phone into his pocket and glanced back at Correk and Leira as he took off after Charlie Monaghan, the older Wizard right behind him.

Craig gave a shudder and pulled his vest's collar closer around his neck. "Whew! Just had a chill run down my back. That was weird."

"It's spring, dude. Cold happens." None of the others seemed to notice the remains of the darkness.

"You need to air out those dogs of yours once in a while. I could smell your feet the entire ride."

"That was not me."

"Quit your complaining. You guys could have driven your-self." Mitzi's mouth was pulled up on one side and she was busy giving all of her passengers the side eye.

"Mitzi, we're buying your beer tonight." Craig grabbed her by the shoulders, smiling. "Thank you for driving us."

Scott elbowed Mike. "Right, yeah, we're buying your beer." He put his hand up to his face and whispered to Scott. "But I'm taking an Uber home."

The women got out of Cassidy's blue Dodge minivan, parked just down the street clapping their hands and chattering amongst themselves.

"Love road trips."

"Not much of a road trip from Rainey Street. More of a short jaunt."

"Take my picture under the sign. Can you get it all in? Stand further back."

"Oooh, let me get in there too."

Estelle slid out of the front passenger seat and walked up, taking a long look around as she lit a cigarette and stood near the curb.

Correk watched the street as the other men gave up and went on inside. He saw the two Silver Griffins and felt himself tense. *This is getting to be a crowded street. Who was that man?*

"I can use a beer and a burger. After you…" Mike held open the door, waving in his friends as a couple holding hands slid in behind them. The man had a tattoo of an ancient battle down both arms and the woman had roses tattooed along her neck.

Leira waved at the women, trying to get them to move along. "It's like they've never been on 6th Street before." Correk stayed by her side, a wave of anger rolling through him. *I failed her. I didn't even sense it.*

"I'm fine, really. Let it go. We're here to have a good time. Whatever it was, it's passed." Leira watched Estelle blow perfect round O's as she looked up the street sensing the trail of dark magic that still lingered. *Can't check it but I know you're there.* Leira shook out her hands and brushed her bangs off her face. "No work tonight if we can help it. I'm going to have to insist on that. Besides, too many regulars hanging nearby."

Estelle looked up at Leira and gave her a wink as she blew out a long stream of smoke.

"You think Estelle is okay? I mean, she's family to me. All that smoking."

"That's at least one thing I can do for you tonight." Correk looked to see if the women were paying attention to him but their backs were turned away and Estelle was looking out at the street. He pulled in enough energy, shading his eyes to hide the light in them and let the magic slowly roll up and around Estelle.

"What are you doing? That's kind of a creepazoid move. If she ever catches you." Leira was shaking her head at him. "Stop before she finally proves she's some kind of magical force we never heard of and turns you into a frog."

"Still not magical and no ill effect from all those cigarettes. Not a bit." He pulled back the magic and dropped his hand, watching her. "Like a force of nature."

"That's not human. Not a single bad something?"

"Not a one. Don't know what to tell you. She's the exception."

"That part makes sense. She's the exception to just about every rule."

"Gribbet."

"Too soon." Leira gave a crooked smile. "I still want you by my side in any kind of fight." Leira held up her fist. "Come on, fist bump. Yeah, it's a thing. Hold up your fist."

Correk smiled and held up his fist as Leira bounced her fist off his, and opened her hand wide, pulling it back. "Kapow...."

"That's awfully close to Hagan's magic hands."

"Not even."

Correk did his best to shake off the feeling of darkness that still lingered. He looked up at the metal sign. "Ambitious. Burgers known round the world. You would have thought we'd have heard about them on Oriceran. What? Why are you poking me?" Correk frowned and held out his hands to defend himself from Leira. "I'm happy to be here. Always willing to try a good burger."

"That's been well established."

Estelle looked unfazed by the swirl of activity around her. Her cat-eye sunglasses with the sparkles in the corners were planted firmly on her face and dramatic dark brows drawn on just above them. Leira noted that Estelle had broken out the bright red lipstick and some of her taller platform shoes. Her red bouffant was as usual, firmly in place.

"Estelle looks like she came to play hard tonight. There have been plenty of days when she's been my inspiration to go kick some ass and believe in a better day."

"I'm glad she was there to stand in the gaps."

"Okay, enough of this. The dark willies have passed. Party on, come on." Leira opened the door as Estelle stubbed out her cigarette and picked up the butt, following behind them.

"I thought we could use a break and take a night off from rock 'em sock 'em world battles." Leira stepped into the darkened bar despite the bright sunlight outside. She stepped aside for Hagan to come through, followed by Correk and Estelle. "Welcome to Casino El Camino…" Leira held out her arms in a grand, sweeping gesture.

Correk watched Hagan turn in a circle, a smile growing across his face.

"This was very nice of you to find him another dark, questionable bar with I'm assuming its own charm."

"And then some. He's going to wonder why he stayed so long at Barfly's when this place existed right on 6th Street. I did some checking around to find it. Look at the place, it's perfect!"

There were gargoyles of every size placed strategically around the room, some hanging from the top of the bar. Correk smiled at Leira, an eyebrow arched. "Reminds me of a pub Perrom took me to in the Dark Forest."

"Just wait…"

In the center of the room was a fountain of a stone Aztec skeleton statue with water pouring out of his head. The bar was fairly empty with a few tables filled with millennials in various stages of piercings and tattoos mixed in with some who could remember Nixon and Agnew.

"Upstairs they show old B movies and this juke box plays music I didn't know I had to hear till I found this place and stayed way too long." Leira's words all ran together in her enthusiasm and her hands danced around as she talked. Correk felt himself relax even as he scanned the bar looking for any possibilities of trouble.

Leira followed his gaze. "Relax. You're here with two agents and one crafty old broad and at least one retired Marine. The building is secure. You can enjoy yourself. Now, look at this juke-box! There's a song in here by the only blues guy to get in the Rock and Roll Hall of Fame for playing the harmonica. The harmonica, dude. Fucking blows my mind."

"Great, I've been around you so long that I feel better when you're swearing. It's like a thermometer at this point."

"There's even a single from Jackie Venson. Best young blues guitarist in Austin. Saw her at the One 2 One Club."

Hagan was up at the bar leaning over someone's shoulder looking at their plate in front of them. "That's one burger?" He bit his lower lip. "Looks pretty good."

The man was wearing a short-sleeved shirt despite the season and his muscular arms were covered in tattoos of an olive branch with olives on one arm and doves in flight on the other. He put out his calloused hand to Hagan and said, "Take a seat. This joint's been waiting for you. What are you misting up there? Are those tears? I feel ya. Had the same reaction when I found the place."

Correk nudged Leira. "It's like you gave him an early birthday present. Look how happy you made the big man."

"Wait till he tastes that burger. It really is the best one I've ever had, and they burned the fries just the way I like them."

The bartender was wearing a porkpie hat, his sleeves rolled up to the elbows. "What'll you have?"

"What he's having, medium rare." Hagan felt his breath catch in his throat. "A new hidey hole," he said in awe.

Estelle stepped up to the bar, her chest barely clearing it. The bartender looked up and a smile creased his face. "Estelle! Now I know it's gonna be a good night. Look everybody, it's Estelle!" A general cheer went up as everyone raised their glass in her direction and yelled out, "Estelle!"

Estelle gave a gracious nod and said, "I'll take the usual. Put it on my tab."

"You have no tab here, Estelle. You know you're like family."

"Of course they know her." Leira threw up her hands. "This is way too cool a place to not have met Estelle. Only thing left is to convince Hagan to never bring the troll here."

"I don't think anyone here would notice. All these gargoyles, he'd fit right in. I have a feeling the patrons would roll with it."

"Oh man, look ACDC's first US release. How does one person know to pull all this together? Best mashup ever."

"This has got to be the only place on 6th Street that isn't crowded with drunk college students."

"The Jackalope never gets crowded. Of course, Jack put that magic aura around the place. You don't think…"

Leira pulled in a flash of magic and saw the room light up with different colored lights pointing out the different Elves and Wizards and even a Gnome sitting in the back. "I just found Hagan a magical hidey hole."

"It's like you were drawn to it. Come on, let's go find a table. Leave Hagan where he is. He's making new friends."

"With a Wizard."

"So much the better. We'll take two of those burgers with fries on the side." Correk called out to the bartender as they sat at a nearby table. The bartender held up two fingers as Correk saw the small tattoo of two trolls swinging from a vine. "You know,

Leira, I think you were right. The troll would fit right in here. This is the perfect hidey hole for Hagan. Good job."

"Speaking of Yumfuck, where has he gotten to?"

"Are you worried?"

"Not so much about him… I'm sure it's nothing, wherever he is."

CHAPTER NINETEEN

The small park on the South Side of Richmond, Virginia was dark and deserted with one lone streetlight shining down on an aging swing set. The decorative streetlights on the other side of the park were either out or blinking rapidly, giving off almost no light. They had shorted out as Louie walked underneath and the sword strapped on his back sucked in the electrical energy in a sizzle and shower of sparks.

Louie was standing in the deeper shadows near the edge that abutted tall wooden fences around homes away from the pool of light. The dark-haired Wizard standing next to him was holding out his wand to create a glamour, hiding them from anyone walking their dog so late at night.

"I won't screw it up. Look, this is what I do. It's why the PDF was so hot to get their hands on my services." Louie gave an easy-going smile despite what he was being asked to do. "Big bad Axiom Corporation is looking for an Oriceran guide to survey the mines near the mountain Gnomes. Not a problem. I've been crawling through them avoiding the shorties for years. You guys have an idea who's selling out our natural resources from Oriceran to some corporation?"

"That intel is not part of your briefing. Focus." The tall, lean Wizard bundled in a puffy green coat and running shoes impatiently tapped at a patch of ice along the grass.

Louie's hand rested lightly on the hilt of the magical sword relic he had rescued from near Dead Man's Crawl. He had been spending all his time practicing with the sword whenever he wasn't out looking for relics for the PDF. He felt the hum of the energy from the sword passing down his back and making him anxious for a fight and a chance to pull out the sword. He had yet to use it in a battle but was anxious to see what it would be like.

"What are we doing in small town America anyway?" Louie wrapped his cloak tighter around his shoulders, shifting his weight as the small stones from his table at the Dark Market shifted and clacked together. The Wizard looked at the pocket where the stones were and back at Louie.

"Good luck charms. I took a liking to them," said Louie.

A cold wind blew through the small park, rattling the chains on the nearby swings.

The Wizard grew concerned and tilted his head, scrutinizing Louie, taking in the large, ancient sword on his back. "You going to take this seriously? I mean, you could get some people killed, including yourself. A good weapon isn't enough. These people may be without magic but they're playing a very mean game. Whatever they're about to do next with so much Oriceran ore…"

"I get it, very bad mojo about to go down."

"Has been going down." The Wizard shifted his wand and lit the end momentarily to show a red stain along his neck. "Got this tangling with them over an attempted robbery at a zoo."

"Hope the other guy looks worse?"

The Wizard gave him a cold stare and let out an exasperated breath. "If this wasn't coming from the top brass I'd be tempted to tell you to go fuck yourself about now. But people with more juice than I have keep swearing you're the best for this job." Without saying another word, the Wizard tapped his wand against Louie's head and a thin beam of blue light circled his ear, pouring a magical earworm into his head.

Louie gave a shiver as images appeared before him and he heard the details of the mission run rapidly through his mind. He focused on the meeting time and place letting it seep into his memory. "Next time, dude you're gonna have to buy me dinner first."

"Hell, if you live through this, I'll rent a nice hotel room, too."

"So, you do have a sense of humor or was that for real?" An image flashed by inside Louie's mind, catching his attention. "Wait, what the hell was that? Did I just see some kind of cow with moving parts holding together the front and back ends? What the fuck have you guys been doing on this planet? You guys are taking fast food a little too seriously. That is some very troubling shit…"

"The humans have been busy. Now you're getting an idea of why everyone's a little on edge. If they're after Oriceran ore it means someone on Oriceran pointed out to them how valuable it is and could incite a lot of scavengers to work for them."

"Not me, of course. I'm spoken for till further notice. Even have this convenient tracking device following me around everywhere." Louie lifted up his pant leg to show the marble-sized balls of light encircling his ankle. "Clever little bastard. Haven't been able to figure out how to disable it… yet."

"Not all fun and games anymore. Sides are starting to play in ways that will leave a more permanent mark on history for both sides. Make sure you lead them astray and nowhere near any real ore."

"And bring some of the ore home to the PDF…"

"Only if the opportunity presents itself. Not mission critical."

"When did you guys get so formal with the lingo? Aren't you a bunch of moms and dads wielding wands for the greater good or some heroic bullshit like that?"

"Speaking of which, spill with the questions or I'm going. I have kids and a home to get to and a warm bed."

"No wife, huh? That explains the nervous leg there." Louie smiled at him, but his eyes were cold as he looked at the Wizard. "I thought you guys only stopped Oricerans from letting the magical cat out of the bag."

"You're mistaking us for the Silver Griffins. The PDF missions are more wide-ranging."

"Code for whatever the hell the Feds want, I get it. That is some really dark magic going down there, even if non-magical humans are behind it."

"I never said no magicals are involved." The Wizard grimaced at the memory of the pictures he had seen. "We're all depending on you, you know. Screw this up and the balance could definitely tip in the wrong direction. Don't want to see what this planet looks like with dark magic getting the upper hand."

"I've got this. I've been in tighter places, believe it or not. I mean, even the undercover part isn't that big a deal. I'm a scavenger by trade and we tend to lie a little." He held up his fingers just inches apart, still giving an icy smile to the Wizard. "Hope that's not a surprise. I gotta go if I'm gonna meet these guys. They don't sound like they would appreciate tardiness. Besides, there are a lot of posers out there these days promising to find you a little treasure. They would definitely get themselves killed just trying to find some ore. Even the Gnomes are a little tricky when it comes to traveling through their land. Turns out, they think all that ore belongs to them. Something about land rights, sacred plots. Testy bunch."

"Don't let me keep you. Use a portal. You have government approval for it and the Silver Griffins have been alerted to look the other way." The Wizard looped his wand in the air in a small series of circles, creating the glamour around himself, leaving Louie out in the open.

"I take it we're done, then." Louie smirked, pulling his collar up around his ears, pink from the cold.

"Report back when you have an update and no later than two days from now, either way. Use the spell I gave you to ping me. Better than a cell phone. Can even leave a message." The Wizard took off at an easy lope across the park, headed for his car parked along the street, the wand still held out in front of him, his other hand in his jacket and his shoulders hunched against the cold. Louie watched him go, giving him a chance to be out of the area.

Once the Wizard drove off, Louie wasted no time, quickly building a ball of light between his hands, blowing into it the coordinates now firmly planted in his mind. He teased out the light with his hands till there was an opening large enough to step through, wasting no time. On the other side he found himself in a dimly lit boardroom on the other side of Richmond facing a row of aging men fully outfitted in LL Bean gear that was clearly bought online earlier that week. They stood on the other side of a long boardroom table.

He landed on top of the smooth wooden table, stamping with his dusty boots, taking joy in watching their eyes widen and a smattering of them backing up from him. The gust of warm air from an overhead vent felt good on his cold face. Not a bad entrance. Give it an eight.

"Gentlemen…" Louie clapped his hands together, a smile spreading across his face. It wasn't his first time meeting a group of dangerous investors. A Kilomea with a toothache and a pickaxe is more dangerous than this bunch. He easily leapt down from the table, landing lightly on the floor. The sword made a sharp, metallic thud against the floor as he touched down, kneeling against the tile floor. The men backed up even further against the far wall to give him more room. "Hear you're in need of a scavenger. Who's in charge and can get this party started?"

He stood up, his hands on his hips, the hilt of the sword just over his shoulder.

No one moved as Louie shook his head, looking around the room. "Take a deep breath folks. Come on, who…"

The door opened abruptly, and Charlie Monaghan breezed in wearing a well-fitting suit and hard soled shoes. "I'm in charge… everyone getting to know each other?" Charlie looked like he was losing weight and his skin was grey and mottled. He had lost more time and woken up in an airport in Texas, wondering how he got there. He smiled harder, doing his best to maintain control. Never let them see you sweat. His head was pounding. That was happening most of the time now.

Okay, another one of these that doesn't apologize for much, like showing up late. Louie kept his eye on him as Charlie pushed his way through the group to vigorously shake Louie's hand in a tight grip. Ah, a manly man, got it. Louie gave a sly smile, waiting for Charlie to go first. Jackson, you are saving my butt once again. Always let the predator go first and show his hand.

Charlie hesitated, waiting to see if Louie would say something. He looks like an over-muscled man. "A Wizard, right? What does that mean? You memorize spells?"

"We're magical beings who can channel it through words and objects. Simple." A magic snob, great. Come on, tell me your spiel.

Charlie let out a disappointed breath, pushing forward. "I hear good things about you. You can act as a guide for all of these men?"

Louie tried to hide his surprise. These jokers want to go with me to Oriceran. That is a fucking bad idea that will end badly. "Sure."

"We pay you half now and half upon delivery. Gold coins I hear is the preferred currency." Charlie went to the credenza, pulling a key out of his pocket to unlock it. He opened a sliding wooden door and pulled out a leather pouch, heavy with gold coins. "There's more where this came from and an increase for your next job if you get them all back safely." He let out a chortle slapping the nearest man on the back even as the color drained from the man's face and he started to protest, sputtering, his finger raised in the air.

Charlie cut him off, speaking for the group. "They're ready to go. I gave them a list of must haves and told them all to be here prepared to have their minds blown. Don't worry, they won't slow you down. All of them are pretty active, play tennis, walk the golf course. Jeff here is a runner."

So a shit show then. "Sounds good but not necessary. I can retrieve the ore and bring it right back here. No muss, no fuss."

"I like my way better. Besides, you'll need help carrying the ore back and the more we retrieve on the trip, the faster we can get our endeavor closer to reality. I have partners with short attention spans."

"What exactly would that particular reality look like?" Partners. That's interesting. Need a little more intel I can deliver to my handlers. The small balls of light whizzing around Louie's ankle hummed against his skin as a reminder.

"Where dreams come true…" Charlie smiled, his even white teeth all showing as he waved his hand in the air. It was his usual signal that he was done talking. The men around him knew it and bunched up together as if they were expected to transport somewhere. "Beam them up." He tossed Louie the bag of coins and Louie easily caught it, feeling the heft of the gold in his hands. Not a bad payday.

Louie resisted rolling his eyes as he pocketed the pouch full of coins. "We'll be moving through some rough terrain. The ore is along the base of the mountains near a deep ravine and then up to a place called Dead Man's Crawl tucked into the mountain."

"Great story," said Charlie, his smile straining. "I'm sure you keep them hanging on every word around the campfire making s'mores. Times to get going so you can get back."

Louie shrugged his shoulders and without another word created a ball of light letting the energy build between his hands as he quietly sang into it. He wanted to get them as close to the edge of the Concha as possible without falling over a cliff. Two days to get this done… Fuck me. Drag a bunch of men who look like a long walk would wear them out through Dead Man's Crawl. Louie jangled the bag of gold coins on his hip to make himself feel better. The portal opened wide over the center of the Concha as the wind blew back Louie's hair. He looked over the side at the vast drop below, tossing an Oriceran penny from his pocket and counted till he heard a faint splash below. "That's pretty fucking far. It'd be awhile before you'd splat. Have to hope you pass out." He pulled his head back inside just as one of the men threw up into a nearby trash can.

Charlie Monaghan looked at him, his lips pressed into a thin pale line, his eyebrows knitted together.

"Nobody got hurt. I was only about a yard off. Hang on." Louie closed the portal as sparks noisily spilled over the shiny table, sizzling in spots. Louie started another ball of light, singing into it again, adjusting the coordinates just enough. He opened the portal and smelled the nearby poisonous vines, smiling. "I love the smell of dung vines in the evening! Look the two moons are rising over the mountains. Good time to get going. Come on men. Portal won't stay open forever, but the world in between will… and I mean forever."

Louie stepped through the portal, holding the opening as the men scurried through, tripping over themselves and standing up, wide-eyed in an inadvertent imitation of baby birds. Louie looked at them, laden down with supplies in their backpacks. Better I scare 'em straight now. "You might want to look more confident or a flying harpy might mistake you for dinner and swoop down and grab one of you." Louie chuckled as the portal closed and he turned and walked down the path toward Dead Man's Crawl and what lay beyond that. "Come on men, better keep up. You wouldn't want to get lost on Oriceran with no way to go home."

He glanced back and saw them bunched up in the middle. "Single file would be best. Too many things jump out and this way we even the odds of getting most of you home in one piece." *Too funny.* Louie took a deep breath, settling himself down. *My fine-tuned sense of humor is going to be the death of them. Stay focused, Louie. That little general will not appreciate it if you lose some of his kind. They're very touchy that way.* "Hope you packed some food in those packs. We're about to pull an all-nighter and I tend to get a bit peckish." Louie let out another laugh and a howl at the moon as the hair on the back of his neck tingled. He held out his arm for everyone to stop, holding up a fist in the air and evening out his breathing. *Ugh, that's one ugly familiar odor. Just what I needed.* He waved his arm in a motion to get everyone to crouch down and hug the side of the mountain.

"Has to be a few Kilomeas passing less than a mile away. They get an odor on them that acts like an early warning system," he whispered. "Tense kind of warriors, always acting out. Best to let them pass."

"Should never have come. My sciatica is acting up already. Told my wife I was going camping." The man was fumbling with his pack to keep it straight on his back. He went to stand up straight to get a better hold on the backpack, despite Louie waving at him, just as a high-pitched whistle sounded loudly in the distance. The others pulled the man down just as an arrow whizzed where his head had just been.

"Kilomea greeting card. Must be scavengers. They think this is their corner. Stay down and keep moving. This is gonna be a bit of a pickle for about a mile."

"What happens in a mile?"

"We go inside the mountain. Different set of problems. We'll deal with that when we get there." *Thank God I have the sword.*

CHAPTER TWENTY

Blake Johnson heard the sound of a bird tweet telling him he got a text on his phone. He flipped it over on his lap as he drove, trying to watch traffic while keeping an eye on the street, hunting for a tiny hairy mythical beast no one else believed in. It was really wearing away at his nerves. The picture on his phone caught his eye immediately. The troll was lying back among red and white pansies next to a garden gnome.

"What are the odds?" A flood of relief ran through Blake as he turned the car around, squealing his tires as other cars honked in frustration. He chattered away to himself as he drove, calming his nerves as he convinced himself everything was actually going to work out for him. Just this once.

"He's at the goddamn garden show! I can get the story done and get the best story of my life. Aliens are real… magic is real… The invasion has started!" He yelled out his car window, startling people on the street as they turned to see if the driver was crazy, rolling their eyes at the sight of a disheveled Blake. His hands shook as he steered the car, careening down Lamar Boulevard, peering over the dashboard.

He was straining at the seatbelt, yelling at the cars in front of him, waving his hands in frustration. An older woman in the SUV in front of him gave him a very slow and polite middle finger while smiling in her rear-view mirror. She lowered her sunglasses a moment to give him a wink before rolling forward an inch. He honked again as she slowly raised her hand again and danced her manicured finger around like it was a puppet.

"Nice! You talk to your kids that way?" He threw up his hands and slapped his thighs for good measure. "It's too late. No way he's still there." He looked over to the side of the road and considered leaving his car and jogging the couple of miles left to get to the Palmer Center where the Garden Show was being held. He looked down at his hard-soled shoes with the inserts. "Thanks Mom. Your poor arches and a complete set of a 1955 Encyclopedia Britannica. Hawaii wasn't even a fucking state yet. No wonder I'm a journalist covering a garden show!"

The light ahead finally turned green and Blake inched forward till he could edge out a small truck, turning to wave to the other driver who eagerly waved him ahead just to get him out of the way. His phone let out another sharp tweet and he looked down, gasping at the sight of the troll mugging for the camera in a fountain, spitting water out of his mouth with one leg lifted behind him. The text underneath read, See you soon, with a smiley face emoticon.

Blake looked up in time to see the traffic stopped directly in front of him and slammed on the brakes, jarring himself against the shoulder strap and hitting his car horn with a loud, sharp blast. "Fuck! He's playing chicken with me! Okay… okay…" Blake drummed his fingers on the wheel, quickly moving in and out of lanes till he could turn on Riverside Drive and gun the engine, headed for the large open parking lot.

He parked the car in the first open spot he saw, not wanting to take the chance on circling and ending up right back there. More precious time lost. He took off running, getting winded after a few car lengths and slowing down to a fast walk, swinging his arms in the hope that would propel him faster. His phone tweeted again and he stopped, winded to take a look. It was a message from his editor. Need the inches double-time.

Blake typed furiously with his thumbs, letting autocorrect take over, texting, On the harp for a big storefront. At Garden Show. Will send stork soon. "Damn, good enough. Says Garden Show." He slid his phone back in his pocket and started walking again, picking up the pace, swinging his arms as the phone tweeted again. He took it out, the phone bobbing in his hand as he walked, and tried to keep his eye on where he was going.

It was the troll. A giggle escaped him as he looked at the picture for clues. "Please be in the Garden Show still. Yes!"

The troll was in another stone fountain, this time doing the backstroke with one arm while holding the phone out in front of himself with the other. The text read, Come on in, the water's fine!

He held the phone out in front of him yelling, "Aha!" as he banged into the oversized fender of a large Chevy truck and squeezed his eyes shut, waiting for the pain to pass, leaning on the truck.

"Don't be touchin' my truck." A deep baritone voice coming from an oversized cowboy in boots and a hat holding a large potted purple orchid.

"What?" Blake looked up into the sun at the shadow of the cowboy hat and the muscular arms and quickly peeled himself off the hood. "Sorry..." he mumbled, as he ran by the man, making sure he didn't brush against him. He finally got to the door and fumbled in his pocket for his press pass, flinging the lavalier around his neck and waving it at the ticket taker inside the cavernous room.

"Bad day?" asked the gray-haired man, looking up and down at Blake's sweaty appearance, his bangs sticking to his forehead.

"I've had better. Can you tell me where the fountains are?"

"Gonna do an article on fountains? Well, that depends..." The man sat down on the wooden stool behind him, rubbing his scruffy beard as he thought about where to send Blake. Tucked in the back pocket of his baggy khaki pants was an old wand made from willow that to the casual observer looked like a worn stick. "There's the commercial fountains. That's a show! Or the ones that have lights and take up a little piece of land. Might make a good article."

Blake pulled out his phone and held up the picture of the troll. "Like this!"

"Oh, the do it yourself displays. I kind of recognize the fountain but never seen that particular floating rodent before. That's kind of new. I suppose it takes all kinds, huh? Follow the banners overhead to aisle 800. Those fountains are over in the far western corner to your left along the yellow brick road. Not an actual brick road, mind you…"

Blake was already striding into the show, hearing the bits of a story the old man was determined to tell even though Blake was already gone. The old man gave a chuckle and a thumbs up to Toni standing nearby. "Always glad to get pulled into a mission every now and then. Can make an old Wizard feel young again." He let out a snort and got up from his post, strolling into the show to his next assigned post. "Feel a little like Dean Martin," he said as he pulled out a small black comb and brushed back his thinning gray hair into perfect straight lines.

Blake was long gone from the entrance, hurrying toward the fountains as he glanced up at the tall banners hanging overhead. The excitement of finally getting a good story distracted him from the Witches and Wizards keeping careful track of him as he hurried toward the fountains.

He punched the camera icon on his phone, ready to video the troll. This truth is gonna set me free. Everyone will finally treat me with the respect I deserve. No more stupid assignments to cover school meetings and garden shows… The litany of complaints ran through his head as they did most days but this time with a feeling that he might just be about to get his.

"Okay, he's here." Toni said into her phone. She smiled at Blake as he passed her. Her wrist jangled with silver bracelets catching his attention, but he barely gave her a glance as he hurried inside.

"Yes, Jack he saw me, but he doesn't actually know who I am." Toni's large, fluffy afro bobbed with her head as she talked to the Jackalope owner. "We're good. Man your station. Operation Troll is a go. I know, I named it. I like saying it. Over and out." Toni moved to her next station over by the succulents and waited for word from Mara. "This is what family does for each other," she said to no one in particular, smiling as she gave a wave to Eric across two aisles. He moved into place behind the outdoor sheds carrying a brown paper bag and made a point of looking at the sturdy patio furniture, testing out the rocker. "Not bad…"

CHAPTER TWENTY-ONE

Yumfuck was enjoying a theme of sorts and was thinking about posing with the gargoyle fountain next while he waited for the reporter. He was in the last display of the Do It Yourself section that featured four scenarios of outdoor living that homeowners could attempt to do themselves. A middle-aged woman with streaks of purple in her hair stopped to watch the troll do a cannon ball off the edge of a fountain with a small spray of water. "A swimming rat. I love Austin. Even the rodents are digging the place. Rock on tiny dude." The woman held up two fingers giving Yumfuck the peace sign.

"Rock on motherfuckers!" chirped the troll, holding up his paw and matching the symbol with two small claws.

The woman let out a laugh as she walked away. "I have never felt so optimistic about this goddamned planet."

The troll waved and spit a thin stream of water doing the doggie paddle back to the edge. He pulled himself out and shook all over, spraying the water. "Time to go," he chirped.

He knew time was running short before Blake Johnson would come barreling into the displays.

The plan was already in motion.

The troll scrambled to the next section, one aisle over to the stylish outdoor bars, while still holding on to his phone. He scrambled up the side of a grass tiki hut and waited, perched on the top above the crowd where he had a panoramic view of most of the show. He waved to Jim, another regular from the Jackalope who picked up the end of a fishing line and gently tugged on the line to make sure it was still secure.

"All set!"

The troll let out a cackle and waved at a tired child in his mother's arms, his head on her shoulder. The child perked up and pointed a small finger at the troll, his mouth forming a perfect o in surprise. The troll waved and gave a wink, holding his finger to his lips. The child waved excitedly, jiggling against his mother.

"What is it? Why are you so excited? Did your dad give you his soda?" The mother did her best to hold on to her son, looking around to see what had caught his attention. The child covered his mouth with both hands, taking side glances at the troll, his eyes wide. "Mickey is real," he finally said, covering his mouth with his hands in excitement.

"That was just a dream, sweetie. Go back to sleep." The mother patted her son's soft head, relieved it was nothing more.

The troll gave a last wave and an okay sign as Blake came running up to the nearby exhibitions, skidding to a stop and turning in a tight circle, looking down at the ground and in all the fountains. Yumfuck watched his frustration grow as he took another selfie, sending Blake a tweet. He watched as Blake looked at his phone and spun around, spotting the troll and holding up his phone, barely able to take a breath. He looked as if he had forgotten how to breathe and was in danger of passing out.

The troll stood up on the top to give Blake a better view as he clicked away, waving at him to come closer.

Just as everyone was starting to look in the same direction Jim gave a sharp tug on the line catching Blake around the ankles and sending him flying into a nearby kiddie pool. He slid across the top, landing in the middle with a splash, his phone still in the air. Two teenage girls giggled and took a selfie with Blake as the background. Jim quickly rolled up the transparent line on his hand and slid it all into his pocket, walking away as the crowd around Blake built to two rows.

Yumfuck slid down the side of the grass hut and landed neatly on the ground as Blake quickly pulled himself out of the pool, ignoring the two guards who were coming over to see who was playing in the displays. The troll was already off and running in a zigzag pattern as a dripping Blake followed in pursuit, weaving in and out of different backyards, hopping across flagstones as if he were playing a heated game of hopscotch.

The troll tucked and rolled near a display of tall grasses and lost Blake long enough to crawl among a collection of lawn ornaments. He ran between a flock of pink flamingos and slid cleanly into place among several smiling monsters made of grey steel, their mouths wide open and thin grey arms outstretched. As Blake ran by the troll opened his mouth in a grimace holding still and waited till Blake was almost out of earshot before calling out, "See ya sucker! Aloha!"

"Huh?" Blake turned so fast his wet shoes flew out from under him and he did a high-stepping dance for a few feet till he could right himself. By now, the crowd had grown even bigger to watch the man playing in the exhibits.

A tall man with a round middle wearing a colorful blue Round Rock Express baseball sweatshirt nudged his wife, digging his elbow into her side. "That's the most entertaining thing I've seen since we got here." His wife rolled her eyes and stepped just far enough away so he'd stop his poking. "Garden shows are not supposed to be interactive. Obviously the man has lost his marbles."

"Probably while waiting for his wife."

Behind the crowd Mara, wearing a floppy hat pulled down

over her ears and large sunglasses moved quickly down the aisle, closely following the path of the troll. She pulled down her sunglasses and gave the troll a wink as he ran right over her shoe on the way to the backyard sheds. Blake came chugging by seconds later sputtering about a furry alien as Mara stepped back to give him room.

"Oh my, are you okay?" she said loudly, looking around at the crowd who were half amused and half standing back just in case. A row of phones were held up in the air as onlookers filmed the whole thing. "Perfect," whispered Mara. "Part one is a success. Okay Yumfuck, part two is up to you and Eric."

The troll had escaped to an aluminum shed sliding in through a small opening near the bottom. He took his time crawling in, shaking his rear end as much as he could, keeping an eye out for the sounds of Blake Johnson tripping over furniture trying to get to the troll. Blake had the presence of mind to film the small dancing furry butt just as it disappeared into the shed.

"At last! You've finally made a mistake!" Blake ran into the shed, slamming the door behind him as he came face to face with Yumfuck Tiberius Troll.

Eric saw the door shut and fumbled with the brown bag in his hands, letting it slide out of his hands as marbles rolled out across the floor blocking everyone's path. "Well a good goddamn," sputtered Eric, looking to all the world as if he was frustrated at himself. He got down on his hands and knees and started scooping marbles toward the bag but only managed to spread them out further sending them rolling in every direction. The two guards who had been following Blake came as close as they could but stopped at the edge of the spill.

The tall man walked back by with a look of surprise as his wife said, "Look at that Gene! He really did lose his marbles."

"Thirty-five years with you and still a surprise every day."

The guards tried to take a step forward as the marbles hit their shoes and they'd take a step back. "You need to clean this up," one of them said sternly, his hands on his hips to let everyone know he meant what he said even if he wasn't moving.

"Maybe a broom would help." Eric was doing his best to sound helpful. "Got 'em for my indoor plants. Weren't cheap, you know. Need to get them all back in the bag or the wife will have a fit." With every sweep of his arm the rolling marbles let out a loud clacking sound, drowning out most of what was coming from the shed.

Toni took her cue and took a look around to make sure everyone was watching the marble spill as she gave a small wave to her wand and whispered, "Louder please." Barry Manilow's voice crooning Copacabana poured out of every speaker in the ceiling further covering any other sound.

Inside the dim light of the shed Blake feverishly held up his camera, licking his dry lips as he collected himself quickly, drying his hands on the front of his pants. At the last moment he realized he was soaking wet from head to toe and gave out a giggle. "All worth it... This is Blake Johnson, reporting on the sighting of an alien or tiny Bigfoot..."

"Or small Cheetos..." cackled the troll as he squeezed his eyes shut and let out an orange fart that slowly rose toward the ceiling.

Blake tried to move his phone around to capture the cloud. "... that has been sighted all over Austin, Texas. Oh man, what is that smell?" He tried breathing through his mouth as he kept talking, his words spilling out. He held the phone as close to his mouth again to be sure he could be heard over the loud music playing outside of the shed. "I've tracked him to the Home and Garden Show at the Palmer Center and have successfully trapped... Yaaaaaa!"

Blake let out a high-pitched squeal as the troll cackled again and grew till he was towering over Blake, hitting the tin roof with a thud. He stood over Blake, hunched against the roof, his hot breath pouring into the reporter's face as he smiled wide. His once tiny sharp teeth were now the only thing Blake could focus on as his phone pressed up against the soft, wiry hair of the troll.

"Homina, homina, homina, homina…" Blake babbled loudly trying to find the words to yell for help. "Don't eat me, please." It was all he could think to say.

The troll snorted and shrunk back down to the size of a small child, gently taking Blake by the hand as he whispered to him, looking him straight in the eye. "You're not a half bad reporter but you could work on being a better human being. Good stories are going to come your way but ask yourself first if every one of them needs to be written and always do your best to err on the side of doing no harm." Yumfuck patted his hand. "You might even manage to do a little good. Now, fair warning, no one is going to believe you on this one. Not yet, anyway. Let it go or live with the consequences."

Blake shook his head hard. "You're talking to me. Wait! Wait!" He pulled his hand away from the tiny troll. "It's the truth. I have to tell the public. It wouldn't be right to hide it. Shit, I'm arguing with an alien. Is my phone still recording? Sweet! It is!"

"Not always about right or wrong. Nature doesn't know right or wrong, only consequences. I have to be going but remember what I said. Look for where you can add to the common good. That'll never steer you wrong." The troll ran to the same hole he had used to get in the shed and shook his furry hind parts at Blake while looking over his shoulder and throwing him a raspberry. At the last moment he threw back his head and let out one last cackle. Yumfuck slid through the opening making sure to stay close to the nearby potted plants, shimmying along a wall. He got to the end of the wall and heard a familiar voice.

"Hagan!" The troll let out a chirp and a trill.

Hagan almost dropped the soft pretzel in his hand as he quickly took a look around to see who else might be watching.

"How in hell do you show up everywhere?" Hagan crouched down, pretending to tie his shoe.

"Those are Velcro, dude," chirped the troll.

"Oh, like you know what Velcro is now. Great. Should I ask what you're doing here? I'm guessing all that commotion had something to do with you."

"A little," chirped the troll. "I'm fixing our little problem." The troll held his finger up to the side of his nose with a smile showing his tiny pointed teeth. "Things can go back to normal."

"Can you let me in on what normal would look like since magic got here?" Hagan held up his hands, waggling his fingers.

The troll let out a cackle and scrambled into Hagan's hand, taking a bite of his pretzel. "Yum…."

"I've taken off a few pounds lately and I swear it's from all the food I've shared with you." Hagan stood up, brushing off the knees of his jeans and looked up the aisle. "Can't keep you with me today, little buddy. Rose is along for this trip. These shows are her crack and we're busy planning her next big garden." Hagan rolled his eyes. "Ever since Leira did that winter bloomfest for her she's been on a kick to do it again. She thinks she has a green thumb or it was something about the Texas dirt."

"Sometimes magic will bite you in the ass," cackled the troll, as he took another bite of the warm salty pretzel.

"Exactly. Hey, hey, slow down. I'll give you more if you stop licking the pretzel. Otherwise I guess I'll give you the whole thing."

"I think you have a friend of mine." Mara smiled and held out her hand. "Thanks for the assist."

"So, you're not working alone on this one. So tempted to ask…" Hagan held out the troll who was clinging to the pretzel. "Fine, it's yours. I'll get another."

"Got you." Mara scooped him up and put him in her pocket. "Pardon me a moment. Have to tidy up." She pulled in enough energy, her eyes aglow and sent all the marbles rolling toward Eric till they came to a stop in a pile near his bag.

Hagan sputtered in disbelief, patting the top of his head. "What the…"

Eric looked up at the surprised guards. "Must be a foundation issue. Might want to check into that." He opened the bag and shoveled the marbles into it with a sweep of his arm, getting to his feet and waving to the crowd. There was even a smattering of applause as he took a short bow.

"Okay, nothing to see here," said a relieved guard. He nudged the other guard, tapping him on the arm. "We should find that nut who was breaking apart the displays before anything else happens. What a day!"

"And you said this would be an easy gig. No problem, Joe. Walk around a bunch of flowers for eight hours, Joe…"

Toni and Jim came to the end of the aisle, waiting patiently for Eric who was walking toward them, the bag safely tucked under his arm. He was whistling as he walked, a smile on his face. "You look pretty pleased with yourself," said Toni.

"Been awhile since I've gotten to do a caper of any kind."

"You think the Silver Griffins will mind that we used a little bit of magic to cause a little mayhem?"

"Definitely. Fortunately for us they have more important things to worry about these days. Been hearing plenty of rumors about all the trouble with artifacts. Even weird stuff I don't know if I want to believe. Hijinks at a local home and garden show won't rate even a flyover in our direction."

"Nice. Flyover. Old school with the whole broom thing."

"Thought you'd like that. How'd that one get started anyway?"

"Probably some Witch levitating holding onto a broom. Who knows? Let's go get Elmer and head out for something to eat. Beer's on me."

Hagan spotted the group and shook his head. "I don't know what this adds up to, but it looks like a regular Ocean's Four plus a troll kind of operation."

The door to the aluminum shed shook as Blake nervously

pried it open, his legs shaking as he came out into the bright light.

"There he is!" shouted one of the guards, quickly bustling over and taking Blake by the arm. "Hey, look at this. He has a press badge!"

The guards each took Blake by an arm and marched him toward the offices as Blake babbled about a talking troll. "A talking doll, you don't say."

Hagan's eyes grew wider. "Isn't that the reporter…" He put his hands up in protest. "Never mind. I don't think I want to know this one. I think I see a loaded down dolly being pushed in my direction. That's my signal to go. Rose has managed to exhaust our savings at last."

"We should leave too. Look, I found some moss we can put in a pot for you at home. Nicer place to sleep than in a shoebox wrapped in underwear."

The troll shrugged. "Why not both?" he chirped.

"You're a weird little dude, but I get that. I come from a long line of women who do things with their own kind of style while kicking a little bit of ass. Leira gets that from our side of the family."

CHAPTER TWENTY-TWO

Turner Underwood stood at the entrance to the executive airport building dressed in his favorite dark cashmere coat and a black homburg squarely on his head. The mother of pearl cufflinks neatly matched the tie pin in his blue silk tie. "Makes me look a little like Churchill, don't you think? One of the finest Gnomes I ever had the pleasure of knowing." He leaned on his favorite cane with a silver robin as the handle.

"You knew Churchill? Even I know who that is." Correk looked incredulous. He was dressed in his old boots from Oriceran that went over his knees and his long tunic. The area was mostly empty except for a few travelers waiting for their planes to be ready.

"I've been the Fixer for a long time now. Things come up that required my attention. Those years were particularly busy. Could have used someone like you back then but rules are rules. One Fixer at a time and you were somewhere on Oriceran probably playing a rousing game of Lutea ball."

"What am I right now if I'm not some kind of Fixer."

"An ordinary Light Elf in training. Were you hoping for a

better title? How about Chief Bottle Washer? Keep your humility close at hand, you're going to need it." He clapped Correk hard on the shoulder. "I won't be gone long but till I get back you need to stay close to Leira. Keep her magic in check," he said sternly, his furry brows knit together as he stared into Correk's eyes, his chin tucked down on his chest. "There will also be times that I will send you on short missions to help someone else in the magical community and I will stay here to be close to Leira."

Correk's face grew darker but the Fixer cut him off before he could protest.

"You must start to learn your new role and you can't learn the entire scope of it by standing next to Leira Berens. Granted, she is a unique case. Once in an Elf lifetime but there are other things that must be tended to as well. Spells to learn, potions to make, energy to channel. And that's just the beginning. There are worlds under this world teeming with magical folk. All of them fall under your purview and when you are exactly what's called for, you'll start to sense it and need to go." The Fixer held up his hand. "And I will be here to guide and protect Leira even if that young woman is determined to fight her own battles. Although, I must say she has come a long way in asking for help."

"What about Jackson and his meddling?"

Turner smiled, the dimples in his cheeks growing deeper. "He is a necessary element who will fulfill some of his fatherly duties at last, if only to annoy you."

Correk shook his head in protest, his blue eyes flashing with anger, which only caused Turner to put back his head and laugh, one hand on top of his impressive black hat. "I'm really looking forward to this stewardship of your learning. Has so many damn flavors to it." The smile dropped from his face as he lowered his voice. "But do not let emotions get the better of you, Elf, in any direction. Anger or affection. Look for balance in all things and you will have a better chance at keeping everyone in one piece and on this side of the veil. Remember there are two hurdles here, neither of them are really enemies."

"I wouldn't call the Dark Mist neutral…"

"And yet in some ways it is. It doesn't think for itself. It's fulfilling some dark, forgotten curse, I imagine…" He tapped his cane against the sidewalk. "It only knows to go toward extreme darkness and extreme light and gather both back into that damnable void. I don't believe we know the real reason even yet. May we never find out, frankly." A shudder passed through him and his eyes briefly glowed, startling Correk.

"You're afraid of the Dark Mist. I don't think I've ever seen you afraid of anything."

"Only a foolish Elf is not afraid of anything. Stay very aware and alert, Correk."

"Is the Light neutral as well?"

"Ah, the Light. That one is even more confusing. It fills Leira with an overwhelming sense of joy and peace. Who wouldn't call that good? And yet, it asks everything of her. To join with it and become one till she disappears from this plane all together. Beyond that I don't know what that means. But I don't wish that for Leira even if I'm pulling her away from what the humans would call heaven. Let it wait a few more hundred years at least for her. Selfish of me, probably."

He saw the pain flash across Correk's face and his expression softened. "The Light serves a purpose but in the extreme it becomes the problem. Some amount of grounding is required. Jackson may prove very useful in that area. He's a Jaspar Elf after all and he may know more than at least you give him credit for."

"He looks like he's homeless and his magic ran out a long time ago."

The Fixer gave a low chortle. "That's a lifestyle choice. It happens to Elves sometimes. We go big in whatever we do. I have to go but I'll be back, and it'll be your turn. Don't hover too much or she'll refuse your help. Knowing Leira she'd lose you in a crowd. Don't let that happen. I'll be back soon. Till I get back keep everyone alive and in one piece. Your first assignment. Last two things I need to tell you and they must stay between us. I'm going to need your word on it."

Correk nodded but Turner pressed his lips together in frustration. "Use your words, Correk," he said in a low tone.

"Of course you have my word. I'll tell no one."

"That includes Leira and even the troll."

"Everything with a beating heart."

"Good. The first is that I placed a tracking ball of light under the Mustang that will stay close to Leira in case she gives you the slip. Follow my energy trail and connect with me and you'll be able to see where she is. The energy will find you if she's in real danger. Don't bother arguing about this. We both know she's a damn good detective and if she senses you're babysitting her, she'll make a point of leaving you somewhere desolate just to prove a point and then go looking for trouble."

"She's already done it once."

"Funny at any other time. God, I love that girl. The second is even more important and a long held secret among Fixers. If everything becomes a shit show, use this whistle." He pulled a thin silver whistle the length of his palm out of his coat pocket and held it out to Correk. A fancy F was engraved on one side and on the other was an inscription. Fight with honor and to the end.

"That's the Oriceran battle cry."

"That was created by the first Fixer a very long time ago. Each Fixer pours a little of his magic into it that keeps it powered and ready to go. The same Fixer gave it only one purpose. To help a Fixer in training if things ever get to the point…"

"Of a shit show."

"Yes, and not before. Not one moment before. Heed that warning."

Correk looked down at the whistle. "What happens if I use this too soon?" But when he looked up the Fixer was gone.

"Hate it when he does that." He clenched the whistle in his hand. "May I never have to use this damnable thing." Even though I probably will.

CHAPTER TWENTY-THREE

Correk followed the trail and found Leira at her office watching the screen for traces of artifacts. She was wearing her running clothes with her favorite blue and orange shoes and her hair was damp along the back of her neck. She was focused on the symbols, her eyes moving quickly.

He stayed back by the door, watching her. *She's learned how to read them in no time at all. I wonder if the energy is teaching her.*

She let out a deep sigh and narrowed her eyes, putting her hands on her hips and her chin out.

He had known her long enough to know that look on her face. *She's determined to get into the fight.* "Where's Hagan? Doesn't he work on these cases with you?"

Leira tilted her head to the side watching him, her dark hair tucked behind an ear. "You worried about Hagan or me?"

"Not worried about anyone. Is there something to worry about?"

"Nice deflection and if you mean above and beyond the fucking horror that's already going on, no. But come here and look at this. See those symbols? There's some increase in activity but it's hard to tell who's doing it. I could ask my own energy the question…"

"Bad idea." Correk blurted it out faster than he had intended to and tried to cover by striking a casual pose and smiling at her.

"Oh, now I know something's up. That's a pretty creepy look you've got going on there. What the fuck are you doing? Who's been talking to you? Was it Jackson? Nana and Mom wouldn't bring the drama…"

"The only one bringing the drama right now is you. Not everything rises to the level of an investigation. Take your beady eyes off me, Berens. This is a normal Light Elf mood."

She gave him a crooked smile and waved to him. "Are you actually coming in or are you staying by the door? What is up with you tonight?" Something about him is different. "You'd tell me if something was wrong." She said it as a fact, waiting to see if he flinched at all.

He held her gaze, remembering her standing on the battle-field, one leg broken and realizing she didn't have the energy left in her to strike down a fireball from someone as powerful as Rhazdon. It was so easy to make that one decision. He smiled easily at her. "I'm hungry and you're taking too long." Partial truth, at least.

"Pizza and popcorn night?"

"How does that work? Not both at once, surely. Although…"

"I don't food judge. You do you," she said. "Let's go get food and take it home. Share with the little furry guy. You seen him lately?" She waved her arm, her eyes glowing for a moment catching him off guard as she erased the screen.

He shook his head, watching her. It's become second nature for her. A growing sense of something bigger coming for both of them took root inside of him. Then we'll face it together. Fight to the end and with honor. Leira looked up at him and he forced a smile. Stay by her side. If it's the last good thing we do. He swallowed hard and felt for the whistle in his pocket. "Good run? Take anyone down on the way?"

Leira got her coat, breaking into a smile. "That would have made it perfect. It wasn't bad as it was. Perfect running weather. Just a little cold and the sky seemed so big and wide open, turning all sorts of colors. Gotta love Texas." She put an arm around him, giving him a hug.

"You're very damp."

"I earned it. You can take a little sweat, can't you?" She raised her elbow in the air, doing her best to try and rub more sweat on him.

"Are you really trying to rub your armpit on me? Back, back." He put the palm of his hand on her forehead holding her at arm's length, smiling as he shook off the feeling. Leira let out a snort and a laugh swinging wildly, trying to land a soft blow and only catching air. "I could take you down if I wanted to."

Correk laughed bending his arm slightly to let her get closer and pushing her back out again at the last moment. "Fake out!"

Leira laughed, gulping in air. "What movie did you get that from? My favorite Martian? Are TV antennas about to come out of the top of your head?" Leira swept a leg around catching him in the back of the ankles and sending his legs out from under him. He landed in a sitting position, laughing out loud, the creases around his eyes deepening as Leira fell forward onto her knees, her bangs sticking to her forehead and a broad smile across her face.

"We make a pretty good team!" She laughed, her head rocking back, her face flushed, nudging him with her foot.

"Quit kicking my butt!" He sat up taller and pulled her by her foot, sliding across the industrial carpet till she was right up against him.

Leira found herself inches from Correk's face, looking closely into his eyes as the smile froze on her face. Correk let out one last laugh as he looked at Leira and let go of her leg. "We should get going," he said, as he pulled himself back up to a standing position and straightened out his tunic.

Leira stood up, stretching her tight back, her arms overhead as her thoughts spilled one over the other. Okay, put it away. Back in the little box in the back of my mind. No can do, Berens.

"I pick the movie tonight," said Correk.

She picked her jacket up off the floor and slid into it. "No, nope, no." She put up her hand as she headed for the door. "Last time you and Yumfuck picked I had to sit through a Vincent Price triple feature. I want something from this millennium."

"You know, I haven't seen Yumfuck. Should we be concerned?" Correk glanced back at the screen just as a message popped up, rolling quickly across the bottom and then disappeared, leaving it blank again. A team was spotted heading for a possible relic site in Wyoming. A PDF team out of Chicago was headed there. He turned back around and kept moving for the door. Let this one fight be someone else's. We'll pick the ball back up tomorrow.

"He's probably hanging with Nana. He'll turn up when he's ready. We're cosmically attached and he's wily. I'm not worried. How about pineapple on the pizza?"

Correk grimaced. "I'd rather stuff Cheetos on the top than pineapple."

"That could be arranged."

CHAPTER TWENTY-FOUR

Leira was in her favorite soft UT sweatpants and hoodie headed out to the patio to sip her coffee and watch the sun rise. There was one spot out there, if she angled her chair just right she could see the sun as it rose. Correk was still asleep on the couch, his face buried in the pillow. Yumfuck had turned up just as they had opened the pizza boxes in the kitchen last night.

"It's like we rang some kind of cosmic dinner bell for you," Correk had said, giving the small troll the once over. "I don't see any signs of mayhem still clinging to you." The troll had laughed as Correk scooped him up and perched him on the edge of his own paper plate.

Correk rubbed his soft green head. "Glad you're home." Leira noticed how bone weary Correk looked. I will have to get it out of him. It's not like him to keep secrets from me.

"I know," the troll had trilled.

Leira checked on the little troll before she came outside and found his nest lined with soft, furry green moss. She went to her bedroom and opened the old dresser that had once belonged to her grandmother and pulled out a new pair of underwear, tucking it around him as he curled up into a tight ball and let out a soft trill in his sleep.

"You look so innocent in your sleep," she whispered. The troll's legs churned and a smile came to his face as he ran in his sleep. "Are you running toward trouble or away from it?" Leira smiled and waited for him to settle back down before she headed outside. He lifted a leg and let out a soft, airy fart, cackling in his sleep.

"Oh gawd, way to kill the sentimental moment." Leira waved a hand in front of her face and quickly covered her mug just in case it was possible to have fallout. "How does Correk sleep through that? I don't know whether or not I should be impressed or check his pulse," she whispered. "Okay, I'm done, moment over." She opened the door to the cottage and used it like a large wooden fan for a moment before stepping over the threshold and gently shutting the door behind herself.

She stood still, breathing in the fresh air, the bricks cold against her bare feet. "May have singed a few nose hairs. How does such a small creature churn out so much gas." She held the chipped Best Grandmother mug up to her face and let the steam warm her cheeks before she took another gulp. "Nectar of the Gods…"

There was a plume of smoke billowing out from just inside the restaurant. Estelle is here early. Wonder what inspired that. Leira dragged a seat over, across from another one and settled in, putting her feet in the other chair. "Wish I had brought the pot out here."

"Then I'm right on time."

She looked up to see Turner Underwood in dark slacks and a shirt and pullover sweater using a cherrywood cane with a brass handle draped over his arm and was carrying a cardboard tray with two large cups of coffee.

"What is that on your head?" Leira set down her nearly empty mug and held out her hand for one of the cups.

Turner pulled off the white boxy hat with no rim as he held out the tray. "This? It's a kufi. A grateful patron gifted it to me in my travels through Africa."

"I don't think I've ever seen you out of a suit."

"Everyone needs a day off now and then."

"I figured you had pajamas that looked like suits."

"Your impertinence always cheers me up. Too many people are too fucking scared to even make a joke these days. Rumors of magic and gates opening have bled into the human world and everyone is on edge. That's for another day, of course." He set the tray down and pulled over a chair. "Watching the sun rise?"

Leira narrowed her eyes, studying him as she took a long sip. The coffee was still hot and felt good going down. "How do you do that? Show up just when someone is in need, apparently even for coffee and know what I'm thinking?"

He tapped the side of his head with his finger. "You're facing east at the crack of dawn and I've seen you guzzle this stuff like a man who was lost in the desert. Didn't even use any magic."

Leira smiled, holding on to the warm paper cup with both hands. "Best way to drink hot coffee is when I'm just this side of too cold."

"Explains the bare feet."

"Doesn't explain why you're here." She looked at him over the top of the cup. "You've gotten Correk involved in something. Not a question, by the way. Did you put him at risk?"

"Being born put him at risk."

Leira sat up, a scowl on her face. She put her feet back on the cold ground. "Don't be clever with me. I know I need your help, but I won't take it at the cost of my friend. I'll take my chances. Hagan and I made a pretty good team long before any of this shit started happening. I'm very comfortable going back to that situation."

"But you'll keep the coffee."

"I have my limits… Tell me the truth or our association ends here. If I can't trust you, I can't work with you, much less learn from you."

"Fair enough and admirable." Turner leaned forward on the handle of his cane. "I am old even in Elven years and not quite as fast as I used to be." He slapped his leg and chortled. "Still faster than most, mind you. But a Fixer has to be so quick that there is no thought, there was no hesitation at all. I can feel myself losing that small, infinitesimal fraction of a second. At the wrong moment that could end up costing someone very dearly."

Leira put down the coffee, one hand still on the warm cup and slid forward on the seat, anger filling her as the scar on her belly heated up, causing a twinge of pain that went through to her spine. "No, you didn't. That's not fair, you know Correk well enough to know he couldn't say no. You asked him to take your place as the Fixer." She turned so her face wasn't visible from the window as her eyes glowed, the magic getting the better of her. The mug slid across the table, crashing against the bricks and splashing her feet with tepid coffee, breaking into bits from the force of the energy surge.

Turner sat back in the chair, patiently waiting as he watched her. "You need to get something to ground yourself." His words came out slowly and evenly as he took in one deep breath after another, holding it for a moment and letting it go. "I'm not the enemy," he said at last. "And you don't get to decide the steps on Correk's journey. Besides, I don't think he'd be very happy if you got to keep him in a neat little box. Remember, he was originally sent here on a mission because he is a trusted and skilled Elven warrior. He has already stayed far longer than expected. Isn't the necklace already back with its rightful owner?"

Leira felt the magic subside and glanced up at the bar, watching the plume of smoke move through the dining room toward the kitchen. "It's probably the Cheetos and Dr Pepper keeping him here," she said, without looking at Turner. *He's right. Fuck, I let Correk hang around because I wanted him here.*

She bent down and picked up the shards of the mug, placing them on the table. "Favorite mug…"

"It's alright that you wanted him to stay. It's alright that he didn't want to go. You know…" He leaned forward, tapping his cane on the ground.

Leira looked up at him. The tapping was a sign to her that he was making a point.

"Some think that being asked to be the Fixer is a privilege that's only bestowed on one Elf every millennia. The chance to serve in a greater capacity and learn far more about magic, honorable magic." He smacked his lips together in irritation, mulling something over. "He will still have a life full of family and friends and adventures that don't always involve a battle or fireballs."

Leira winced at the mention of fireballs as understanding came over Turner Underwood. "It's not your fault, what happened to him. He made a choice, which is his right. It's what gives life its flavor and without it, we're all just puppets." Turner leaned forward and held out his fist, rolling out his fingers one at a time. The broken bits of mug on the table and scattered along the ground came back together in the glittering glow of a stream of purple light, till the mug was whole again.

"You even got rid of the chipped edge."

"I like to give a little extra when I can. I don't know if you've noticed but I'm a bit of a showman." Turner paused, shutting his eyes for a moment and holding a finger in the air, testing the direction of the wind. "Change is coming. Can you feel it? It's impossible to stop it and you either get on board or get dragged. You don't strike me as the kind to try and hold back anything. Including Correk. Mark my words, though, you're not letting him go…"

"I didn't say…"

"You didn't need to and neither did he. You're letting the truth free and it will do its own work out there in the world. Your journeys will continue to unfold and knowing the two of you will be full of a lot of kicking ass and fucking around with dangerous things. This is your destiny."

"You don't mean fate."

"Not at all." Turner raised his cane in the air, his voice growing louder. "Fate is for fools. It's like knowing you were out here to see the sunrise. You will never be content to sit at home and watch Hoda and Jenna, wondering what to make for dinner. You'll always be out there seeking adventure because you believe in something. The basic good of everything there is. Otherwise, the light would not have found such an amenable home within you. Light doesn't go where it isn't welcome. It's very polite in that way."

"Most people don't think of former homicide detectives as optimists."

"It takes a powerful optimist to face down the worst a human being can do and still believe in justice. If you weren't an optimist, you would be in the revenge business. That will darken your magic faster than anything I've ever seen, and I've seen a lot in my travels. Do this for me. Instead of wondering what you may be losing, look for what may be gained. Look for it in every step. You have nothing to lose and you may find you don't miss the moments of joy in between fighting the Dark Mist or hunting for artifacts or whatever ghoulish adventure is waiting out there for you."

Leira took another sip from the coffee Turner had brought her. "It's still hot. If this is magic, you really have to teach me this one. I know you're right. I wouldn't let anyone hold me back. I won't do that to anyone else..."

"That you care about..."

Leira sipped the hot coffee and didn't answer him, watching the sun finally climb higher into the sky. This coffee is one of the best magic tricks he's done so far.

CHAPTER TWENTY-FIVE

Eireka and Mara sat at the stone entrance to the underground city of Hilldale near the Enchanted Rock kemana. The door was open and Eireka could see the beginning of the glowing lavender stones that lit the long, stone staircase down to the bustling city square. She looked up at the plateau, remembering the battle and shivered. We all came too close to a bad ending. Some of us slipped right over the line. Still can't shake the feeling something worse is building and headed our way.

They heard a shuffling from below and someone taking the stairs at a fast clip. A Swamp Kilomea came up the stairs, a large crate on his shoulder, grunting as he got to the top.

"This door's supposed to be kept closed. Too many curious eyes around these parts."

Mara lifted an arm, sweeping it around her head, making the transparent glamour around them shimmer.

Outside the protective bubble the wind was blowing hard even though the sky was clear, kicking up dust and the occasional small tumbleweed. The Kilomea gave another grunt, shifting the heavy wooden crate on his shoulder as he passed through the glamour to the other side, shifting into a glamour of his own.

"Not bad," said Mara, watching the Kilomea disguised as a muscled, dark-skinned man pick his way over the rocky outgrowths toward the parking lot.

Three hikers passed by, stopping to watch the man for a moment.

"I totally get that."

Eireka let out a hush with a stern look but Mara smiled at her and kept right on talking. "What, you think this is my first glamour? I know how to soundproof these fuckers. Watch…" Mara stood up and jumped up and down, waving her hands and screaming as loud as she could.

Eireka turned to watch, ready to push the stone marked with the infinity symbol to hurriedly close the opening. She bit her bottom lip, looking back and forth. The one on the right. Not the circle or the square symbol. Can't afford to be knocked out or electrocuted.

The hikers kept chatting easily among themselves as one of them tossed a rock that easily passed through the glamour. Eireka froze right where she was, looking back and forth between the rock and the hiker.

Mara toed the rock, raising her eyebrows at Eireka. "I'm a very experienced Elf and even part Witch, if you'll recall. A bit of a magic mutt, my dear. The glamour suggests to anyone who has no magic the very image they expect to see. Hell, I couldn't even tell you if those three all saw the same thing. But they'll believe it till their dying day. Pretty clever, huh?"

One of the women pointed toward a stream to the other side of the opening to Hilldale and they set off, passing just by where the women sat without ever knowing they were there.

"Never quite get used to a good Texas wind under a blue sky." Mara shielded her dark brown eyes from the sun and gave up and put on her sunglasses. "How long did the Jersey Willen say this would take? He's been gone for well over an hour."

"I'll answer the question you're really asking. Yes, he's coming back. They're thieves but they're not liars. It's an odd kind of virtue. You can go wait back in the car if you want to. I don't mind. Jackson said we have to find this artifact for Leira's sake."

"You're still really good and pissed off at me. I suppose I get it."

"I don't think you can. I spent Leira's entire life thinking her father never really cared about me. You could have at least changed that for me."

"You were taken away…"

"There were ten good years where we were all crammed together in a small house and you had plenty of opportunities."

"I'm sorry, I was wrong. I should have said something. I let my own fear about what might happen get the better of things."

"That's all I wanted was a damn apology."

"You really need to learn to swear more. That particular gene must have skipped a generation."

Eireka smiled despite herself and looked out toward the tall kemana. "There's not enough time for what needs to be done. The signs are all there. We're all getting ready for some damn war. These artifacts, everyone wants them, and every day there's more rumors of magic being real. Can't call it fake news much longer. Have you ever read the symbols along Leira's arms when she's channeling magic? They're growing more cryptic, like it's more than even that much energy can comprehend."

Mara patted the seat next to her. "Come sit by your weird mother." Mara put her arm around her daughter, passing her calming energy through to Eireka. "You've always been good at calling things, so I trust you that there's trouble brewing. God knows we've already seen our share. But if we're going to make it, we'll need to slow down to just this day we're in. Not sure I can take worrying about what's not happening every day."

"This can't be all you want. Mom, the truth is I'm okay, Leira has plenty of allies these days. You can think about you a little. What do you want?"

"That is a great question that I've been pondering more and more lately. Maybe a change of scenery. Visit Virginia again. I always did like the different seasons and the Blue Ridge Mountains have some of the most beautiful spots I've ever seen. Not today, though. Today, I'll be here with you…"

A cold wind blew up from the stairs and the Jersey Willen scrambled to the top, his whiskers twittering. He was still wearing a worn black jacket in mourning for his mother and looked a little thinner than the last time they saw him.

Eireka stood up and went to see what he was pulling out of the folds of his skin. "Do you have it?"

The Willen held out a long, thin metal armband of two snakes intertwined and rubies for eyes. "Got it, but not sure if it'll do what you want." He handed over the artifact, rubbing his paws together eagerly. Eireka lifted the cloth HEB bag with the silver teapot. "A deal's a deal," said the Willen.

"You earned it. Don't want to know the details but you earned it."

She handed him the bag and saw his eyes widen with delight when he felt the heft of the silver inside of it. It was the first time she had seen him smile since the battle. "Oooh, the good stuff. Till we meet again." He hoisted the bag over his shoulder, the teapot too big to hide in his folds and scampered down the stairs, anxious to get home and hide his new treasure. "A real find," echoed off the walls as the door slid shut with a firm click.

Mara took a good look around before wiping away the glamour and the wind at least reached their faces, blowing back her hair. "Good Texas wind. Would be hard to leave this place but might be time for a change. We'll see…"

CHAPTER TWENTY-SIX

"Everybody stay together!" Louie yelled louder than he needed to at the men to keep them moving along. There was already a couple of stragglers at the back of the pack, which didn't bode well for their survival in one piece. The first night they pitched a tent and all slept in thick, down-filled sleeping bags while Louie slept under the stars with his bag under his head for a pillow and his cloak pulled tight around him. He heard a pack of wild dogs with luminescent eyes venture close to the camp site, but he easily cast a spell, scenting the area with wild wolfsbane and they fled for parts unknown, baying at the twin moons. He saw the tents bulge out in places and shake. "This is gonna be a long fucking trip." He shook his head and rolled over. "I blame Leira Berens. If she had left me alone, I wouldn't be in this mess. I would have just walked away the second they said I had to wander around with a bunch of magic-less greenhorns from a whole other world. But no…"

The dogs howled again followed by a loud yelp and the sound of a sharp crack. "That's definitely not good. Kilomeas are still in these parts. Apparently dining on wild dog tonight." We might have a little competition on our hands.

They got up with the bright Oriceran sun the next morning and Louie dined on blue poppy beetles he found under the rocks, roasting them over a small fire and crunching on their hard shells. "Want some? No?" The men scrambled through their packs and chewed down on Kind bars and beef jerky, sipping water from Earth. None of them offered him a bite or a sip and seemed determined not to share, even with each other.

"Might want to ration out that water. We have another full day ahead of us and I don't know how you'd take to Oriceran hydration." Louie gave a one-sided grin. Okay, that was at least a little fun.

They hiked along the base of the mountain till they got to the entrance to the Gnomes kingdom that burrowed deep into the lower parts of the mountain. Louie put two fingers in his mouth and let out one sharp whistle. A Gnome came waddling out of the darkness, shading his eyes, a scowl on his face and a stocking cap on his head to protect against the cold winds that blew through the mountain. Some suspected a dragon lived in its depths, but Louie theorized the magical whirlpools that had sucked in more than one careless scavenger and drowned them had more to do with it. Still better than death by harpy, thought Louie as he took in a deep breath, steeling himself for the negotiation.

"Louie! I thought you got your ass kicked the last time you passed through these parts. Heard the caves almost won that round. Usually takes you a good month to build up your courage to do the same dumbass thing again. Why the rush this time?" His eyes grew wide as he looked behind Louie and saw the pack traveling with him. "You must have taken a bigger blow to that head of yours than I realized." The Gnome squinted into the light to get a better look as he wrinkled his forehead and snorted. "Humans! You brought humans up here who have no magic! Might as well have brought them on a spit and made it easier for the Kilomeas! Do they know they're considered prey by some of them?"

Louie shifted his weight resisting the urge to punch the Gnome square in the face just to shut him up. That would hurt negotiations. Don't do it. We have to get by here. Remember the last time you got in a fight with one of them and a hundred of the shorties chased you for a good mile. There's a reason they call this the ant hill and they are fast little fuckers. "I think you're worrying the livestock," Louie said with a smile. "If you could keep it down…" He pushed down with his hand, doing his best to look relaxed.

"Wait till I tell my cousins. Hey! Hey Mannie, you'll never guess…" he yelled over his shoulder.

Louie rolled his eyes and took out a shiny piece of gold, flipping it in the air to catch the reflection of the sunlight.

That caught the Gnome's attention and he whipped back around, the smile gone from his face.

"We would like the privilege of passing by your door," said Louie, still flipping the coin.

The Gnome looked at the coin and peered around Louie to look at the men behind him. They were all huddled closely together doing their best to not just grab each other's hands and hold on tight.

"I've heard stories from other scavengers that there's something new and slimy up in the higher caves. Must have crawled out of the whirlpools and has taken refuge higher in the mountain. Two coins."

"Not the first time something like that has happened. One coin and I leave you alone for a week."

"This one may have eaten one of your competitors. Two coins and I punch you in the nuts."

"I'm pretty sure that's not how you negotiate shortie. Not much of an incentive for me, and my kind get eaten all the time.

It's why I don't like making friends with them. Too hard to keep figuring out who's still around."

"Call me shortie again and I'll punch you free of charge. Besides, those things have to be withering on your puny vine. You're not getting much use out of them."

"Not sure why you're so fascinated by my junk. Apparently I'm what you dream about at night, and seems we've gotten a bit off topic." Louie flipped the coin again and suddenly felt the sword warming his back, sending a flood of energy through him. Focus.

"One coin and I use your head for a tabletop." Louie felt his palms becoming hot and itchy. This cannot be good.

The Gnome's eyes grew glassy. "Okay, deal!"

Louie gave a small shake to his head, replaying what just happened. The sword felt like it was branding his back, pushing him forward. He quickly put the coin in the Gnome's hand, shifting the weight of the sword on his back.

The Gnome bit down on the edge of the coin, looking pleased with his deal as he turned and walked back into the depths of the mountain without looking back. Louie waited a moment to make sure none of his hundred brothers or sisters were about to pile out of there, but the entrance was quiet.

"That was fucking weird. What just happened?" He clapped his hands together and turned to face his small entourage. "Okay, don't question good fortune, especially on this trip. That has never been that easy. Maybe it's an omen. Come on gentlemen, let's move our asses. We have a ways to go before we get to the hard part. Let's get away from the shorties' entrance before whatever that was wears off."

It took hours but eventually they made it to the high cliffs, winding their way to the mines. They were inching along the cliff face toward Dead Man's Crawl with Louie in the lead, taking constant looks over his shoulder to make sure no one had quietly slipped over the edge.

It was Louie's first time being responsible for anyone other than Ronnie, and even Ronnie wouldn't come near this part of Oriceran. Jackson was the one who originally showed him the route but even he thought long and hard before venturing up there. This was fucking stupid. There was a sheen of sweat across Louie's forehead. He wasn't used to worrying this much before trouble showed up. Even then, he was always too busy working at a solution to get involved with worry. This is definitely fucking stupid.

He heard a yelp behind him and the sound of gravel spraying and turned around to find one of the men on his knees and the others frozen around him, not even helping him up. "Come on, aren't some of you supposed to be at least weekend athletes? Help the guy up. Look, let's try this from an angle you can understand. You survive this little adventure, you'll be richer than all your little friends and can tell them about this epic trip for the rest of your lives. Even better, I won't be around to call you liars about the details."

"What if we wait for you here?" The tall, thin man who was pointed out as being good at tennis and a weekend runner stepped forward.

"Spokesman for the group? Okay, I get it. No can do, though. You're just bait out here. You think this has got to be safer, especially after all the trash that the shortie was saying but here you're like antelope sitting too close to some very hungry Kilomeas who actually know how to use weapons besides having way more strength than something with that small a brain and short a temper should have. Don't tell them I said that. Some of them are friends."

The men stood there, looking around nervously, not moving an inch.

"Come on guys, I kid… Except about the getting eaten part. You really need to keep moving." He waved his arm, shooing them along like lost sheep. "Come on, get moving. Not my idea but now we gotta see it through. Life lessons, am I right? Think about how you'll spend the money on the honeys."

The men started moving again and Louie deftly wove through and around them, balancing on the edge of the cliff at one point with his heels over the side, till he was back at the front. "Almost there, lads. Just a couple more hurdles." The wind briefly shifted and the smell of something rancid filled his nostrils. The smile dropped from his face momentarily as he listened for any unfamiliar noises knowing full well the mountain could easily insulate the sound of tearing or screaming. Nothing. *I wonder if that's what something slimy would smell like.*

He heard the sound of retching behind him but didn't look back. *So I lose one or two. Leira is just gonna have to understand.*

CHAPTER TWENTY-SEVEN

Correk opened his eyes to see Leira standing over him. "Are you out of coffee again? That can't be it. I can smell it on you." He shut his eyes again and sank back into the pillow. "What time is it?"

"Creeping up toward lunch."

He opened one eye to look at her face. "You look serious. How is that possible? The little furry beast usually pulls at my hair at some point. I've found dried Cheetos stuck to my hair on some mornings. There was that one Raisinette that gave me a real start till I figured out it was chocolate. That would have been a new low, even for a troll. You know he actually took it out of my hand and ate it. I think I tasted my own Pop Tart coming back up. Hang on." Correk gave the center of his chest a few hard taps with his fist, swallowing hard at the memory.

"He took off out of here early this morning. I feel fairly confident he's not planning anything that could go boom." Leira shrugged. "Okay, I admit it. I've lowered the bar when it comes to the troll and it's freed up a lot of my time." Leira pursed her lips, picturing where the troll might be. "I should ask my grandmother what's going on. I feel her fingerprints all over this one."

"Why are you standing over me? Are you bored? That's good news. You're only bored with what everyone else calls an ordinary day. It means nothing is blowing up and no one is waving a gun or an artifact."

"I got it out of Turner. What you're up to. I know all about it." Leira stood there with her hands on her hips, her chin sticking out. "You should have told me."

Correk sat up on his elbows waiting to see exactly what Leira knew.

She tilted her head to the side, arching an eyebrow. "So, it's like that? Okay, I know you're his pick for the new Fixer. Were you ever planning to tell me?" Leira paced the floor in front of him. "I tell you everything…"

"Not true."

"And bring you in on every case…"

"Not true."

"I even take your advice most of the time."

"You're deeply in denial."

"I trust you with my life." She pushed his feet aside and sat down on the end of the couch.

"Alright, that one is true." Correk pulled himself up to a sitting position, wrapping his arms around his knees. His long silver hair was tied back in a braid. "But trusting me with your life doesn't mean an obligation to tell you everything that's going on in my life. You're not doing that either and I don't expect it."

Leira glanced over at Correk as the blanket slipped down to his lap. "Are you wearing a Demogorgon sweatshirt?"

"The troll found Netflix. Reminds me of a game I loved to play when I was a young Elf."

"Of course you played Dungeons and Dragons. You live among the real thing."

"I knew you would know what that is."

"You know, this right here," she said, pointing back and forth, "this is why we don't have the time to tell each other the important stuff."

"Or it's because you want to hear information more than you want to share it. I'm listening now."

"Things are changing, again." She shook her head. "It's to be expected but something big is rolling toward us. Whatever it is, it's dark and ferocious."

"We'll stop the beings behind the animal mutations and the sanctuaries will get built."

"It's not that. I can feel the edges of something dark and massive, some event getting closer." Leira pulled in a small amount of magic, enough to light up her arms as the symbols slowly turned, giving out a message. "Look at that. It makes no sense. Best I can tell, it's talking about an invasion from within. A darkness that smothers. I don't know, maybe I'm reading them wrong. I need to show Turner." She looked up at Correk, her eyes still glowing with magic. "Usually I can feel the answer in here." She pressed her fingertips against the large scar on her belly. "All I can feel this time is the edge of something and it fills me with the same feeling I get when faced with danger. I'm ready to kick some ass."

Correk smiled and leaned against the couch. "That's your normal resting state. I approach you with caution at all times. Too soon? Look, your ability to channel energy is so great that magic actually talks to you about what's ahead. But we don't live by fate, so these can only be the possibilities, not the reality that hasn't happened yet. Apparently, one of the possibilities is troublesome."

"More like a new enemy." A shiver passed down Leira's back as her eyes glowed silver, the symbols changing to something Correk didn't recognize.

"I wonder if the message is that one enemy is coming who's powerful enough to throw the odds in his favor that we're headed straight for his reality." Correk watched Leira's eyes brighten even further. "Focus on that idea."

The symbols rippled across her skin again. Correk impulsively reached out and grabbed Leira's hand to connect with her energy and felt a sharp icy cold fill his chest. He opened his mouth to speak and his breath turned to snowflakes as it hit the warmer air. An image filled his head and he instinctively gripped her hand harder, pulling some of her energy toward him.

"Harkin," he whispered. "But the magic doesn't tell the past."

"Only possible futures." The chill swirled through Leira, watching the images of Harkin. A rogue version of Correk.

"No, that's not possible."

"We passed impossible about one battle ago with Rhazdon. Maybe it's time to find out."

"There's no time to chase fairytales. He's dead, there were witnesses." He let go of her arm and felt the warmth gradually return. "Do you feel how cold that is?"

Leira saw the pain on his face and let it go. For now. "I do, but the magic is protecting me from it at the same time. Fucking cryptic icy future behind door number one. Feels more personal."

"Whatever it is, I've got your back. We fight with honor and to the end."

"Was this Oriceran battle cry worthy?" She pressed her lips together and reached for his hand. "I'm more interested in finding the solution that steers us away from having to fight the icy future. I love a good battle as much as the next guy, but I'm not tied to it. I could find some other ways to fill my time. Get ready for the gates to open. Learn more magic so I don't become a living light bulb. But I was planning to do that with you and Hagan. He's my official partner at the PDF but..."

"Choosing to take on the responsibility of being the Fixer is me stepping up my game so I don't get blown away by another fireball. The more I learn about magic, the more I can help choose a different door for the world to go through or at least be ready if we do end up in the deep freeze, or whatever that icy grip meant. It's not enough to go on and is only a feeling. Our plate is full…"

Sparks shot across the room as a portal opened up in the living room.

"Need to get an Oriceran doorbell for those things…" muttered Leira. "Friend or foe," she shouted, as her father, Jackson stepped through the opening. The Dark Forest of Oriceran was behind him, a gentle rainfall hitting the leaves. Jackson clapped his hands, shutting the portal as he shook off the rain drops running down his hair and back.

"This looks cozy." Jackson stood in the center of the small living room, a rucksack tied to his back. "Not sure what my role is here."

"Elf who doesn't call first." Correk scowled at him and threw the covers off, swinging his legs around and putting his feet on the floor.

"You don't have a role here. I'm a grown ass woman. Is this a social call? You look ready for something."

"I have a lead on a relic. It might be the one we need to ground Leira's energy, but I'll need some help to get it. I was actually going to ask tall, blonde and brooding here if he'd be willing to go along for the ride."

"I'll be coming along on this hunt. I don't get left behind in my own story. Give me five minutes." Leira easily bounded over the side of the couch and disappeared into her bedroom, leaving Jackson and Correk alone in the living room.

"So, you and my daughter…"

"Are none of your business…" Correk created a small fireball in his hands and just as quickly extinguished it, glancing up at Jackson who smiled and made two appear in his hand, blowing on them to put them out, a wisp of smoke rising in the air.

Leira came back out dressed in jeans and a t-shirt with her leather jacket. "Smells like burning hair in here. Don't want to know." She held up her hand before they could say anything. "You two have the silence thing down. Let's get going…" Her phone rang just as Jackson opened the portal and stepped through. "It's the general. I have to take it. Looks like you two are on your own. Duty calls. Try not to kill each other."

Correk reluctantly stepped through, looking back at Leira as she shrugged and the portal closed with a sizzle and pop, leaving her standing alone in the guest house. I wonder if he'll find a lead on Harkin. "Hello sir." She held the phone up to her ear, listening intently. "I know the place. I can meet you at the office and we'll leave from there." Leira hung up the phone and slid it back into her pocket. "Maybe they can bond hunting for the artifact. Nah, one of them is coming back with a scorch mark."

CHAPTER TWENTY-EIGHT

The general was waiting for Leira when she got to the warehouse. He was sitting at Hagan's desk, surrounded by Alan Cohen and two other familiar PDF agents, Mark and Gail. His hat was neatly placed on the top of the desk. "This must be big. You brought reinforcements." Leira waved to the two witches, Patsy and Lois who looked grim and had situated themselves on the couches, not saying a word. I feel better when those two are talking like magpies. They only grow silent when magic is running amok.

The general held up his cell phone, waving it in the air. "We have a rather delicate problem. Patsy, run it again, please."

Patsy raised her wand toward the overhead virtual screen and images started to form in the air.

"Looks like they're here with us in the room," said Mark, stepping closer, his mouth hanging open. He was wearing a blue nylon jacket with large PDA letters in white on the back.

"That's Charlie Monaghan, the CEO of that corporation Correk and I visited." Broke into, took their seeds away, destroyed a lab, pissed off Monaghan. A good day at the office.

"The men sitting next to him are several US Senators and

they're brokering a deal from hell." The general drummed his fingers on Hagan's desk angrily. "Fortunately for our side, a Wizard was sitting nearby and recorded the whole thing without anyone noticing. Lacey Trader was good enough to pass it along through channels."

Lois gave a wave. "We're the channels."

"There was a vote recently on Capitol Hill that gave a childish kind of finders keepers to whoever finds artifacts first, giving Axiom a right of way I would have sworn they'd never get. Nasty thing about these kinds of votes is that once the right is given, it's harder to convince others to take it away." The general gave a curt nod to Lois and Patsy.

Lois swirled her wand in the air, enhancing the sound quality so their voices became audible.

"I'm not interested unless this technology is coming online soon, and I mean within the next year." The Senator was jabbing his wrinkled finger against the white linen tablecloth. The knuckles of his hand were swollen and twisted. "I don't have the luxury of investing in green bananas."

"New technology..." Leira stepped closer to the screen to watch.

"We're getting close to being able to enhance humans with the machinery and prolong life, improve mobility..."

Shock grew over Leira's face. Enhance humans... "He can't be talking about using relics on human beings."

"He's negotiating to use it on them to keep them alive long past their expiration dates, enhance their skills." The general watched the men plotting, his mood growing darker.

"Too late, looks like their milk already curdled," muttered Gail.

"This is worse than magic running loose. This is politicians with magic. If they figure out how to do that there's no telling where it would all end."

"She gets it!" Patsy threw her hands up in the air as Lois sent a pea-sized ball of light flying across Patsy's head. Patsy saw the glowing volley just in time and ducked, smirking at Lois as the ball turned and knocked her in the back of her head and a half-eaten M&M popped out of her mouth.

The general was distracted by the virtual images playing out in the middle of the warehouse.

"Looks like we could just go over and join them," said Mark, putting his hand in the air and watching it pass right through the screen.

"We need to know more about Charlie Monaghan's intentions. This just isn't enough information. I'm sending Lois and Patsy to follow him. He's already seen you, Leira and it has to be someone with magical capabilities. He'll never see those two coming and they're a lot cagier than they look."

"Let's hope so," whispered Gail, leaning closer to Alan.

"You are going to pay these Senators a visit." The general got up from the desk and came to stand opposite Leira as he put his hat back on his head. The agents fell in behind him, ready to leave. "I've been able to pull a few strings and get them together in one room without overplaying my hand. I need you to make an appearance and put the fear of magic into them. Leave a lasting impression that will overcome whatever riches Charlie Monaghan is promising."

"Of course, general. I can put on a shit show that will leave them checking under their beds for the rest of their lives." Leira looked up at Charlie just as he got up from the table and turned to get the waiter's attention. She stepped closer, looking at the back of his head, narrowing her eyes. *I've got it! Wait… he was on the streets of Austin.* Leira let the image play through her mind, looking for more details. *Headed up 6th Street walking alone.* She shook her head. *Nothing. Why would he be in Austin.* "There! Did you see that? Lois, can you replay that part and… stop it right there. Look at his eyes. What is that? His eyes turn totally black there for just a second."

"We noticed that too and were hoping you'd have some input."

Leira looked over at Lois who quickly shook her head and swirled her wand just enough to draw the Silver Griffins symbol in light that faded just as quickly before anyone else could see the gesture.

"I'm still new to a lot of this. That one is new to me, but I can't imagine it's a good sign."

"Then we move on and gather more information. Here are the coordinates for the meeting. They should be gathered within the hour. Make it a good entrance." The general turned and headed for the door without another word. The events of the day were weighing heavily on him.

Alan took Leira by the arm, whispering, "We need to talk. I'll find you after the meeting is over." He looked like he wanted to say more but the general was already in the parking lot.

"I'll text you when I'm back at Estelle's. We can meet there."

He gave her arm a squeeze and took off in a quick jog to catch up with the others.

Lois and Patsy hung back, closing the door behind Alan as Lois held out her wand in the air. "Should have done this the first time I came here. You need your own human detection system."

"You need to explain, Lois."

"Look, I know you were raised like you were one hundred percent grade A human but face the facts. You're a magical being working with humans. We're all getting along really well right now but there are limits."

"Sometimes harsh ones," said Patsy, drawing a line across her throat. "We kid around with each other, but we never forget we're playing in their sandbox. They decide we've overstayed our welcome and things get bad pretty fast."

"Charlie Monaghan is showing signs of having arrived at that point." Lois pursed her lips and held up her wand to replay the scene again. "Those dark eyes. Never seen them before but heard about it from an old Witch I mentored with a long time ago. Its darkness is filling every square inch of him. I think you like to call it the Dark Mist."

The color drained from Leira's face. "I thought the Dark Mist only went after magical beings…"

"Normally, that's a true statement." Patsy found an old blue peanut M&M in her pocket and brushed off the fuzz, popping it into her mouth. "But Charlie Monaghan's been handling a lot of very powerful artifacts. Using those artifacts, even."

"Humans who mess with artifacts tend to do so with less than honorable intentions. The more they do it, the worse the intentions become. It gets to be like an addiction, filling them up inside."

"They don't see the shortcut as a problem, they see it as a solution to all their ills."

"Till it's not. But by then, living in this world on its terms has taken a backseat."

"The old Witch told me that there were stories from when she was young of the darkness taking over some humans. Artifacts were getting dug up and tossed around in the last century, infecting some of the humans and stirring up magic."

"It did not end well for anyone and took the Silver Griffins quite a while to clean up the mess and lock all of the artifacts in their vault."

"It was really what got the vault going. One small catch, though was that the world talked about our kind like we were the devil."

"Drew us with warts and giant noses. What's that about? Seems a little discriminatory, if you ask me."

"We had to go way underground. The Silver Griffins came up with rules to protect magic that were a lot harsher. A lot…"

Lois gave Patsy a sidelong glance. "All of that is our way of leading up to this." She went into her green leather handbag shaped like a trapezoid with a gold clasp on top and pulled out a red-checkered dish towel. She held it in her palm, unfolding each side carefully. "We heard through the magic grapevine that you may be in need of some grounding, being a Jaspar Elf and all." In the center of the dish towel sat a bracelet, sparkling even in the low light.

Leira put out her hand to touch it and felt a rush of wind in her lungs. The bracelet rose into the air and hovered just near her hand.

"That's a pretty fancy trick right there. Your eyes aren't even glowing."

"I'm not doing that," said Leira.

"We know. It's the power in this artifact. It's filled with some very old, pure energy of a different kind."

"Lacey said that it was beings who were half magical, half human who filled the bracelet for a moment just like this one."

"They saw it coming. It's always been rumored that Jaspar Elves still existed. But, boy, Jackson did a good job of hiding his true self. Hunkering down in the woods of Oriceran and living like a hermit." Patsy shook her head.

"And we knew that the spark of humanity was in the occasional person."

"One in a few million but it's there."

"Eventually, the two might come together..." Lois moved her hands closer together. "Creating you, but with a tricky kind of catch. Mara was right to worry. Yes, we heard that whole sordid tale. But that whole melting into the light thing. Whoa!" Patsy felt the outside of her pockets but there was no spare bit of candy anywhere.

"Toni saw what you could do, and stories started getting back to us and we wondered."

"The bracelet is telling us we were right. You have the spark. Don't worry, we'll keep that one within the community with as few of our kind as possible."

Leira moved her hand around slowly and watched mesmerized as the bracelet changed direction to keep up with her.

"You two are weirdly good at getting the good dirt on what's going on." Leira smiled, her eyes wide, fascinated with the bracelet.

"Thank you kindly. We may act the fool but it's more of a cover than anything else. Human beings don't fear what they don't really respect."

"The general respects you."

"Until the day he doesn't… Granted, he's definitely one of the good ones but times change. Besides, people talk more around us because they see us as harmless."

"Especially me," laughed Patsy.

"She wields a wicked wand, trust me."

"I remember you two at the seminary. I saw what you could do."

"Oh, that was just a taste. You're right about the general. He's no fool and he hired us. Think about it."

"This artifact will ground me…"

"No, this is only half of what you need. Notice it's missing its stone and that's a necessary component. The right kind of stone channels the energy in a loop, creating the grounding."

"You need to get on finding one of those. We don't have it, or we'd give it to you but it's rare. Mostly because we haven't figured out how to tell when we're holding one."

"We'd have to hand one stone artifact after another over to you and wait to see what happens with you, the bracelet and the stone."

Lois carefully covered the bracelet with the washcloth again, capturing it in the air, and rolled it up as Leira hugged her around the neck. "Thank you, thank you."

"Heed our words though. You possess more power than even magical beings have been able to stomach at times. Be careful of who you trust."

"Patsy, we had best be going. We have an assignment to get to and that meeting will just be getting under way. I'm sure those

Senators must be wondering right about now who's the guest speaker." Lois let out a snort of laughter and handed the bundle over to Leira. "We hope this helps. Lacey's not keen on letting you run through the vast collection they've locked up but if it comes to that, we'll work on her for you."

"Others are looking too," said Leira.

"Not surprising to us at all. You are part of a large network that has your back. Remember that and call on us when you need us."

It's going to take all of us to defeat what's coming. Magical and human had better come together. I can just feel it.

CHAPTER TWENTY-NINE

The two moons were rising by the time Louie was able to get his band of humans all the way to the entrance. He stood back from them to get a better look

A loud screech echoed overhead as some of the men ducked and others pressed themselves harder against the wall. "Wish the earth would just swallow me up," said a wiry man wearing protective goggles.

"You'd have to be on an entirely different world for that to work. Actually, I take that back. Oriceran would be more than happy to oblige, especially in these parts." Louie silently counted down from five, holding out his fingers. "Right on time," smiled Louie, as a harpy appeared, flying directly overhead, screeching and making ever smaller circles right over their heads.

"I have more confidence in my motley crew than that harpy," he muttered to himself.

He thought better of taking stock of everyone outside of the entrance and ushered them all into the cool darkness, keeping an eye on the harpy. She looks big enough to pick off the short bald one in the back. "No, don't leave your backpack outside here. Any number of flying, crawling, walking creatures will make off with it. You want to keep it, you keep it on or kiss it goodbye." He rolled his lucky stones around in his hand, in and under his fingers as he assessed the scrapes and bruises. "No broken bones, few good scrapes and one good bump on the head. Not bad at all. Turns out all that jogging and playing golf really did pay off for you guys. I would not have believed it if I wasn't here with you."

The men looked at him as if he was too dangerous to be in charge. Louie clutched the stones in his hand and held out his arms as he shrugged. "Again, this class trip was not my idea." He slid the small stones back in his pocket and clapped his hands together. "Now, here comes the hard part."

A loud collective groan went up from the men.

"Yeah, I feel the same way but we're here and we've already been through Ricky's rockslide and John's dry retching. The ore is close gentlemen." Louie turned to lead them further into Dead Man's Crawl but stopped abruptly and turned. "Just in case I'm the one who dies on this little trip, which means we all die, tell me why this ore is so important to the rest of you that you'd follow me straight into hell to get it. It's precious on this planet, not on yours."

The men looked at each other, not saying a word till the tall runner spit out some blood from an earlier fall, clearing his throat as he stepped forward.

"Okay, that's dramatic." Louie leaned back on one foot, waiting.

"There's one thing that unites both our worlds. Something we have in common. Greed. We know about the gates and in just another generation they'll start to open. Magic will pour in and the balance will tip away from us." The man waved his arm, chopping the air. "None of us are prepared to become second-class citizens on our own planet."

"So, you need ore to buy our services."

"Money talks, everything else walks," The man said, holding

his head high despite the smear of dirt down the side of his face and the long tear in his cammo jacket.

"I appreciate you holding on to your dignity like that in these surroundings. I mean, that's what matters at a time like this, am I right?" Louie looked at them, barely disguising his disgust. "What happens if Elves or Wizards or Gnomes stop caring about your precious ore?" *There's something else. I can see it on their sweaty, sunburned faces.*

No one would look at him and the spokesperson had backed up till he was shoulder to shoulder again with the others. "Alright, I get it. Courage is a tricky thing. Sometimes it burns out pretty fast. Well, gather it back up again, men! We're on the last leg and about to set out. Stay close, as usual. Who's last in line? Calvin's back there. Call out every two minutes Cal, no more than that so we know you didn't disappear on us. Okay, let's go!"

Louie pulled his sword out of its sheath on his back and felt the hum shake his hands as he held it out in front of him. The men backed up from him until Calvin pushed from the back and they followed him into a narrow passage too tight to go more than one man at a time and in places, they had to shimmy sideways. Louie got out his wand and held it in front, letting the blue glow shine forth to light their way in the total darkness. "Nobody afraid of small places, are they? Keep it to yourself at this point. We're in it deep, men!" His shout echoed in the narrow chamber. *This is fucking bad. I may have to take a break for an entire month after this.*

Louie's head rocked back as a familiar wave of foul air rolled over him, making his eyes sting. *Same smell from before. What the hell on Oriceran can cook up a stench like that and still call itself alive?* He crept forward holding out the sword and slid the wand into the pack on his back, the light still shining from it. *Can't leave them by themselves. That's a definite no. They will just have to come with me.* Louie's heart was beating faster as the sword grew warmer in his hands. Shit is just up ahead. Literal shit. The smell grew stronger and Louie looked back for a moment at the sweaty faces behind him in the glow from the wand. They had come this far and there was a chance that smell was the worst part. "Fuck this day," he muttered.

They came to the antechamber where the ore was the easiest to find and piled into the larger space, grateful to be out of the closeness of the passageway. Louie stood in the center, his sword still out in front of him, listening for any sound at all this deep into the mountain. "Quiet! Quit moving around!"

The air was still and every muscle along Louie's back and arms was tense, waiting for something to happen.

"I don't hear anything," whispered Calvin.

Louie gave it another thirty seconds, finally lowering his sword. "Guess I'm a little jumpy too, gentlemen. We appear to have made it to our destination without loss of limb or life and I don't mind telling you now, I did not see that happening." Louie pulled out his wand and shone all over the walls, lighting up shining black stones jutting out from the dirt. "There is your precious ore. Careful though, don't be in such a hurry. Those edges to the stone are razor sharp and will cut your hands into ribbons. You're going to have to dig around them and let them drop into your bag. Nobody said robbing a planet was going to be that easy."

The men got out folding shovels or spades and set to work, grunting and swearing as they dug. A rock the size of his palm came loose and plopped into one of the men's backpack. "I got one! I actually fucking got one!" He dug faster, his enthusiasm building, dreaming of the riches and the magic he would be able to use. His shovel slipped down the sleek side of one of the rocks, slicing open his finger. "Aaaah! He dropped the shovel, clanging against the ground and grabbed his finger, applying pressure.

Louie looked up, the stench filling his nostrils again. "Everybody stand back…"

It was all he got out as a long tentacle reached out of the darkness, wrapping itself around the man, winding its way up his torso and whipping him backwards, splitting him in two as he opened his eyes in surprise. He came apart with a loud pop and a crack. The tentacle dragged off the bottom half leaving the top half to stare lifeless back at them, the entrails hanging out in the dirt like fleshy rope.

Calvin retched in the dirt and the others turned round and round in the center, backing away from the darkness where the tentacle had emerged.

Louie held up his sword and took a deep breath. He was always at his best in moments like this one where death was far closer than actually getting back to his home.

He felt the sword start to vibrate and gave into it, turning and swinging in the opposite direction, cutting away at a tentacle that unfurled itself into the light. The red, meaty flesh fell to the ground of the cave and liquid oozed out of it, sizzling as it made contact with the dirt. The men all shifted, coming behind Louie as they stepped over the monster's limb, most of them holding up their shovels as makeshift weapons.

Duck! Louie crouched down instinctively, wondering where the command was coming from as a tentacle flew over his head and wrapped itself around the runner, crushing his head and pulling his entire body back into the depths. This is fucking bad.

Louie stayed crouched down, the rest of the men following his lead but still looking more like prey than warriors. A tentacle whipped out again and Louie caught the edge of it nicking the long, deep red appendage, lined with round, sucking, puffy flesh down the entire underside. The tentacle bucked as the sword made contact, coming down on top of a backpack that was still strapped to Calvin and lifting him into the air.

"Get it off me! Get it off me!" Calvin struggled to work his arms out of the backpack as the fat tentacle came down to wrap itself all the way around him. He slid out just in time, falling back to the ground, flattening himself against the earth as his back-pack zipped into the darkness at remarkable speed. Calvin stayed where he was hugging the dirt, pressing the side of his face as hard as he could against the cave floor.

The tentacle immediately unfurled again as the stench grew in the room, coming out a different side of the cave, slicing another man open and dragging only pieces of him into the darkness.

Is there more than one of these fucking beasts or is this just one big motherfucker? Roll! Louie rolled to the right as a series of tentacles came sliding out grabbing two men around the ankle, sliding them through the dirt as they clawed at each other. Louie ran forward and sliced at a tentacle, only managing to save one of the men. The other let out a scream, his voice getting shrill until it ended in a watery gurgle in the darkness.

"That could not have been pretty." Louie held out his hand to the man he saved, kicking the tentacle away as he examined the red welts along the man's skin. "I thought it had you…"

Louie was whipped around, the muscles in his arms tensing as the sword swung of its own accord. Louie hung on for dear life as the tentacle came at his face and he sliced it right down the middle. The acid dripped down, burning Louie around the ankle.

"How many goddamn arms can one goddamn monster have? Come on, we have to get out of here!" He dragged Calvin by the collar as he scrambled to his knees, crawling behind Louie. The only other man was already running ahead of them toward the narrow passageway.

Just as the man got there a tentacle reached out and grabbed him, twisting his head off his shoulders as it rolled across the ground like a hard ball and Louie jumped over the body and into the passageway. Calvin climbed over the body and pulled in his foot just as the tentacle appeared again, wrapping itself around the head and lifting it into the air, the lifeless mouth still hanging open.

Louie held out his sword, not sure what direction the beast may come from as he whispered, "Light the way."

Calvin was hiccupping wildly, trying to take in air and stay on his feet as they clambered through the passageway. "Looked hic like hic octopus arms hic from the ocean."

"Yeah, well somebody should let it know that it's a few miles off course and to get the fuck out of here."

Louie felt the warm air hit his face and moved faster, finally bursting forth into the sunlight with Calvin right at his heels. "That was fucking bad." Louie held out his sword still, not sure if the danger was over and rested his other hand on his knee, trying to catch his breath. "At least I got one of you out of there."

He looked up at Calvin who was holding his throat, smoke coming between his fingers. He peeled back his hand to show a red welt that was burning a hole through his throat. He reached out to Louie as his face reddened and his throat continued to smoke, stumbling over his new hiking boots and tripping over the edge. His arms pinwheeled through the air as he fell backward toward the Conca and the waters below. By the time his body hit the bottom the sound barely reached Louie where he stood, his hand still out to grab Calvin, his sword still raised.

"I did not see that coming." He straightened up, his eyes wide and ran his hand through his hair, turning around in a circle to see if anything else was about to happen. He pulled up the leg of his pants to check his ankle and saw that the magical tracking device had saved most of his skin and was burned to a crisp. He nudged it with the sword and watched it fall to the ground.

"I'll say it again. That was one big, badass motherfucker. What the hell? I lost them all, got no ore and still have to go back by the Gnomes and the Kilomeas just to report my failure. On the bright side, I have some gold left and no one tracking me. Shit, they may think I'm dead."

The stench wafted out from the passageway as Louie made his way down Dead Man's Crawl, making a lot better time. He got to the entrance to the Gnome's cave and saw that his ankle was swelling. Great, now I'm the fucking prey. He ran past the entrance, not willing to stand there and negotiate while his ankle got worse and hoped no one would notice.

"Hey, someone's trying to get past without paying!"

"I'd know that high-pitched whine anywhere," muttered Louie as he took off at a run. Something jumped down past him as he raised his sword, ready to fight his way out of there.

"Don't kill the one friend you've got in this world!"

"Ronnie! Mother of the oceans, am I glad to see you!"

"I can see that." Ronnie put himself between the herd of Gnomes hustling in their direction and Louie held out his arm. "Not another step, Sigfried or I'll tell your wife about the last two moons party at the Green Vines Pub. You too, Liam. I know about your little fetish and I'm happy to blab about it if you keep harassing my best friend, here."

"You're friends with a Wizard! Against your own kind!"

"Give it a rest. You guys are just bored and were going to chase him till he was winded enough to puke. You've done it a thousand times."

Sigfried gave a low chuckle. "That is a good one. Fine! We'll let him stroll out of here but just this once. Next time he pays or pukes!"

"Deal," said Louie, the pain growing in his ankle.

"See you at the next family dinner, Ronnie?"

"Not sure I can make this one. Pretty packed calendar. I'll stop by soon."

Sigfried waved his arm, annoyed but shrugged as they all turned to go back to the cave. Ronnie turned his attention to Louie, concern on his face. "You okay?"

"Nope. Today was one of my less fortunate scavenger days. Big, hairy monster with long flesh-eating tentacles ate the crew I brought. Well, except for Calvin. He took a flight off the cliff." Still have some gold, at least.

Ronnie leaned down and looked at his ankle. "That's gonna leave a mark. Woof." He stood up and let Louie lean on him as they made their way down the path.

"What the hell are you doing out here anyway?"

"Jackson keeps coming by looking for you. He had that Leira chick with him. Do you know that's his kid?"

"No shit! Jackson with a kid…"

"Yeah and she can capture light inside a stone! You know what that means. Hey, you're getting heavy. Oh, yeah…" Ronnie snapped his fingers. "Jackson said to tell you, it's go time. Said you'd know what that means and then he did the usual threatening me if I didn't keep it to myself routine."

"He said it's go time? You're sure?" Louie did his best to pick up his speed, hobbling along.

"Yeah, why that mean something?"

"Yeah, that means something. We need to move it."

CHAPTER THIRTY

Hagan walked up the steps to his bungalow, whistling as he brushed a few leaves off the steps. He opened the door calling out, "Rose, I'm home! Something smells good! There you are, I've got a little extra time today before I have to be back at work." He followed her down the front hall and into the kitchen. "How about you stop stirring whatever that heavenly smell is coming from and come sit down here with me. Come on. I have a few things I need to tell you." He tapped the top of their old Formica and wood kitchen table as it wobbled. "Meant to fix that already. Hang on, I can fold up a napkin under the leg."

Rose reached out and laid a warm hand on top of his and looked into his eyes, smiling. "Just tell me, Felix. It'll be okay."

Hagan smiled nervously and sat back, still holding hands with Rose across the table. "It's a doozie, Rose but I had to wait for clearance before I could tell you anything. Just came through. That's why they gave me the extra time today. I told them it was just getting to be too hard to go out on these adventures and not have you to tell them all to. Well, not all the details. I had to agree to leave out whatever they decide is classified."

"Take a breath, dear."

"Right. You see, this is why I needed to fill you in, Rose. Like the old days when I was still a homicide detective. Who knew that would look so innocent and simple? Okay, here goes. You trust me, right? Well, I work for the federal government, that part is true. But it's kind of a black ops division that most people will never hear about if we do our jobs right. We're tasked with keeping magic a secret for as long as possible while protecting the U.S. interests in the whole thing. Kind of a big deal. Let me show you."

He held out his phone to Rose and ignored that she was looking at him as if he had finally had the long awaited stroke from too many doughnuts. The video played showing Yumfuck and Leira's eyes glowing and the virtual screen.

"One of the people I work with, Lois put this together. You'd love her. Great gal. Also a Witch." Hagan pulled out his handkerchief and mopped his forehead and wiped his mouth. "She's willing to stop by if you need some direct proof so you don't have to worry that I've lost my marbles." Hagan took a deep breath. Almost home with this one. "And Leira Berens, my partner of a number of years now. Well, it turns out she's a human being of course, a fine one. But also a mixture of a bunch of other things that are really out there magically. Mostly magical." His voice got louder as he talked. "I'm still not really sure what the hell is going on there. You doing okay? Okay, well there's more."

Rose got out of her chair and leaned forward, kissing her husband on the forehead before settling back in her chair, leaning her chin in her hands, hanging on every word.

"There was this bad guy named Rhazdon, who turned out to be some ancient woman..."

Yumfuck perched on Mara's shoulder watching as she clicked on the mouse, altering pictures to show the troll water skiing, and another with him walking a red carpet. The troll cackled as he jumped up and down on her shoulder.

"This ought to do it. Frankly, I don't even think this part of our plan is necessary anymore. Whatever you said to that reporter seems to have done the trick. Not one word about you anywhere on the web except for the bar brawl of course. Blake Johnson even took down all the different photos he had of you. Still…" Mara made another one with Yumfuck posing with the Kardashians. "…if we can get people to believe it's all photo shopped and fake news then we don't have to worry about this at all. This was a good idea you had, little furry dude."

"Make that one my Facebook profile picture," he chirped.

"You have a Facebook page? I told you to stay off my computer when I'm not here. Leira will have my hide." Mara typed in Yumfuck Tiberius Troll and found a picture of the troll smiling too close to the camera. "Not your best selfie. What the hell? You have almost a million followers. I think I have a total of thirty-four friends, you little asshole." She plucked the troll off her shoulder and put him on the desk where she could see him. "You're a worldwide phenomenon! Alright, I'll change your profile pic. Why not? This will only help us convince people it can't possibly be true that a tiny little magical swearing creature from another world is actually real and living in Texas." Mara shook her head, brushing her long hair off her shoulder. "Just when you think you've seen it all. Oh look, your last post got a thousand hits. You posted a picture of a doughnut that looked like Ed Sheeran. Yeah, I can see that. Oooh, they're asking for a plushie of you. I wonder if we could figure out how to make their dreams come true."

"I'd like to teach the world to sing in perfect harmony," chirped the troll.

"I see you've switched brands from Dr. Pepper. Alright, this is America, you're allowed… Imagine that Coke commercial…"

CHAPTER THIRTY-ONE

Leira opened a portal using the logistics the general had given her and found herself looking into a group of men and women staring back at her, their eyes wide. So far, so good…

She leaped out, landing on her feet in a crouched position, quickly pulling in enough energy to light up the symbols along her arms and neck, her eyes glowing. *Let's get the show started early.*

Several people gasped while one man with a pointed nose and a shock of dark hair stood up abruptly demanding, "What in blazes is going on here? Do you know who we are?"

Leira let the energy surge through her just enough as she let out an electrical pulse that knocked him back into his chair and made his hair stand up on end. "You are self-entitled bitches who thought you could pull a fast one on the very government you were elected to serve." Leira wagged her finger at them, the symbols turning over on her skin. "Not so fast, though. As you are all in a unique position to know, the world is changing." Leira stood up straight and leaped onto the table in front of them. "Magic is fucking real and it's making a return and I'm its first ambassador and your worst fucking nightmare."

She gave into the magic just a little more, careful not to let it go too far, aware of the risks as she felt the edges of the bliss. "This is power…" Just as she expected a dark mist started to curl around her feet and turned, as if it were curious about the others in the room. The mist swirled around them, probing into their own darkness.

This is a thin place in the veil. Did the general know? Leira let the light shine through her, blinding them all as a tear emerged in the world in between, startling even Leira. Might as well work with it. The scar on her belly burned as the light passed through her. She yelled over the roar coming from the light. "This is the world in between! There will be no jury, just your disappearance and your stain upon our world removed."

She could feel the energy starting to get away from her and she clamped her hand down hard on the shoulder of the nearest person, grounding her energy through him and scaring him further till a dark wet stain grew on his pants. I reached him at least. She clenched her teeth, ratcheting the energy back. The Senators all looked into the gaping hole of the world in between and saw the drawn faces of people trapped in there, clawing toward the small opening as it closed.

"What was that?" asked one of the Senators, his hands shaking as they gripped the arms of his chair.

"Literal living hell with almost no escape that can go on forever. That's what you're toying with when you play with magic that doesn't belong to you. Dark magic wants to own you and make you its permanent bitch more than it will ever reward you." Leira remembered the trick she pulled off the first time she went to the Jackalope and slowly levitated inches off the floor, her eyes still glowing. "This is your only warning and the friendliest one you'll get. Back away from Charlie Monaghan, back away from magic, back away from Oriceran and leave this to those among us who can use it for good without getting ourselves killed or worse. Yes, that was a glimpse of worse."

Leira could feel her arms shaking from the effort of holding back the energy and let it subside to a slow trickle, forming a ball of light between her hands that opened into the warehouse back in Austin, Texas. "Don't make me come back here." She stepped through, still glaring at the men and women who weren't moving as they stared back at her.

The portal closed, spraying sparks across the warehouse floor and she collapsed to her knees, breathing hard, her arms still shaking. "That was close." There was a sheen of sweat across her face as she sat back on her heels and smiled. "And fucking fun." She took in a deep breath and let it out, laughing. "I think that was mission accomplished. For now."

The general sat at his desk looking through the classified material the PDF had gathered on Charlie Monaghan, his face growing more sour with every moment. "The son of a bitch thinks he can run for office in my country." He looked stricken as he clicked through each file seeing the donations already pouring into an independent Political Action Committee to support a race for Senator. "Not as long as I have a breath left in my body. You will not defame this great nation." The general's teeth were clenched as he made a mental note of who was already on the Monaghan for Senate bandwagon. "Traitors, every one of them." He rubbed his tired face with his hands and looked back at the screen. "I'm coming for every last one of you but especially you, Charlie Monaghan. Not revenge… won't sink down into the gutter with you. Good old fashion justice and a nice cell locked away where no one will ever find you. Someone is backing you, too. It's as clear as day. I'll find them too. Enjoy your time while you can because your time is coming to an end."

CHAPTER THIRTY-TWO

Leira drove home in the green Mustang, her legs still feeling weak from the power surge. For once she was grateful for the open parking spot right in front of her gate as she opened the door and waited a minute before lurching out of the car.

"Leira? Sorry I couldn't wait, and it was getting late so I thought I'd take a chance." Alan Cohen was standing patiently by her gate, waiting for her.

"How long have you been here?" The muscles in Leira's body were slow to respond as she made her way toward home. The sudden highs and lows of the power surge had spent her own energy.

Alan saw how weary she was and reached out his hand. "I take it that was no simple assignment."

"I'm okay," she said, turning down his offer of an assist. "I can still make it under my own power."

"Never doubted it." He smiled, looking away for a moment. "I had a feeling it was going to be a rough one. The general probably did too, which is why he sent you in. Those are all seasoned politicians who've seen the worst of what humanity has to offer and have been willing to dish it out pretty badly as well. It would take a lot to scare them back into their cages. Worth the wear and tear on your body and soul?"

"Always worth it. Not really a question I ask myself. It's more about accomplishing the mission." Leira stepped past him and opened the gate. The patio was jumping with the late night crowd. Estelle would be shooing them all toward the door in another hour. She was standing behind the bar on her stool, pouring out a set of shots, cigarette firmly clamped between her teeth, one eye closed against the swirling smoke. She gave a brief wave to Leira as she took the cigarette out of her mouth long enough to blow a long stream of smoke to the side. Her reading glasses were securely tucked into her towering red bouffant, ready for when she needed them. Ashes drifted from the end of the cigarette as she squinted, watching Alan and Leira make their way to the gate house.

Leira stopped at her door, her hand resting on the doorknob. "I'd ask you in but everyone's probably asleep by now." Her forehead wrinkled as she watched him shift his weight and study the nearby bushes, glancing over at the people gathered around the cornhole game. "You okay?"

"I haven't been this nervous since I was back in eighth grade. He smiled and dug his hands in his pockets, unsure what to do with them. "I'm better at arresting people, even fighting that thing that wanted to suck us into nowheresville."

"There's a chance you're making it worse…" Leira smiled and let out an easy laugh. "You're sweating at night in the early spring. Outdoors."

"Okay, right… Would you go out to dinner with me? On a date. It'd be a date, no work. This isn't about an assignment." The words spilled out of him.

Leira gave him a crooked smile, her eyes opening wider. "A date? Oh… Sure, yeah, okay. That's something we could do." Damn, just say yes.

"Okay... great." Alan looked relieved and let out a breath he'd been holding. Ugh, I can breathe again.

Leira nodded, waiting for more... How long has it been since I was on a date? Months? Fuck... years? No... Has it? No... Yeah, I should definitely go.

"Right... okay... How about next weekend? Saturday... Saturday is good. Unless the world comes apart or magic blows something up." Way to make it romantic. Think of something to say besides work. Nothing, I got nothing.

"Saturday works. I could do a date on a Saturday." She smiled and tucked her hair behind her ear.

"What about the Lucky Robot? I hear good things. Pick you up at seven. I'll drive... drive you, of course." Fuck me, I'm babbling. Someone please shoot me now. Or shoot someone else and I'll chase them.

Leira laughed. "This is really awkward, isn't it?" She patted him on the arm, laughing. "I have no idea how to get out of this moment."

"I'll put us out of this misery and back away slowly," he said, smiling. "Think I'll go read some reports, go for a run..." He walked backwards for a few steps till his heel hit against a loose slate tile and he threw his arms up instinctively. Leira put out her hands to help him but he steadied himself. "Okay, now I'm really going. Bye..."

Leira smiled, nodding. "Good night." She opened the door and went in to make it easier on both of them.

Estelle blew out a perfect round O blowing a steady stream of smoke right through the center. "About time that girl did a little something normal that didn't involve a gun." She poured half a glass of beer and took a slow sip looking out over the patio. "Not a bad night, all in all."

General Anderson poured himself two fingers of Knob Creek whiskey in a cut glass. "Cheers." He held the glass up for a moment, clinking it against the other glass and took a long slow sip. "Just the way I like it. No ice to bruise the flavor. But you already know that. You know everything there is to know about me. That's hard to replace. I'll bet you could even finish all of my sentences for me. Hell, you put most of the humanity into me. I think I'd be a certifiable jackass without you." He had changed out of his uniform and was wearing an old pair of comfortable flannel plaid drawstring pajama bottoms and a faded Wu-Tang Clan t-shirt. His oversized Citadel ring clinked against the glass of whiskey.

He shook his head as he took another sip. "But hot damn the world has changed. It would curl your hair if you knew half of what I've seen lately. Hell, if I had enough hair left it would curl mine." He let out a chuckle and set the glass down, still holding on to the edges. "Thank God for you and this refuge of a home. A place to go where the world makes sense even if it's a simple home. It's a damn fine good one and that's all thanks to you. I know, I know, don't be so damn modest. Okay, well I think I did a good job of standing up for America today. Put the interests of the average citizen above the power brokers. That will most likely come back to bite me in the ass, but we'll deal with that on the day it happens." He took another sip, feeling the smooth liquor warm his throat. "That felt pretty good. Oh, and did I tell you about the wildlife sanctuaries that are being built? One in Alaska and one in Hawaii that will serve to keep a lot of precious cargo on this planet alive. There's already a pretty nifty one in Texas. Score one for mankind." He sat back against the padded Caribbean blue cushion tied to the kitchen chair and rested his arm against the table as he lifted the glass. "Just for tonight, in this small hour all is right with the world. Goodnight my love." He rubbed his hand against the shiny brass urn as he did every night. It was inscribed with the words, *Some love lasts forever.*

Jessica Anderson. Beloved wife. Rest in eternal peace. "Till we meet again."

A cicada landed on the table at Estelle's crawling over to Mara and stepping onto her plate. Estelle stood behind the bar, holding a wet rag in one hand, a cloud of smoke passing in front of her face.

Mara gently brushed the cicada off her plate and heard the whirring and clicking. She looked down and watched the wings flapping, revealing her initials carved in small letters underneath. A chill passed through her and she picked it up and held it to her ear, listening to the worried voice of the young Light Elf. "We're at the top of Enchanted Rock. We've been followed by Oriceran rebels… Wait! What is that?" The words faded into squeals and squeaks before sputtering out altogether. Mara looked up and licked her lips. "Looks like I'm heading for a fight. I wonder if I can find some reinforcements."

CHAPTER THIRTY-THREE

Turner Underwood stood on the back lawn of his estate slowly lifting his arms to the sides, his arms slightly bent at the elbows.

"You've been on this planet too long." Jackson stood in the wet grass behind him, smiling broadly, his thumbs hooked in his belt. "You look like one of their antennas. Signaling aliens? No, wait, that's us."

Turner moved his arms to a different position, breathing deeply. "Good morning, Jackson. Still as impertinent as when you trained under me, I see." He moved his arms through the tai chi position. "It's called the white crane spreads its wings. You should try it sometime. Would help you get rid of a lot of that hostility you claim you don't have." Turner shut his eyes and felt the warmth of the early morning sun on his face. He let out a deep breath and moved to another position.

"Is your slow jam going to take much more time? It's not like me to be early so I have to figure you knew I'd be here by now. Is this your backward way of teaching another important life lesson?" Jackson walked over to the nearby table set up with a hot pot of coffee and several mugs. "Best thing this planet has come up with. Hot coffee."

Turner pressed his palms together against his chest and bowed to the sun, opening his eyes and making his way slowly to the table. "And your daughter."

"That's a recent bit of knowledge I'm still getting used to." He picked up a croissant and turned it over, giving it a sniff. "Leira know you and I are old pals, yet? No, I didn't think so. The inscrutable Turner Underwood likes to parcel out the information."

Turner took the croissant from his hand and put it on a small white plate edged in silver for him. "How is fatherhood going so far?"

Jackson ignored the question and counted the coffee cups, touching each one just to annoy Turner. "Looks like we're expecting a lot of company. Who else is coming to this party?"

Turner smiled slowly and stood back, getting his cane from where it rested against the stone wall.

A portal opened out on the lawn, the gold and silver sparks fizzing against the morning dew. Louie stepped cautiously onto the firm ground, testing his weight on his ankle. The portal snapped closed behind him and he hobbled toward the patio, a broad smile on his face. "I may need to borrow one of those fancy canes of yours, Turner. You have a spare?"

"What happened to you?" Jackson dug his fingers into the bowl of strawberries, stuffing some into his mouth and talking while he chewed. "You look like something finally managed to snack on you. Rough day at the office?"

"Something like that. Turns out there are a few beasts I still haven't heard of and don't have a name for them. Shouldn't there be a list by now?" Louie made his way to a seat and lowered himself heavily into the chair as he watched Jackson push a few more berries into his mouth. "Uh Jackson, what the fuck are you doing? I know you have a thing for free anything but slow down. There's plenty."

"I believe that is for my benefit so he can let me know how little he's retained from what I poured into him. He's hoping I feel regret for giving him so much of my time." Turner lowered his eyelids and looked at Jackson. "I do not. Some things take longer to grow and mature, but in the end, the plant flourishes or dies. Either one is acceptable."

Jackson swallowed hard, laughing as Louie smiled, the creases in his face deepening.

They could hear the sound of a car approaching as the green Mustang came up the long driveway and parked in the front. Leira and Correk made their way around to the back of the house as Louie pulled a chair in front of him and rested his bandaged leg. Jackson glanced down at the swollen ankle, his eyebrows raised. "Don't ask," said Louie. "Eyes popping out, bones crushing, heads rolling across a cave floor. This was the least of it."

"The usual shit, then." Jackson shook his head. "You'll have to tell me later. You'll buy, of course."

Leira headed straight for the coffee, pouring herself a cup and drinking half of it down, refilling the cup. "Best invention ever. What?" She looked up at Turner's smiling face as she took another gulp, topping off the cup again. She poured another cup and handed it to Correk. "He gets the really good beans from Hawaii. It's like a coffee experience."

Correk took the cup and went to lean against the stone wall. Leira went and stood next to him as Louie winked at her and said, "Morning." Correk rolled his eyes and sent a small pea-sized ball of light to nudge the chair with his leg in it. Louie winced but smiled as he sat up straighter in the chair. "That one was probably earned," he said.

"Did you bring it?" Turner Underwood held out his hands to Leira as she fished the dish towel out of her pocket and gave it to him. "Very good. We are halfway there." He unfolded the towel and laid it on the table, exposing the bracelet. "A rarified artifact full of both Elven, Wizard and human magic. Very rare and interesting combination." He rubbed his chin, feeling the day's growth against his skin.

"The stone is missing." Correk turned the bracelet over, looking at the empty setting. "How important is that piece?"

"Vital," said Turner. "Without it, this is a useless half measure. And it's not just any stone. It must be one that has more than the usual power to fuel the bracelet. One that has the same mixture of elements but in higher doses. They exist but…"

"We're looking for a stone among a billion stones on two planets." Leira looked out toward the lake, watching a pair of ducks swim around each other. In the distance a kayaker forged a path resolutely across the water.

"How would we recognize the stone?" Correk stood back, his hands on his hips.

"That part is actually relatively simple. Few would be able to handle it, even among the magical community and even among humans. It would spark or burn their hands. To someone who can channel more energy, more efficiently it would give off a strong hum or vibration. Might even make someone feel lightheaded or stoned." Turner tapped his cane against the ground and let out a deep sigh. "This is our next quest."

Jackson sat forward and thumped Louie on his good leg. "You think you can do this?"

"Time is of the essence." Correk turned to Leira. "Your ability to channel energy only grows stronger and you won't always be able to find someone to help you tamp it down." He brushed a hand against her back, putting it back down by his side but not before Jackson noticed.

Louie was ignoring all of them, staring at the bracelet. He reached into his pocket and pulled out his lucky stones, rolling them through his hands. Zaps most, burns a few. Sounds familiar.

He looked at the size of the setting and down at his hand. Only one of the stones from the estate sale managed to give a few customers at the Dark Market a jolt. The large, blood red stone with a thin sliver of gold running through it. Contact high first time I squeezed it in my hand. My luckiest stone. First the sword, now this. Okay, I can do this. Without saying a word, Louie leaned forward and took the bracelet, turning the stone around and around till it dropped neatly into place not quite meeting the sides. The stone rattled in the setting, melting into a liquid and spreading out till it filled the edges. Light glowed from every side as it bubbled, slowly hardening until it fit the setting exactly. Louie looked up to see everyone standing closer to him, their eyes wide. He held up the bracelet to Leira, a crooked smile on his face. "Something like this, right?"

"Absolute miracle. Exactly as it was described." Turner urged Leira. "Go on, take it. Put it on."

Leira put out her hand and was surprised to see her fingers shaking. She picked it up and barely felt the hum as she slid it onto her wrist.

Correk took her hands and looked her in the eyes. "Okay, this is where you take it for a test drive. Danger is minimum. We're all standing here, ready to ground you if things don't go as planned. Think of a task for the magic and let the energy lead the way."

Leira looked up into his eyes. "I trust you." She squeezed his hands and let go, pulling in energy from the ground as the symbols burned brightly on her arms, spreading up her neck. She relaxed into it, focusing on a task. Show me the sanctuary. Keep it safe.

She gasped and arched her back as the energy rushed through her in a gust, billowing out in a widening stream of light as she watched the images emerge in front of her. The energy sought out first the sanctuary in Texas, circling around the grounds and running over the mossy areas, sensing all was well. With another surge, Leira relaxed her shoulders and felt it cross the veil into

Oriceran without using a portal. She let herself be swept up into it, all worries falling away as the light sought out the Dark Forest.

Correk's muscles tensed as he watched her eyes glow like embers, her mind somewhere else. *I trust you, too.* He waited, encircling her with his own energy, sensing if she was going too far over the edge.

The symbols along her arms flipped over faster and faster as Turner did his best to keep up, reading them as they sought out their target.

Leira felt the energy rushing through the dense trees into the darkness under the thick canopy. It had found its task. Leaves rustled and animals lifted their heads and turned to run as they sensed the magic flowing rapidly through the woods. Just at the far edge near the Land of Terran Leira could see smugglers moving elephants into large pens to transport across the nearby ocean. The magic burst forth, splitting the pens in two as the elephants reared up, curling their trunks and trumpeting an alarm. The Elves and Wizards tried to calm the elephants, spinning the same magical spell to soothe them that had worked just moments ago but were horrified to see it had no effect.

Leira opened her hands wider, taking long, deep even breaths as the energy swirled around them, sucking the air out of them and throwing the thieves to the ground. The elephants trumpeted their distress again, running toward the deeper parts of the forest as the men did their best to stand or crawl toward their carts. "Get out of here! The Gardener will be here soon!" yelled a Wizard.

Kyomi stood on the edge of the swirl of magic and watched, his muscles straining to hold him up as he scowled even as he marveled at the magic blowing around him, his tunic clinging to his frame. *Charlie Monaghan will not be happy about this turn of events. Neither will Fleeker. Someone with more power is playing with us now.*

The energy made a sharp turn, racing along the forest floor

toward a deeper part of the forest till it came to a long, low slung building and sought out one corner, shut off from everything else. Leira sensed something there that was not quite sentient. Definitely angry.

Peyton felt the currents swimming around him and stood up to his full height, roaring with frustration. There was a pulse in the room that held his bed and a few belongings, neatly knocking the concrete door off its hinges and neutralizing the old spell that had contained him till now.

Leira watched the beast moving through the forest, trying to determine what he was. Elf? Not a Kilomea.

She felt the magic pull back on its own, her left arm where the bracelet sat, shaking visibly. Jackson reached out to touch her, but Turner gave a sharp, "No!" and knocked his hand away with the top of his cane.

"It's working," said Correk relieved. He could feel the magic subsiding inside of her, draining back into the earth. Leira curled her fingers into fists and let out her breath in a gasp as she fell forward into Correk's arms.

"It worked," she said, smiling as the symbols finally faded. She pushed herself off Correk and found her footing. Correk managed a smile as Jackson watched the two of them together. Turner leaned closer to Jackson and whispered, "You've missed far too many years to make a comment. Focus on the win here."

Leira looked down at the bracelet. A thin wisp of smoke was coming from it. "Thank you, Louie. I owe you big for this. I owe all of you."

"Don't say it." Jackson put his hand on Louie's shoulder. "This one was gratis."

"Leira, it's only a temporary fix. This doesn't solve the issue long-term. It only buys us time."

"Just like you, Turner to bring the party down at your first opportunity," Jackson scowled. "How about we take the win?"

Leira was still smiling, relieved and still feeling the remains of the bliss from the magic. "This is enough for today. I can take this for now. I'll dig in for a longer solution, but for now, I'm grateful." What was that beast?

<hr>

Peyton stumbled, confused and stopped at the threshold, putting his hands out to see if the door was really gone, batting at the air. He took a step out, a rumble of laughter emerging from his chest as he came into the lab. He felt the ribbon of magic rolling away, receding back into the forest and followed it, grateful for his rescue. Not sure what else to do.

He pushed through the branches and ferns till he got to the first clearing and felt the sunlight on the top of his head. He looked up, brambles caught in his long, tangled hair, blinking at the light and let out a roar that was an even mixture of joy and agony.

The Gardener heard the different cries in the Dark Forest and rode toward Peyton, sending a pack of grey wolves to push the elephant thieves that survived the pack further out of the forest. The injured Light Elf was a much bigger threat. He had never been out on his own in over twenty years.

The story is far from over. Leira's adventure continues in *Enemies of Magic.*

Get sneak peeks, exclusive giveaways, behind the scenes content, and more. PLUS you'll be notified of special **one day only fan pricing** on new releases.

Sign up today to get free stories.

Visit: https://marthacarr.com/read-free-stories/

Here we are, halfway through the year of change that feels like its own decade. Okay, not the cheeriest opening. Let's try again.

Here we are discovering a lot of things about ourselves that we never knew before and can embrace or hide in the pantry. In some ways, this is not my first rodeo. I went through so-called terminal cancer (the cancer was real, I'm happy to report the terminal appears to have been exaggerated), losing all the possessions during the Great Recession, and the slow build back that comes with that and probably a few things I've forgotten. All of these life events overlapped each other – a lot like now. I was reduced down to nothing left to lose, which may have made it easier to quit staring at it.

I have some perspective. The biggest difference this time is I've never done it as a group sport with the *world*.

When it seemed like I had very, very limited choices I realized I still had one. To choose to be happy and work with what I had right in front of me. I worked harder on creating a positive tribe around me and I made sure I stayed in touch with people as much as possible. I found affordable fun and asked for help, a lot, from the right sources. Translate that last one for you. It means I stayed away from people whose focus was on what was going wrong and headed straight for those who chipped away at solutions for me. No wonder Leira does the same.

So, here I am again and this time with a billion other people, chipping away at finding the good. Hopefully, I will pile up the same wonderful memories that center around all the friendships that grew deeper. More adventures to follow.

Original Author Notes written January 28, 2018

The start of the New Year opened with a bang for me. I ended the year wondering if I should go back to Chicago (the place I consider my hometown) or move into Austin, closer to the Offspring, Louie. Eeny, meeny, miney, mo. So, I took off for my old hometown to get a little Chicago Christmas under my belt and be surrounded by old friends. Maybe it would help me decide.

It was a wonderful time that showed me how connected I am to people in the world. My family is mostly made up of people I'm not blood related to – some of you can probably relate. But I also saw that my life had moved on and somewhere in there I became a Texan. Plus, navigating icy wooden stairs is tricky and walking the playful Lois Lane on ice seemed like a no go.

So back in Texas and on a whim my realtor friend, Sheila and I took off to look at a subdivision in Southeast Austin one Sunday afternoon two weeks ago. Didn't really see anything… the best offering would have meant I'd spend most of my day in a dark room. Sheila looked at me and said, "It's like a cubicle." On another whim with only a half hour to go I said, "Let's go across the main street and look at the fancy houses in that other subdivision."

You can probably see where this is going, but hang on… It gets better. We went in the model home and noticed that the garage was already converted. BIG CLUE. They were almost sold out. The ceilings were super high, and the finishes were fancier than I'm used to and we walked around with our mouths open, laughing and touching everything. Okay, 3rd whim... I asked the realtor who had an Eastern European accent so thick we had to lean in and listen carefully – was there anything left? Yes, one rancher...

Then she listed everything about the house, and I could see good ol' Sheila glancing at me sideways because the woman was listing everything I hoped for... including a bay window in the bedroom. Long and short, Sheila talked them down by A LOT over the next few days, figuring they were done and wanted out. And... I bought a house! (It's being built, and pictures will keep coming on my FB page and in the Martha Carr Fan Group) It's a better house than I have ever lived in as a child or an adult. I keep taking deep breaths and telling myself, all is well, you pre-qualified. It's okay.

BIG TRUTH is I am able to do all of this because of all of you. This past year has changed my life inside and out, and now it's going to help change my address. I'm a kid who grew up in a kind of public housing (rectory, campus housing) and then lived in a variety of apartments... and this wonderful house. But as Sheila's husband said... this house is a whole other level. One dream after another keeps coming true as if magic were real. And like I've said before... we're just getting started.

There's the Open House for Austin-area Veterans the day before this book comes out with a Kindle raffle, giving away some stickers and books and food and of course cake. There has to be cake. If all goes well that will become a model for a strange US book tour that will wind through where you guys, THE FANS said you're mostly located. One fan made a great suggestion to do a signing in a bar that resembles Estelle's. We're looking into adding that...

In the meantime, Michael is hard at work on The Amazing Mr. Brownstone series in the Oriceran Universe. I'm really looking forward to that one... and we have a few other ideas up our sleeve. Thanks for making ALL OF THIS POSSIBLE!

More adventures to follow.
Martha

First (well, again maybe?), thank you for not only reading this story but reading the *Author Notes* here at the back as well.

I just messaged Martha that I think her comment regarding the terminal part of terminal cancer was perhaps the funniest poignant comment I've read in a long time. If there is anyone I know that has the ability to cut through the darkest part of life with a humorous remark...

It's Martha.

Unfortunately, she has had so many opportunities to practice her art, it isn't even funny (as you will read in her future *Author Notes*, as well.)

If you get a chance (and haven't already), go and subscribe to her emails.

In them, you will find additional moments of life's efforts to be ugly cut through the heart with her clarity of thought. Often disarming whatever is negative and reminding us all that life can be completely enjoyed (even in the hard parts) by DECIDING to allow what we dwell on to become who we are.

Remember, your conscious thought(s) are the filter to what your future holds.

Or, you can just read our books and allow your mind to dwell on a cursing six-inch-tall troll.

And doughnuts.

Original Author Notes written January 29, 2018

First, thank you for not only reading this story, but reading the author notes here at the back as well!

I've said this before (probably in previous author notes in this series) but it pleases the ever-loving-fuck out of me to have played a part in Martha's success.

Why you ask?

Because I am a firm believer that leaving behind those older in our society is a stupid-assed, short-sighted strategy.

Granted, some of those older people are pains-in-the-asses (but so are some of the younger people in our world.) There is no minimum or maximum age limit for someone to say, "I know what the hell I'm doing, and I don't care what you tell me."

Sixteen or sixty-five, the same attitude can be found in *both*.

However, rant aside, Martha is a talented author who had toed the line for the traditional model for so many years and did it 'their way.'

Until she tossed off the shackles of the system, gave them a "Heigh-ho, fuck you Joe, I'm off to write about..." A female Austin, Tx detective that swears like a sailor and a troll named *Yumfuck*

Yeah, cause *THAT* would have made the agents and editors / publishers at the big houses stand on their chairs, screaming that they wanted to publish this series!

(Yes, I know, we are both shaking our heads at that actually playing out.)

However, *we* did it. She and I worked out the story, the world (Universe) and she believed enough in me to take some of it on faith.

And some of it by hard-headedness.

Either way, Martha is just about seven (7) months into her Oriceran Universe effort and together, she and I can smile, wave our middle-fingers to those who didn't believe in her and enjoy the fact that we DID create a fan favorite swearing detective with a troll who has a penchant for causing mischief.

And it has been a best-selling series, with over 15,000 books sold and 8,000,000 pages read in Kindle Unlimited.

In just half a year.

More is coming from this dynamo, so thank you for cheering her on in her 'old age' and please, try to keep her attention with you on Facebook. Because if you don't, she will turn that attention back to me and I've had enough little arrows stuck in me when she's bored.

Thank-you-very-much.

Now, before you start harassing me about calling her old, SHE is the one who likes to point out that she is often the oldest in the group (I'm 50 – but she calls me just a child.)

It's when Stephen Campbell (Zen Master Walking ™) is around that she keeps her mouth shut about age.

Ok, I'm off to continue falling asleep. Except, this time I'm going to fall asleep in my bed, instead of using my laptop as a pillow.

Love you guys and gals!

Ad Aeternitatem,
Michael

For Hire: Teachers for special school in Virginia countryside.

Must be able to handle teenagers with special abilities.

Cannot be afraid to discipline werewolves, wizards, elves and other assorted hormonal teens.

Apply at the School of Necessary Magic.

AVAILABLE ON AMAZON RETAILERS

If smart phones and GPS rule the world - why am I hunting a magic compass to save the planet?

Austin Detective Maggie Parker has seen some weird things in her day, but finding a surly gnome rooting through her garage beats all.

Her world is about to be turned upside down in a frantic search for 4 Elementals.

Each one has an artifact that can keep the Earth humming along, but they need her to unite them first.

Unless the forces against her get there first.

AVAILABLE ON AMAZON AND IN KINDLE UNLIMITED!

OTHER SERIES IN THE ORICERAN UNIVERSE

SOUL STONE MAGE

THE KACY CHRONICLES

MIDWEST MAGIC CHRONICLES

THE FAIRHAVEN CHRONICLES

I FEAR NO EVIL

THE DANIEL CODEX SERIES

SCHOOL OF NECESSARY MAGIC

SCHOOL OF NECESSARY MAGIC: RAINE CAMPBELL

ALISON BROWNSTONE

FEDERAL AGENTS OF MAGIC

SCIONS OF MAGIC

THE UNBELIEVABLE MR. BROWNSTONE

OTHER BOOKS BY JUDITH BERENS

OTHER BOOKS BY MARTHA CARR

JOIN THE ORICERAN UNIVERSE FAN GROUP ON FACEBOOK!